"Such little hands to be so talented.

"They not only fashion exquisite dolls, but they soothe a small daughter's fears and hurts," Clint murmured. "I'll bet they could drive a man mad."

The tingle turned into pinprick flames, and Elyse was in imminent danger of melting. No man had ever affected her like this before with just a touch and a few huskily spoken words. She had an overwhelming urge to find out just what her hands *could* do to him.

She felt a gentle tug on her arm as he pulled her toward him, then the hot flush of embarrassment as her face flamed. He was seducing her—and without even half trying. She jerked her hand from his and jumped up. "Go away, Clint," she rasped. "I don't want you here."

He rose, too, and stood behind her. "I'm not sure I can," he said simply.

Dear Reader,

Sophisticated but sensitive, savvy yet unabashedly sentimental—that's today's woman, today's romance reader—you! And Silhouette Special Editions are written expressly to reward your quest for substantial, emotionally involving love stories.

So take a leisurely stroll under the cover's lavender arch into a garden of romantic delights. Pick and choose among titles if you must—we hope you'll soon equate all six Special Editions each month with consistently gratifying romantic reading.

Watch for sparkling new stories from your Silhouette favorites—Nora Roberts, Tracy Sinclair, Ginna Gray, Lindsay McKenna, Curtiss Ann Matlock, among others—along with some exciting newcomers to Silhouette, such as Karen Keast and Patricia Coughlin. Be on the lookout, too, for the new Silhouette Classics, a distinctive collection of bestselling Special Editions and Silhouette Intimate Moments now brought back to the stands—two each month—by popular demand.

On behalf of all the authors and editors of Special Editions,
Warmest wishes,

Leslie Kazanjian
Senior Editor

PHYLLIS HALLDORSON
Cross My Heart

Silhouette Special Edition

Published by Silhouette Books New York

America's Publisher of Contemporary Romance

For our other sons and daughters:
Bob, Dwayne, Manuel, Jan and Linda.

 SILHOUETTE BOOKS
300 East 42nd St., New York, N.Y. 10017

Copyright © 1988 by Phyllis Halldorson

ISBN: 0-373-09430-2

First Silhouette Books printing January 1988

America's Publisher of Contemporary Romance

Printed in the U.S.A.

Books by Phyllis Halldorson

Silhouette Romance

Silhouette Special Edition

PHYLLIS HALLDORSON,

like all her heroines, is as in love with her husband to-day as on the day they met. It is because she has known so much love in her own life that her characters seem to come alive as they, too, discover the joys of romance.

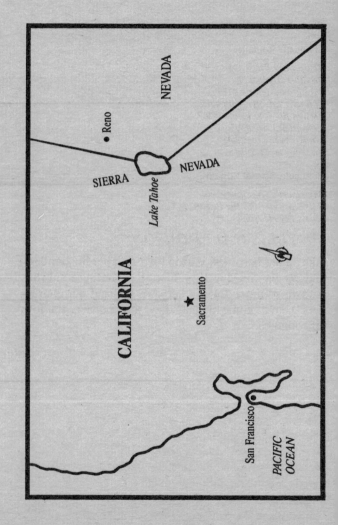

Chapter One

For the third time in as many days California State Senator Clinton Sterling reread the report from the private detective agency. It told him nothing he couldn't have found out for himself and was a waste of their time and his money.

He took off his reading glasses and rubbed his tired eyes. Mary Elyse Haley. What kind of woman had his younger brother, Paul, gotten himself mixed up with this time? All Clint had before him were statistics. Age: 24. Height: 5′5″. Weight: 118 lbs. Curly auburn hair. Brown eyes. Two years of college. Owner of Mary Elyse's Fairy-tale Angels, a custom-designed doll shop. She'd been born in the foothills town of Placerville, known during the gold rush days as Hangtown, and had lived there all her life.

Her neighbors and friends thought highly of her, and her handmade porcelain dolls won prizes every year. She sounded almost too good to be true—with one exception. She'd never been married, but she had a four-year-old daughter named Janey.

Clint frowned. Twenty-five years ago that would have been a glaring flaw, but today it was almost commonplace. Obviously he was going to have to go and see for himself if Paul's taste in women had matured any since the last time.

The disagreeable thought made him shudder. In spite of the fact that he was a politician, Clint was a private person. He firmly believed that everyone was entitled to privacy in his personal life, and the thought of prying into his brother's made him squirm.

Damn Paul, anyway. He was twenty-six years old, and it was time he grew up. Instead he was still addicted to fast cars, fast women and a fast turnover in both. The last glory-seeking bimbo he'd romanced and then dropped had taken her sad story to one of the tabloids, and the resulting notoriety had been embarrassing to the Sterling family and potentially harmful to Clint's political future and Paul's law career.

Now thirty-eight, Clint had never married, and the tabloids were always speculating about his love life. When he'd proved to be dull copy, they'd gleefully jumped at the unsavory firsthand story about the playboy brother of the esteemed lawmaker.

Now Paul was apparently seeing another woman, and Clint's public relations advisers were bringing pressure to bear on him to make sure she wasn't the kind who would make more trouble. This was an election year, and with the primaries coming up in a couple of months, more objectionable publicity could conceivably lose Clint his seat in the Senate. Especially since his closest contender in the party was Mr. Clean incarnate. The man was either a saint or an expert at covering his past sins—and those of his family members.

Clint's ambition reached all the way to the governor's office, and he had no intention of allowing his brother's irresponsible actions to jeopardize his chances.

The ring of the telephone broke into his thoughts, and he dropped the report on his big desk as he reached for the receiver. The call must be important or the switchboard wouldn't have put it through, since it was already long past office hours. He hoped it wasn't something that had to be taken care of tonight. It had been a long busy day, and he still had a thirty-minute drive from Sacramento to his home in the residential community of Cameron Park.

As he picked up the receiver, he made a mental note to call on Ms. Mary Elyse Haley the following day and buy a doll. Surely there must be a lady among his acquaintances who would appreciate an expensive collector's item as a gift.

Elyse reached into the rectangular box, pushed aside the white tissue wrapping and lifted out the little boy doll dressed in blue tweed knickers and a blue linen shirt. His firm cloth body was reclining on its side with his knees drawn up, and his porcelain face, with a sprinkling of brown freckles across his nose, was resting on his porcelain hand. His eyes were closed in sleep, and clutched in the crook of his other arm was a miniature brass horn.

"Here you are, Mrs. Wilson," she said as she held him out to the middle-aged woman on the other side of the counter. "Little Boy Blue complete with horn."

The woman took the doll and cradled it in her arms. "Oh, he's absolutely adorable," she said breathlessly. "I'm going to display him on the coffee table. My husband's building me a stand with hay for him to sleep on.''

Elyse smiled as she took the doll back and again packaged it in the tissue-filled box. The woman continued to talk. ''I have your Little Miss Muffett sitting on top of my television, and everyone who comes in comments on it. I never thought I'd be able to afford another doll, but then I won a thousand dollars in the lottery and this is the first thing I bought.''

''I'm flattered,'' Elyse said warmly as she handed the box to the customer. ''Congratulations on your winnings, and I hope you enjoy my little boy.''

''Oh, I will, and if I ever win again I'll be back for another. I hope someday to have the whole nursery-rhyme set.''

The woman left, balancing the box in her arms, and Elyse grinned happily as she secured the check for two hundred fifty dollars plus tax in the cash register. It was a beautiful warm Saturday in April, the trees had a thick green coat of leaves, and the pansies, daffodils, tulips and azaleas were in full, colorful blossom. She loved spring in the Sierra foothills.

Elyse glanced around the shop. It had originally been the front parlor of the big old family home that she and her sister, Mary Elizabeth, had inherited when their parents had died.

Elyse grimaced. She didn't usually think of her sister as ''Mary Elizabeth.'' She'd always been known as ''Liz,'' just as Mary Elyse was always called ''Elyse.'' It was unfortunate that their mother, whose name was Mary, had insisted on naming her two daughters after herself, and giving them such similar middle names had only compounded the problem. In instances where they had to use their full names nothing but confusion and frustrating mix-ups resulted.

Her gaze skimmed the schoolhouse clock on the wall, and her brown eyes widened in surprise. Almost one o'clock. Long past time to bring Janey in from the backyard, where she was playing on her new swing set, and give her some lunch.

Clint Sterling picked up the business card from his dresser. It was made of heavy bond paper with just a slight tint of pink. The drawing of a little girl doll in a ruffled pinafore filled the right top corner. Centered in the middle were the words Mary Elyse's Fairy-tale Angels and, under that, an address and phone number in Placerville, California. It was an excellent card: businesslike enough to impress bankers and informal enough to attract doll customers. Paul's latest love was apparently a good businesswoman, a departure from the kind of women he'd been attracted to in the past.

On the other hand she could also be smart enough to plot a little mischief if things didn't go her way.

Clint grimaced with distaste. It went against his nature to make quick assumptions, but he couldn't afford another family scandal and Paul had demonstrated that his judgment in such matters couldn't be trusted.

Clint put the card in the pocket of his jeans and slid a lightweight blue pullover over his plaid sport shirt. Paul, a championship golfer, was playing in a golf tournament in Monterey this weekend. It was the perfect time for Clint to meet Ms. Haley face to face and decide for himself just what kind of person she was. If she had nothing to hide, she'd be richer by the price of a doll and he'd have peace of mind. If she was after Paul's money and family prestige, then he'd take appropriate action, with a clear conscience.

An hour later he stopped his cream-colored Cadillac Eldorado in front of a yellow Victorian house on top of a hill in the older residential district of Placerville. There were two doors. The one at the top of the five wide stairs that led to the porch was of heavy beveled glass and walnut, obviously the original. A second one a few feet to his right was solid walnut and new. A tastefully printed sign in the large old-fashioned window beside it announced that this was The Home of Mary Elyse's Fairy-tale Angels.

In the absence of any instructions to walk in, Clint rang the bell and waited. He was just about to ring it again, when the door was opened by a young woman. "Good afternoon," she said in a husky drawl, "I'm Mary Elyse. Won't you please come in?"

Clint stared. No wonder Paul was besotted! Mary Elyse Haley was exquisite.

Her hair was the most startling thing about her. It was a medium shade of auburn and cut to frame her heart-shaped face in a riot of loose curls that lengthened to tumble around her shoulders and upper arms. Her full lips were tinted the exact shade of rose that glowed naturally on her high cheekbones, and her eyes were light brown with a tinge of green and a subconscious hint of seduction.

His undisciplined gaze roamed downward to the slender neck and the full high breasts, which seemed to strain under the avocado cotton fabric of the dress she wore. A matching braided belt encircled her small waist, and her swing skirt suggested gently flaring hips and slim thighs, which tapered to slender calves and trim ankles.

Her small feet were encased in multicolored low-heeled pumps.

Clint felt a stirring in his lower body and dragged his attention back to the business at hand. Good Lord, what was the matter with him? He was supposed to be evaluating her for his brother, not lusting after her for himself. This unpalatable job was going to be even more difficult than he'd anticipated.

He smiled and tried to keep his eyes under control as he stepped inside and directly into her display room, which, no doubt, had been designed as the front parlor. "Thank you," he said a bit belatedly. "I'm Clinton Edwards." He used his middle name but didn't add the Sterling. He didn't want her to recognize him. "I need a gift, and somebody suggested one of your dolls."

Her answering smile lit up the room. "They do make lovely presents," she said as she led the way to a big glass case. "Is the lady a collector?"

"Uh... yes. That is, she loves beautiful things."

"Is there a special type of doll she prefers?"

Clint blinked. "Type?"

Elyse's laugh was as rich and husky as her voice. "There are different categories of dolls, Mr. Edwards."

"'Clint.' Please call me 'Clint.'" He wanted to get things on a more informal basis. It would make it easier to find out what he wanted to know.

"All right, Clint. Some of the classifications are Antique Reproduction, Celebrity, Fashion... I specialize in storybook dolls, my version of children's storybook characters." She opened the glass door and pointed to one about fifteen inches tall. "This is Little Tommy Tucker. He has his lute, and you can see by the shape of his mouth that he's singing for his supper."

She moved her hand and picked up another, dressed in an elaborate ball gown. "This is Cinderella." She held it out to him. "She comes with a change of clothing—a tattered dress and a broom for sweeping cinders."

He took the doll from her and held it. It was perfect in every detail. "Do you make these yourself, or do you just design them?"

"Oh, I make them all, from the design to the finished product, except for the wigs and the shoes. Although I had to do Cinderella's glass slippers myself." She wrinkled her nose and her eyes twinkled with amusement. "I cheated a little, though. They're actually made of clear plastic."

"I'm impressed," Clint murmured, and he meant it.

He sincerely hoped she was the sweet and honest lady she seemed to be. She could break his brother's heart if she wasn't.

Clint spent the better part of an hour examining dolls and asking questions. But it wasn't the dolls that fascinated him; it was their creator. She was a real charmer. But was she also just a little too good to be true? So far she hadn't done or said a thing to make him believe she wasn't exactly what she seemed to be. Yet it was also obvious that she was very bright. Was it possible that she'd recognized him as Paul Sterling's brother, the senator, and was playing along with his deception?

He was running out of questions and wondering how he could move the conversation to a more personal level, when the door that separated the shop from the rest of the house opened, and a little girl appeared, wearing pajamas and looking damply tousled from sleep. "Mommy, my nap's all gone," she said with a yawn.

Elyse scooped her up in her arms and cuddled her against her shoulder. "So I see, sweetheart," she said as she brushed the child's reddish hair back and kissed her on the neck.

She turned toward Clint. "This is my daughter, Janey. Janey, can you say hello to Mr. Edwards?"

Janey raised her head and looked uncertainly at Clint. She was almost as beautiful as her mother with her mop of red-gold curls in disarray around her elfin-like face. "Are you going to buy a doll?" she asked, omitting the preliminary hello.

"Janey!" her mother admonished.

Clint reach out and curled a lock of the fine hair around his finger—something he'd been wanting to do to the child's mother ever since he'd arrived. "Yes, Janey," he said, "I'm going to buy a doll. But they're all so pretty that I can't decide which one I want."

She squirmed out of her mother's arms and ran over to the glass case. "Buy this one," she said, her face glowing with excitement as she pointed to one on the lower shelf. "It's me."

Clint squatted down to get a better view and recognized the child in the doll immediately. It's wig was a profusion of titian curls, and it was dressed in a white party dress of ruffles and lace with tiny hand-embroidered flowers sprinkled across the bodice. He knew immediately this was the one he wanted.

He smiled at Janey, standing next to him. "It looks just like you," he said, "and it's the most beautiful doll in the case. Does she have a name?"

"Her name's Amanda Jane, just like me, and she's going to a tea party."

"I can see that," he said. "She's all dressed up. If I buy her and take her home with me, will you and your mother come and have tea with us sometime?"

Slow down, Sterling, he admonished himself. *Don't bring the child into this with invitations you can't honor.*

Before Janey could answer, Mary Elyse spoke. "I'm sorry, Clint, but that doll's not for sale." She indicated a plaque next to the doll, which he'd missed. "It's one of a kind. I won't duplicate it. If you have a son or daughter, I could make a doll that looks like him or her... but you realize it would be very expensive."

Clint felt an unreasonable sense of disappointment as he stood to face her but silently acknowledged it was just as well. "I'm not married, nor do I have children, but I can understand why you wouldn't want to sell the reproduction of your little one." An idea occurred to him. "Was it a gift for her father?"

She shook her head. "Janey's father is dead."

Dead! That possibility had never occurred to him, but if she was the type of woman she seemed to be, this was the only explanation that made sense. What man in his right mind would walk away from Mary Elyse Haley and leave her to bear and raise his child alone?

"Oh, Mary, I'm so sorry," he said, surprised at the depth of feeling that accompanied the words.

"Thank you, but it happened before she was born. And please call me 'Elyse.' I only use the first name for business purposes. My family and friends have always called me 'Elyse.'

Clint nodded. "I like it. It suits you.

Elyse looked down at her daughter. "If you'll excuse me for a few minutes, I'd better dress Janey. Would you like a cup of coffee while you wait?"

"If it's not too much trouble," he answered as she reached for the coffeepot on the tea table beside her. She motioned toward the love seat fitted into the bay window area at the front of the room and handed him a bone china cup and saucer painted with delicate blue flowers. "Sit over there if you like. I'll only be a few minutes."

Elyse worked quickly as she dressed Janey in slacks and a T-shirt. She was a little uneasy about leaving a strange man alone downstairs. Not that Clint was strange. Actually, he seemed like one of the nicest men she'd met in a long time.

Handsome, too. Tall and muscular, with short black hair and the most astonishing green eyes. Eyes that probed and dared her to hold anything back. He was unique but strangely familiar. She was almost sure she'd seen him before, and yet she knew she'd never met him. Odd.

She ran the brush through her daughter's disheveled hair, so like her own, then sent her outside to her swings, slide and jungle gym.

Back in the shop Clint was just finishing his coffee. He stood as she came in, but she signaled him to sit back down. "Are you in a hurry, or would you like a refill?"

"I have the rest of the day," he said as he held up his cup. "Will you join me?"

He looks right at home, she thought as she took another cup from the tea table and filled them both, then sat down beside him on the small sofa. She was already seated before she realized there was barely enough space for the two of them. Their thighs almost touched, and his size and raw masculinity were nearly overpowering.

Flustered, she quickly said the first thing that came to mind. "Have you decided yet which doll you like?"

"I like them all," he answered, a look of amusement in his watching eyes. "But I think I'll buy Tom, Tom, the Piper's Son for my sister. He looks like my nephew, little devil that he is."

Elyse laughed and tried unobtrusively to put more distance between them. "That's a popular doll. People are almost as taken by the pig under his arm as by the doll itself."

"Did you make the pig, too?"

"Oh, sure. That's part of the nursery rhyme; I couldn't leave it out. If you noticed, Miss Muffett has a spider, Simple Simon has a pie, and so on. How old is your nephew?" The elusive scent of his shaving lotion tantalized her nostrils, bringing with it an urge to know more about this man who did exciting things to her heartbeat.

"Donnie's seven, and he has brothers five and two. They live in New Hampshire, so I don't see them as much as I'd like."

"Do you have other sisters and brothers?"

He seemed to hesitate, but then he said, "One older sister, who has teenage children and a younger brother who's not married. Now it's your turn. How many are in your family?"

She ran her finger around the rim of her mug. "My older sister, Liz, and I are the only ones left. And Janey, of course. Our mother died of cancer when I was ten, and a week later Dad suffered a stroke and only lived another month."

Clint moved to take her hand in his, and for a moment their thighs did touch. His was firm and warm and sent small tingles down her leg. He squeezed the hand he was holding. "It seems you've had more than your share of sadness in your young life," he said gently.

"Yes." She lowered her eyes for a moment. "But I was lucky to have Liz. She's twelve years older and was just out of college when they died. She took over and finished raising me. We inherited this house, so we

weren't uprooted, and there was insurance that helped."
He continued to hold her hand, and she felt oddly comforted.

"Does your sister make dolls, too?"

"Oh, my, no. I'm the dreamer. She's the intellectual.
She teaches high school English and literature."

He was silent for a moment, then asked, "Does she
have a family of her own now?"

"No." Elyse's instinct was to leave things at that, but
those hypnotic eyes of his seemed to loosen her tongue.
"Liz was married a few years ago, but it didn't work out.
She's divorced now and lives here with Janey and me.
She's out of town for the weekend."

It occurred to Elyse that this tall, handsome and *single* man would be a good match for her sister. He was
mature and he had the confident, relaxed style of a man
who had achieved success in whatever it was he did for
a living. Although he was dressed casually, his clothes
were designer quality, and she'd noticed the cream-
colored Cadillac parked at the curb when she'd answered the door.

Perversely Elyse was glad Liz wasn't home. For some
reason the idea of Clint Edwards and her sister as a
twosome upset her. Besides, although Liz vehemently
denied it, she showed every indication of being in love
with Paul Sterling, the young man she'd met on the golf
course in Cameron Park a few weeks ago and had been
dating steadily ever since. Because of the age difference—Paul was ten years younger—Liz refused to consider the possibility of a romance. Still, they'd gone to
Monterey together for a weekend golf tournament, and
Elyse wasn't making any bets they'd still be "just
friends" by the time they returned.

The sound of the doorbell jerked her back to the present, and she looked at her watch. "Oh, heavens!" she exclaimed as she stood. "How did the time get away from me? This will be the lady who called earlier to ask if she could come by and see the dolls." She headed toward the door. "I'll ring up your sale while she's browsing."

Clint didn't move. "That's not necessary. I'll wait. There's something more I want to talk to you about."

Elyse opened her mouth to argue, but the bell rang again, and instead she nodded and opened the door.

Half an hour later she said goodbye to the customer, who finally decided to make a down payment on Little Bo Peep, complete with lamb, and put it on layaway. Clint had joined in on the conversation, pointing out some of the small details and superb workmanship, which Elyse was too modest to mention.

Now Elyse held up her palms and shrugged. "I'm sorry it took so long," she said. "Choosing a doll and then deciding whether they want to spend several hundred dollars for it is a major decision for most customers, and they take their time thinking about it. I didn't mean to keep you waiting."

"You didn't," he said. "Actually, I was waiting for her to leave so I could invite you and Janey to go out to dinner with me."

Elyse's eyes widened with surprise. "Take us out? Oh, Clint, I don't know..."

"I assure you I'm a perfectly respectable lawyer with nothing on my mind but hamburgers and french fries at Janey's favorite hangout." A stab of guilt made him wince inwardly. He *was* a lawyer as well as a senator, but his intentions weren't quite so honorable. They were only just getting to know each other well enough that he felt he could ask more personal questions without having her tell him it was none of his business. He couldn't leave yet. He'd have no excuse for coming back.

Elyse grinned. "Oh, you mean McDonald's."

Clint made a face. "If that's what she wants, that's what she'll get."

Elyse laughed. "Well, how can I resist such a generous invitation? In fact, I'll even supply the dessert afterward. I have three different flavors of ice cream and freshly baked peanut butter cookies."

Janey was thrilled at the prospect of going out to eat, and when they arrived they discovered the drive-in was having a promotional affair, and Ronald McDonald, the clown, was there. Janey shrieked with excitement when he came to their table and picked coins out of her hair. But with all the commotion there was no chance for Clint even to talk to Elyse, let alone question her.

Afterward they went back to the house, where she made hot chocolate and served dessert.

When she got up from the table to put the dishes in the sink Clint knew he couldn't prolong his visit any longer. He'd have to convince her to see him again.

He looked at his watch and frowned. "I'm afraid I've overstayed my welcome," he said, and stood. "It must be past the little one's bedtime. I'd better leave."

Janey protested loudly, and Elyse's impulse was to do the same. Then she remembered that Clint Edwards was a man she'd only met a few hours ago. She really knew nothing about him, and it would be unwise, if not downright foolhardy, to encourage him to stay any longer.

At the front door he picked Janey up and hugged her. "Good night, sweetheart. Thank you for having dinner with me."

Janey, a naturally loving child, hugged him back.

Clint looked at Elyse and seemed to hesitate, then took her hand. "I'd like to see you again, Elyse," he said. "Will you and Janey spend tomorrow with me? We can go to Sacramento and take Janey to the zoo and Fairy-tale Town. I'll even spring for lunch. A fancy one this time."

Janey's happy face glowed. "Oh, Mommy, can we? Please say yes! Please!"

She was bouncing around in Clint's arms, and he was having a hard time holding on to her.

"Well, I . . ." This was all happening too fast.

Her feelings about him were ambivalent. He'd come in here and spent the day charming the socks off her. Janey, too—and that could lead to trouble. Since the child had no father she tended to look for one in every man who was nice to her, and Elyse didn't want to see her daughter hurt.

On the other hand, Elyse was almost sure Clint wasn't acting or pretending. He'd seemed to truly enjoy the afternoon and evening, and he'd been a perfect gentleman at all times.

She couldn't deny she was attracted to him, had been from the moment she'd opened the door and seen him standing there looking at her so approvingly. For the first time in five years she'd felt the warm heady tingle of sexual attraction. Not that she hadn't had her share of dates since Janey was born, but she'd never been tempted to give more than a good-night kiss at the door. The attraction was doubly exciting because it had never happened to her this quickly before, not even with Jerry.

"Say yes, Mommy. Please," Janey repeated desperately.

"All right," Elyse answered with a chuckle, reaching out to take her bubbly daughter from Clint. "Are you sure you know what you're getting into?" she asked him. "Energetic little girls can try the patience of a saint."

His grin seemed a little strained. "Since I'm no saint, we won't have to worry. I'll pick you up in the morning. About...ten?"

Clint stopped for the light, then turned west onto the freeway. Damn it all to hell! He'd almost been convinced that Mary Elyse Haley was nothing like the airheads Paul was usually attracted to. She was a talented, intelligent woman who ran her business and raised her daughter with equal expertise. She'd seemed like the perfect choice for his brother, but then she'd spoiled it by agreeing to go out with him again.

Clint glanced at the speedometer and lightened his foot on the gas pedal. If he got a ticket for speeding the reporters would be all over him. Sometimes being a politician was a pain in the rear.

His thoughts returned to the young woman he'd just left. She'd seemed remarkably mature for her age, and the investigation had indicated a spotless character, unless an illegitimate child was considered a demerit. She was even an active member of her church. But if she was dating Paul on a steady basis, why had she agreed to go out with another man? And worse, a stranger she'd met when Paul was out of town? In fact, why had she agreed to spend the evening with him once their business had supposedly been completed?

He felt an overwhelming sense of disappointment and swore softly. Had he been so bewitched by the sexy innocence she projected that he'd believed what he wanted to instead of what was?

If so, he was a fool. There hadn't been a woman in the past four years who had aroused his emotions. His lust occasionally, but never his emotions.

He was a one-woman man, and the woman he wanted now was the one he couldn't have.

He'd come to terms with his exclusivity four years ago when Dinah had left, and although he'd eventually managed to put her out of his thoughts and get on with his life, he knew he'd never fall in love again. He certainly had better sense than to get involved with his brother's girlfriend!

Trying to think rationally, he admitted he really hadn't given Elyse a chance to decline either time he'd asked her to go out with him. He'd woven his plans around Janey, and the mother hadn't wanted to disappoint her child.

On the other hand if Elyse were *his* love, he'd be furious if she went out with another man when he wasn't around, no matter how much pressure was put on her. He knew Paul would feel the same way.

Maybe spending another day with her was a good idea. If she was intent on taking his brother for all she could get, then he wanted to know it—now. If Elyse was trying to attach herself to Paul for a reason other than love, she'd be smart enough to do a lot more damage than just talking to the press if things didn't go her way.

Yes, he'd definitely see Elyse again, and this time he'd find out just how far she was willing to let him go while her boyfriend was away.

Chapter Two

Sacramento is known as the city of camellias and trees, and although there were only a few camellias still blooming, the lawns, trees and flower bushes of William Land Park, where the zoo was located, were green and thick with foliage. The weather in the valley ranged from warm to hot during the months of March through October before the rainy season took over and the temperature cooled.

On this bright and beautiful April Sunday afternoon, Elyse, Clint and Janey had discarded their thin sweaters and were wandering around the compact zoo with their bare arms exposed to the rapidly warming air.

Clint held Janey on his shoulders so she could see the monkeys cavorting around their island, and Janey laughed and clapped her hands at their antics. On the surface he, Elyse and Janey had spent a delightful two hours watching the elephants, giraffes, bears and more exotic animals, as well as the colorful birds, but Elyse couldn't shake the feeling that Clint wasn't really enjoying himself.

Not that he'd said or done anything to make her think so. When he'd picked them up at the house that morning he'd seemed in a playful mood with Janey, but sitting next to him in the car on the forty-mile drive to Sacramento, Elyse had become aware of a nebulous tension in him. He'd kept up a conversation with her daughter but had made little effort to start one with her.

She walked a few steps away from him and threw a handful of popcorn in front of one of the tame peacocks that roamed the grounds, then watched it peck at the food.

A squeal of delight from Janey brought an answering laugh from Clint, and Elyse frowned. Was she being too sensitive? He sounded happy enough, and he'd certainly been attentive. He'd bought them popcorn and Cokes and even a stuffed bear for Janey, and he'd answered all their questions.

She shook her head as if to dislodge her nagging doubts. She hardly knew the man. It was presumptuous of her to think she could read his thoughts.

He turned to her as she moved back to his side. "It's nearly one o'clock," he said. "We'd probably better go somewhere for lunch, then come back to tour Fairy-tale Town, don't you think?"

Elyse hesitated for a moment. He was probably getting bored. Most bachelors did after several hours with a small child. She'd let him off the hook.

"I think we'd better have lunch and then go on home," she said. "Janey takes a nap, and if she misses it completely she's cranky and difficult. She's enjoyed the zoo, and I can take her to Fairy-tale Town some other time.''

Engrossed in the monkeys, Janey had missed the conversation. Clint eased her off his shoulders and stood her on the ground. ''Come along, honey, we've seen all there is to see here. Now we're going to have lunch.''

Elyse noticed he hadn't objected to cutting the day short.

She was surprised when he shunned downtown Sacramento and drove twenty miles east of the city before stopping at a restaurant in the small historical town of Folsom. It was in one of the old restored buildings on Sutter Street, the town's second attraction. The first was the aging, federal maximum security Folsom Prison, which sat bleak and forbidding on the hill.

Sutter Street was a restoration of the gold rush era. A three-block-long recreation featured restaurants, boutiques and museums, with gaslight streetlamps and a small theater where old-fashioned melodramas were performed to the encouragement of hisses and cheers from the audience.

The café Clint had chosen was on the second floor, and they found a table on the balcony, which overlooked the scenic street. Sunday brunch was still being served, and while they ate, he finally seemed to relax, and became more talkative.

''I'd like to thank you for spending last evening with me, Elyse,'' he said as he cut a bite-size piece from his thick slice of ham. ''I don't imagine you have many Saturday evenings free. A lady as young and beautiful as you must have a busy social life.''

Elyse laughed. ''Well, yes, I suppose so, if you consider singing in the choir at church and helping once a week in the cooperative nursery school Janey attends 'social.' Running my own business and raising a small child by myself doesn't leave a lot of time for party-ing."

Clint didn't join her merriment. "Come now, surely you have dates?"

She could see he was serious. "I date now and then," she said, "but certainly not every Saturday night."

He frowned. "You mean there's no special man in your life right now?"

For the life of her she couldn't understand why this conversation seemed to be upsetting him, and he was venturing into areas that were none of his business.

"Not now, and not since Janey's father died." There was a chill in her tone. "Is there some reason you're asking?"

Clint knew he was handling this wrong, but he couldn't seem to help it. Damn her, she was lying to him. The operative's report had stated that Paul and Mary E. Haley spent a great deal of time together, and knowing Paul, he'd take her to plenty of parties. He and his friends were always carousing.

Clint tried for a nonchalant shrug that didn't come off. "Not really," he answered. "I just find it hard to believe that you spend all your evenings sitting at home, reading nursery rhymes to your child."

Elyse blinked and looked genuinely hurt. "Believe what you want," she snapped, then pushed back her chair to stand. "I'm sorry to rush you, but it's past time for Janey's nap. I'd like to go home."

As they pulled out onto the freeway and again headed east toward Placerville, Clint swore silently to himself. So much for the investigative skills that had earned him such a fine reputation as a lawyer! He'd botched this from the minute he'd laid eyes on his brother's latest little beauty. He'd taken one look at her and let his emotions get involved. Which was sheer lunacy, since even if he wanted her—which he didn't—and she were as pure as the dolls she created, he still couldn't have her. Paul had first claim, which he apparently had no intention of relinquishing. At least not yet.

But the fact remained that she'd deliberately and cold-bloodedly lied to him. Both his public relations man and the private investigator had seen Paul and Mary E. Haley together, nights and on weekends, on numerous occasions. Why had she told him there was no special man in her life? What game was she playing? And how was he going to find out if he'd been so clumsy in his questioning that she'd never see him again?

With a sigh he gripped the steering wheel. He knew what he had to do, and his distaste for the task came close to revulsion. If Elyse was willing to forgive him, he'd have to apologize and romance her a little. Make her think he was jealous. See if he could get her to admit she was seeing another man and what her motive was for lying about it.

When all this was over, Clint intended to make damn sure Paul never put him in such an untenable position again. It was time little brother learned the facts of life: namely, that big brother Clint wasn't averse to kicking Paul's behind right out of the law firm if he didn't stop screwing up and start studying for his bar exam.

Elyse sat quietly in the passenger seat with her hands folded in her lap, while Janey snoozed in the back. She should have known better than to let herself be captivated by a handsome stranger with a winning smile, a smooth line and a way with children. He was just like most of the other men she'd met since Janey was born; sure that because she'd had a child without benefit of wedding vows she must be a bit of a trollop, a hot little number who couldn't wait to jump in the sack with any man who showed an interest.

Her stomach muscles knotted, and she wished she hadn't just eaten. She'd thought Clint was different. He'd seemed so gentle and understanding and genuinely interested in her and Janey that she'd let down her guard. She'd reacted to his charisma with the trust of a wide-eyed fifteen-year-old experiencing the first stirrings of her sexuality.

The faint flutter of nausea reminded her to try to relax. Her sexuality had been stirred up years ago, and it had brought her both ecstasy and anguish. She'd never settle for less than the ecstasy, nor deliberately put herself in a position to experience more of the anguish.

No sense getting so upset over this. Clinton Edwards didn't mean anything to her. Once they got home she'd thank him for his thoughtfulness to Janey, tell him goodbye and never see him again. So why did she feel as though she'd just been kicked in the stomach?

She was so preoccupied with her disturbing thoughts that she jumped when Clint reached over and covered her clenched hands with his big one. "I'm sorry, Elyse," he said when she looked at him questioningly. "I didn't mean to frighten you, nor did I intend to upset you with my questions. I'm sorry if you thought I was probing. Actually, I was just trying to get to know you better."

"By accusing me of lying?" She withdrew her hands from his.

He recaptured one of them. "I wasn't accusing you of lying," he said softly. "I just find it difficult to believe you aren't overrun with suitors."

"Because of my lax morals, you mean." It wasn't a question but a statement, and her tone was bitter.

This time it was Clint who dropped her hand and stared. "What in hell are you talking about?"

He really did look confused. For a moment she could almost believe her statement had shocked him, but she quickly regained her hold on reality.

"Don't be coy with me, Clint," she shot back. "I've had four years of sly innuendos from men who assumed that since I had an illegitimate child I was just panting to go to bed with anyone who beckoned."

She heard Clint's choked denial but was too incensed to stop. "I'll admit you used more finesse, but you were still leading up to the same old thing. I slept with Janey's father, therefore I should be eager to give you the same privilege. Well, forget it. I'm afraid you've wasted both your time and your money."

Elyse had been so intent on what she was saying that she hadn't noticed they'd entered Placerville and were approaching her house. Clint pulled over to the curb, but before he could speak she had her seat belt off and the door open. She jumped out and jerked open the back door to grab her sleeping daughter, but somehow Clint was beside her.

"I'll carry her," he said tersely.

"Never mind. I'll carry her myself," she grated as she hauled the little girl out of the car and over her shoulder.

"Elyse, if you'll just calm down and—"

She didn't wait to hear what he had to say but hurried up the walk to the front porch.

He rushed after her and caught up in time to put his arm around her waist and help her up the steps with her inert burden. When they reached the top, she shook free of his arm and tried to open her purse with one hand. He took it from her and extracted her key, then opened the heavy door and held it for her to enter. She did, quickly pushing it shut behind her. It locked automatically, leaving Clint standing outside, banging and calling to her to let him in.

Elyse ignored him and carried Janey across the shop and into the hall, where she literally ran into her sister, Mary Elizabeth, who was hurrying toward the commotion at the door.

They both stepped back, and Elyse's eyes widened with surprise. "Liz," she gasped, "I didn't expect you back from Monterey until late tonight."

The pretty, dark-haired woman looked askance. "Obviously not. What on earth is going on out there? Do you want me to call the police?"

Elyse shook her head. "No, he'll quiet down in a minute and go away. Excuse me while I put Janey to bed for her nap. Then I'll tell you all about it."

"Please do," Liz drawled as the banging continued.

Still seething, Elyse took Janey upstairs and laid her carefully on the single brass bed in the pink-and-white nursery next to her own bedroom. She took off the child's sneakers and socks and covered her with the hand-knit coverlet that was kept folded at the bottom of the bed, before kissing her on the forehead and closing the door behind her as she left.

Downstairs the commotion had stopped, and a quick glance out the glass door revealed that the expensive Cadillac was no longer parked at the curb. But in the back parlor, which they used as a family living room, Liz had no intention of letting the subject drop. "I take it that was one of your disappointed suitors?"

Elyse grimaced. "Spring seems to bring out the rutting instinct in males."

Liz raised one eyebrow. "Honey, *you* bring out the rutting instinct in males. What did this one do that was so awful?"

Elyse shrugged. "Actually, he didn't *do* anything. It was more what he said."

"So what did he say?"

"Well, it wasn't so much what he said as how he said it." Elyse was beginning to realize she may have overreacted.

"Good grief, woman," Liz exploded, "did the man do anything to warrant getting the door slammed in his face or not?"

Elyse slumped in the old-fashioned leather rocker. "Yes. Oh, I don't know. He was subtle, but . . . well, I made a mistake going out with him. He just wandered in here yesterday looking for a doll—"

She told her sister everything that had happened during the past two days with Clint. "Maybe I did overreact," she said in conclusion, "but he seemed to assume I was just a party girl always looking for a good time."

Liz sighed and brushed a lock of short dark hair off her forehead. "Elyse, you're too sensitive. Everyone in town knew you were engaged to Jerry and making plans to be married when he died. None of them are throwing rocks at you. And as for other men . . . ? They're only reacting to the way you look. Face it, sweetie, with that wild hair and husky voice—to say nothing of all your other natural attributes—you could turn on the proverbial stone statue. Enjoy it, for heaven's sake. Most of us would sell our souls for a little of what you've got in such abundance."

Elyse shook her head. "I don't know. Raising a child alone is such a responsibility. I'd like to marry someday. I need a man in my life and Janey needs a father, but for both our sakes I have to be careful. I'm as susceptible as any other woman to a good looking guy's advances, but I won't get involved in a romance that's not leading to a commitment.''

Liz drew her legs up under her on the wheat-and-brown homespun couch and leaned against the thickly padded arm. ''I wish I had your good sense and your self-discipline,'' she said.

The ragged edge to her voice made Elyse look up. She'd been too preoccupied to notice before, but her sister was considerably more subdued than she should be after spending a weekend on the magnificent and expensive Pebble Beach Golf Course with a wickedly handsome partner.

''Liz, is something wrong?'' Elyse paused, then continued. ''Why are you and Paul home from Monterey so early? You didn't quarrel, did you?''

Liz uttered an unladylike snort. ''We'd have been smarter if we had! Instead we spent the night together—as in one room, one bed and one hell of a lot of fantastic loving.''

Elyse grinned. ''Well, then, what are you moping around about? Sounds like a mutually satisfactory weekend. You and Paul have been dating for several weeks, and Paul's feelings for you have been pretty obvious. You must have known where this was leading.''

Liz looked stunned. ''I'm old enough to be his mother!'' she shrieked.

Elyse's smile faded, and a look of disbelief replaced it. ''Mary Elizabeth Haley, you're an idiot! Ten years is a long way from a generation, and what does his age have to do with anything? Apparently he wasn't too young to perform.''

"Don't be crude," Liz snapped heatedly. "You know perfectly well what I'm saying. He's just out of law school. Hasn't even passed the bar yet. I never intended things to go this far. We started out as golfing partners. We were well matched and I liked him, so when he asked me to go out with him I did."

She threw out her arms. "It just snowballed from there. I knew my feelings were getting out of hand, that I should stop seeing him, but he wouldn't let me. Kept teasing me about my 'absurd age fallacy' as he called it."

She dropped her hands back in her lap. "I must have been out of my mind to agree to go with him this weekend, even though we had booked separate rooms. I'm no starry-eyed virgin. I know all about lust, even if I do have middle-aged spread and crow's-feet." Her voice broke, but she continued. "I've made a damned fool of myself, and I—I've told him I'm not going to s—s—see him anymore." She dropped her face in her hands, and a sob shook her shoulders.

"Liz!" Elyse jumped up and crossed the few steps to the sofa. She sat down and put her arms around her sister. "You do *not* have middle-aged spread and crow's-feet, and we're not talking lust but strong mutual attraction and caring. You're taking this business of age too seriously. It doesn't seem to bother Paul. Why should it bother you?"

"B—b—because I'm old enough to know better. We're not discussing Joe Blow here. Paul's ancestors came to California with the gold rush and have been movers and shakers in state politics ever since. His grandfather was lieutenant governor, and both his father and older brother have served terms in the Senate."

Elyse stroked Liz's back as her sister wept. "What does Paul's family have to do with anything?" she asked softly. "He may be younger than you, but he's certainly no child. He's two years older than I am and more than capable of making his own decisions. He doesn't need his father's permission to court you."

Liz raised her tearstained face and reached into the pocket of her slacks for a tissue. "The problem is, it's gone past courting," she said, and blew her nose. "Paul's asked me to marry him."

Elyse opened her mouth, but nothing came out. She was speechless.

"You see?" Liz wailed accusingly. "You're as appalled as I am."

Elyse shut her mouth and took a deep breath. "I'm not appalled, I'm surprised. Men don't usually propose marriage quite so quickly. Are you in love with him? Yes, of course you are. You wouldn't have gone to bed with him if you weren't."

"It doesn't matter if I am or not, I've no intention of encouraging this lunacy." Liz wiped at her wet cheeks with the palms of her hands. "I told him no and sent him away. I'm just a novelty. The young women swarm all over him. He won't have any trouble replacing me with someone more suitable."

Her efforts at drying her face were in vain as her tears spilled down it once again.

Clint sat at the desk in the study of his large ranch-style house in Cameron Park and tried to work, but his thoughts kept returning to last Sunday and Elyse. He hadn't meant to make her so angry. Obviously she was more sensitive than he'd imagined about her status as an unwed mother.

He hadn't even been thinking about that when he'd questioned her about her social life. He'd only wanted to make her stop lying to him and admit there was a man in her life. He'd wanted her to talk about Paul—where they went, what they did, how she felt about him. Instead she'd assumed he was coming on to her.

He slapped his hand on the desk and stood up. Well, hell, that's what he *had* been doing, and no matter how he tried to rationalize his behavior, they both knew it. His little scheme to investigate her had blown up in his face and left him feeling like the bastard he was.

He prowled around the room. Again, as had happened so often in the past three days and nights, the picture rose in his mind of her sitting next to him in the car, looking as if he'd just accused her of being the town tramp.

He hadn't even understood what she was haranguing him about. It wasn't until she came right out and told him that he realized how his questions had sounded to her. All he'd wanted then was to hold her in his arms and apologize, to somehow take back the pain he'd caused her and wipe the look of bewildered hurt from her delicate face.

He stopped at the window and looked out at the night, illuminated by trillions of twinkling stars and the slender crescent moon. He'd left shortly after she'd slammed the door and it had become apparent she wasn't going to let him in. There was nothing else he could do, and even if she had been willing to talk to him, he'd probably have managed to say the wrong thing.

Early the following morning he'd flown to Washington, D.C. for a conference on national party issues, and he'd only just returned, so he hadn't had a chance to go back to try to straighten things out with her. He knew now what he was going to do, though, and it wasn't harass Elyse. He was going to deal with his brother, as he should have done in the first place.

Clint returned to the desk, picked up the phone and dialed Paul's apartment in Sacramento. Although the home in Cameron Park belonged to their parents, their father and mother used it only as a stopping off place between winters in Palm Springs and summers at Lake Tahoe since their father's retirement after a stroke six years ago. Clint stayed in residence, but sharing a house with his big brother wasn't part of Paul's free, swinging style.

The phone at the other end rang eight times before Clint broke the connection. He looked at his watch. Quarter to ten. Paul was probably out with Elyse. Clint's muscles tightened. Dammit, he was going to get some straight answers—and soon.

He made his decision: he'd stop in at the law firm in the morning and confront Paul in person. He'd had enough pussyfooting around.

Elyse lay on her back in her big old-fashioned four-poster pineapple bed and tried to relax into sleep. It wasn't going to be any easier tonight than it had been for the past three nights.

If only she didn't see Clint Edwards every time she closed her eyes.

It had been three days since they'd quarreled, and she hadn't seen or heard from him. Not that she expected to. She'd made it unmistakably clear she wasn't interested in anything he might propose, so why did her gaze follow every car that went past the house? Why did her heart speed up every time the doorbell or the telephone rang?

She hardly knew the man, for heaven's sake. He might even have a wife. He'd denied having children, but that didn't mean he wasn't married and looking for a little extra action.

She rolled onto her side and punched her pillow into a more comfortable position. She didn't need Clint to haunt her dreams; she had enough trouble with Liz. In fact, her sister was getting to be a real pain. She was obviously miserable, but it was her own fault. She wouldn't talk to Paul Sterling either on the phone or in person, and she wouldn't listen when Elyse tried to reason with her. She just kept spouting nonsense about how totally unsuitable it would be to marry a man so much younger.

Elyse flipped to her stomach and clutched the pillow in her arms. Liz should thank God for sending a man like Paul Sterling into her life. He'd admitted to being something of a hell raiser in high school and college, but if that was true he seemed to have worked it out of his system. Oh, he still had a streak of youthful exuberance, but he was thoughtful and considerate, and he obviously adored Liz. Elyse didn't doubt Liz felt the same way about Paul, so why was she being so stubborn?

There were times when she thought her elder sister was a throwback. Older women married younger men all the time these days, and nobody thought anything of it.

Elyse just wished she had a man like Paul to love her. No, that wasn't quite accurate. She wished she had a man like Clint Edwards to love her. Or at least a man like the man Clint had seemed to be.

She clutched the pillow harder. He'd made her heart race and her imagination soar. Why did he have to turn out to be a skirt chaser like all the rest?

* * *

Clint arrived at the law offices of Sterling, Fernald and Highsmith at eight o'clock the next morning, only to find that Paul had already been there and gone and would be tied up all day in court. Clint left a message for him to call.

The call came at one o'clock just as Clint was leaving his office for lunch. "Sorry I missed you this morning," Paul said.

"No problem," Clint answered, "but I do want to talk to you. When can we get together?"

"I want to talk to you, too." Paul's voice sounded strained. "Are you free for dinner tonight? I can meet you at the Lillian Russell Room at Sam's Town around seven-thirty?"

Clint checked his appointment book. "Fine. Will you be spending the night at the house?"

Sam's Town was a large sprawling restaurant and pioneer town facsimile along the freeway at Cameron Park, thirty miles from Paul's apartment in one of the new high-rise buildings in downtown Sacramento.

There was a pause. "I'm not sure. Tell Alice it's a possibility."

Alice and Grover Irwin had been housekeeper and gardener-handyman for the Sterlings for years. They were both past sixty but continued to live in the apartment above the garage and pamper both the property and Clint. Alice kept telling Clint they couldn't retire until he brought home a wife to take care of him—a prospect that seemed more unlikely every year.

Clint arrived at the restaurant a few minutes late and found Paul in the bar. The two brothers looked nothing alike. Paul was a few inches shorter and several pounds lighter, and his hair, which had been golden as a child, had darkened only slightly over the years. His wide blue eyes were fringed with long thick dark lashes that apparently no woman could resist, and he had a perpetual happy-go-lucky attitude that wasn't always an asset. It was hard to get him to take anything seriously.

The brothers found a table at the back of the dimly lit room, which they hoped would afford a little privacy.

After the greetings were over and the waitress had brought Clint a Scotch and soda and replaced Paul's gin and tonic, Paul opened the conversation. "Funny you should have stopped by the office to see me this morning, Clint. I tried to get in touch with you Tuesday, but Alice said you were in D.C. and she wasn't sure when you'd be back."

Clint was surprised. He and his younger brother lived totally separate lives, and sometimes weeks went by without their contacting each other.

"Alice didn't mention it," he said as his gaze settled on the other man. For the first time he noticed that the usual cocky grin was gone and the twinkle in Paul's eyes had been replaced by a bewildered sadness. "I got back last night and tried to call you, but you weren't home. Is something wrong?"

Paul took a quick swallow of his gin. "Yeah, I guess you could say that. You see, there's this girl—"

Clint's hands knotted into fists. "Oh, hell, Paul," he bellowed, "not again!"

Paul looked up, startled. "No, you don't understand. This girl's different—"

"They always are, aren't they? Right up to the time you drop them. Then they turn vicious. For God's sake, won't you ever learn?"

He felt sick. What was Elyse demanding as her price for not causing a big blowup just six weeks before the primary elections? Damn, he'd hoped...

"Calm down, will you?" Paul demanded. "I don't want to drop this one. I'm in love with her. But I asked her to marry me and she refused."

Clint stared, unable for a moment to understand what he'd just heard. "She refused?"

Paul nodded miserably. "Yeah, and I don't blame her. I've behaved like a jerk. Haven't even introduced her to any of my family. I've bragged about my brother, the senator, and my mother, who owns a string of pharmacies inherited from her parents, but, well, to tell the truth, I didn't want you to know about her until I was sure how I felt. After that last woman I...well, anyway, I'm in love with her. I proposed to her on Sunday, and she not only said no, she won't even speak to me now."

Clint was stabbed at the same time by elation and despair. Paul must have proposed to Elyse when he got home from Monterey on Sunday evening, after Clint had spent most of the weekend with her. She'd refused him. Did that mean she'd recognized Clint as Senator Sterling and decided to go after bigger fish, or was she playing some sort of game with Paul?

Or was there any possible chance that she really was as open and honest as she seemed to be and she just wasn't in love with Paul?

Before Clint could comment Paul continued. "Look, Clint, I want to ask a favor." Clint opened his mouth, but Paul held up his hand for silence. "I want you to go to her house with me tonight and let me introduce you." For a moment his teasing grin was back. "Since Dad and Mom aren't available, you're the next best thing." Again he was serious. "She's a stickler for manners. She won't refuse to speak to me as long as you're there. She's a real lady. I swear you'll like her, and I need your help to get her to listen."

Clint was appalled. He'd never messed up this badly before. He usually had tight control of any situation he was involved in, but this time he'd fumbled right from the minute Mary Elyse Haley had opened the door and smiled at him. Now what was he going to do? If he showed up at her house with Paul and told her what he'd been up to, she'd throw them both out.

On the other hand, if Paul was really serious about her, then it was more important than ever that he find out just what she was up to. This was something he was going to have to face. He might as well do it and get it over with. He just hoped they'd come out of it with Paul, at least, still speaking to him.

Clint gulped the rest of his whiskey and nodded. "I'd heard you were seeing another woman, so this doesn't come as a complete surprise. In fact, that's what I wanted to talk to you about this morning." He stood. "Come on, if we're going to see her we might as well do it now. We can eat later." *If we still have appetites*, he thought grimly.

Paul stood, also. "Great. I really appreciate this." He reached into his pocket and pulled out Elyse's pale pink business card. "She lives in Placerville. Here's the address. It's only a short drive. You can follow me."

Elyse was on her way downstairs after putting Janey to bed, when the doorbell rang. "I'll get it," she called to Liz, who was grading test papers at the kitchen table.

She ran down the remaining steps and opened the door, to find Paul Sterling standing on the porch. It was darker out than she'd realized, and although she could see another man standing a few feet behind him, she couldn't tell who it was. "Paul, come on in," she said. She moved aside to allow him to enter and looked away to switch on the porch light. "Liz is in the kitchen, but I don't think she'll—"

She looked up and blinked. The other man was Clint Edwards! He'd followed Paul in and was standing beside him in the hallway.

Before she could react Paul said, "Elyse, I'd like you to meet my brother, Clinton Sterling. Clint, this is Elyse Haley, Liz's sister." He grinned tentatively at Elyse. "Clint's the family mediator. I brought him along to meet the woman I intend to marry. Maybe he can help convince her that I'm all grown up and haven't worn diapers for years."

Elyse was staring at Clint, but her eyes didn't focus enough to see him. The man she'd known as Clint Edwards was really State Senator Clinton Sterling—Paul Sterling's brother!

No wonder he'd looked so familiar. She should have recognized him. She would have, if he hadn't deliberately deceived her by giving a false name. Which meant that he'd also lied about his reason for coming to see her.

It was then that the delayed wave of pain and disillusion rolled over her.

Clinton Edwards/Sterling wasn't only a senator, he was also a liar and a first-class bastard.

Chapter Three

Elyse made an effort to pull herself together, and her rapidly developing rage was a big help. So the handsome, charismatic young senator wasn't above trampling on his constituents' personal rights to privacy!

But why her? What on earth had she done to merit his dubious attention?

A thought sent her anger skyrocketing. Clint had no interest in her. It was Liz he was spying on, using Elyse to do it. That had to be it, since his only connection with the Haley family was through his brother.

She didn't acknowledge the introduction but squared her shoulders and turned to Paul. "Come with me," she said, and started down the hall toward the kitchen. She was going to stick with them until she found out what was going on. If Clint Sterling considered Liz an unsuitable candidate for the sister-in-law of a state senator, then he was going to get more than he'd bargained for.

Elyse had been gullible enough to think he was special. She'd unknowingly given him access to the family, but she had no intention of letting him hurt her sister.

Liz looked up from where she was sitting at the round oak pedestal table, covered with student papers, as the three of them walked into the huge old kitchen. She was wearing her dark-framed reading glasses, and she'd obviously been running her fingers through her short brown hair while she worked. It stood up in some places and hung limp in others.

Liz would never be considered beautiful. Like most women she was sometimes very pretty and at other times quite plain. Elyse winced as she realized that this was definitely one of Liz's plain moments. She'd changed from the neat skirt and blouse she'd worn to school into a comfortable old pair of faded jeans and a sweater she'd bought years ago. Since then, she'd blossomed, but the sweater had shrunk, so the resulting fit left little of Liz to the imagination from the waist up. And the makeup that had been so expertly applied at seven that morning had faded and melted into an oily sheen.

Elyse groaned as her sister's eyes widened in surprise. Why hadn't she made Paul and Clint wait in the family room and given Liz the opportunity to fix herself up? Liz had always been particular about how she looked when she knew Paul was coming. But Elyse had been so thrown off balance by the appearance of Clint she hadn't been thinking straight.

Liz blanched, but her composure held as she pushed back her chair and stood. "Paul, I—I wasn't expecting you."

Paul walked over to the table but didn't touch her. "I know." His voice wavered slightly as he continued. "I was afraid you wouldn't see me if you knew I was coming. Honey, I want you to meet my brother, Clint. I've told you about him, but I made the mistake of not telling him about you. That was an error on my part, and I'm truly sorry."

He turned to Clint. "Clint, this is Mary Elizabeth Haley, and I'm very much in love with her. I've asked her to marry me, but I'm afraid I was tactless about it, and she's said no. I hope the three of us can sit down and talk and straighten this out."

Elyse was still standing just inside the kitchen door and could see Clint only in profile, but there was no mistaking the shock on his face. To his credit he suppressed it immediately and put out his hand. "Mary Elizabeth, I don't think you'll ever know just how pleased I am to meet you."

Now it was Liz who looked shocked as she put her hand in his. "Th—thank you, Senator Sterling."

"Please call me 'Clint.'" He smiled. "If you're going to be a member of the family, we'd better get on a first-name basis, don't you think?"

Liz shook her head sadly. "I'm not going to marry Paul, but I'd like it if you'd call me 'Liz.' Both my sister and I were christened 'Mary,' so we go by our middle names. Have you met Elyse?"

Both of them turned to look at Elyse, and Clint caught her off guard by moving toward her and taking her arm. "Yes, I have. In fact, I—"

"Paul introduced us at the door," Elyse cut in quickly. "Why don't you three go into the family room, where it's more comfortable. I'll make some coffee."

She didn't know what Clint had intended to say, but if he planned to tell Paul and Liz he'd been spying on them, she had to stop him. That would be the final humiliation for her genteel sister and would make her all the more determined not to continue her relationship with Paul.

"Well, I—" Liz started, but Paul closed the gap between them and put his arm around her waist.

"Come on, sweetheart," he said. "This is going to take a while. We might as well have a soft place to sit."

Liz allowed him to walk her out of the kitchen, like a sleepwalker being guided back to bed. *Or a sheep being led to the slaughter,* Liz thought grimly.

As soon as they were out of the room, Elyse pulled away from Clint. "Elyse," he said huskily, and reached out to her.

"I'd rather you didn't touch me, *Senator Sterling*," she said icily.

He dropped his arm and sighed. "I don't blame you for being upset, but I'll explain everything in a few minutes. I know it's a lot to ask, but could you hold off making judgments until you've heard what I have to say?"

She had to admit he was a good actor. Probably part of the makeup of a politician. He really did look repentant.

"I'm afraid not," she snapped. "I've pretty much figured it out, anyway. You were using me to get information about Liz."

"That's not true," he said anxiously. "I thought it was you Paul was seeing. The names—"

"Ah, yes, the old problem of our similar names." She glared at him. "I don't like people who lie to me, Senator. Especially men who are supposed to represent me in the state legislature. I'm not interested in your explanation, but if you have a shred of decency you won't tell either Paul or Liz what you've been up to. My sister is a very proper school teacher. She believes in setting a good example for her students, and she'd be shattered if she thought Paul's family was sneaking around having her investigated."

Clint muttered an expletive, but she didn't pause. "If it's me you're worried about, if the fact that Liz has a sister who sleeps around and got herself pregnant is going to contaminate your family honor and political reputation, then—"

"Dammit, Elyse! Stop that!" Clint's roar must have been heard all over the house as he reached out and folded her in his arms.

She tried to pull away, but his hold was unbreakable. "Don't fight me," he said through clenched teeth. "Just listen."

He held her so she couldn't get away while he swiftly enumerated his reasons for feeling it was necessary to know more about the woman Paul was seeing. She gradually relaxed as his story began to make a rather botched-up kind of sense.

"I admit I did everything wrong," he said in conclusion. "It just never occurred to me you weren't the Mary E. Haley Paul was seeing. He even gave me your business card tonight when he asked me to follow him here."

Elyse nodded against his shoulder. "He asked for some to distribute among his friends after he saw the shop. But of course it has Liz's address and phone number, too, since we live together."

He cuddled her closer and stroked his big fingers through her soft auburn curls. "You're trembling," he murmured. "I'm sorry I've upset you so. I seem to have a special talent for it. Can't we wipe the slate clean and start over again?''

Elyse had succumbed to the feel of his arms around her, found refuge in the strength of his hard body but his question snapped her back to reality, and once more she tried to push away from him. ''That won't be necessary, Senator.'' Her tone was all business. ''Now that you have the sisters straight, you can deal with Liz directly.''

She took a step back, and this time he let her go. ''You'd better join Paul and Liz. They're waiting for you,'' she said as she turned away. ''The family room is right across the hall. I'll bring the coffee in later.''

She kept her back to him as she walked to the sink and started running the water, but she knew exactly how long he stood there looking after her and the moment he turned and walked out of the room.

Elyse plugged in the coffee maker and leaned against the counter. Clint was right; she was trembling.

She stalled for half an hour, then put the glass coffee carafe on a tray with cream, sugar, mugs and a plate of cookies and carried it to the family room. As she approached the open door she heard Liz saying, ''Wouldn't make so much difference if we were both ten years older, but twenty-six is still very young for a man, and thirty-six is definitely mature for a woman. No, listen to me, Paul. I may not even be able to give you the children you want. A lot of women in their thirties are finding that after postponing childbearing for so long, they're unable to conceive.''

''Sweetheart, don't borrow trouble.'' It was Paul, and he sounded a little frantic. ''We'll worry about that if the problem ever arises—''

Elyse walked into the room. Paul and Liz were seated on the couch, engaged in the heated debate, and Clint was sitting in the upholstered chair, saying nothing, letting them talk.

He jumped up when Elyse came in. "Here, let me help." He took the tray from her and set it on the coffee table.

"I'm sorry," Elyse said as she poured. "I didn't mean to interrupt." She handed a mug to Liz and another one to Paul.

"That's all right," Clint answered as he reached for his mug. "It's time for a break." His glance returned to the tray. "Didn't you bring a cup for yourself?"

"Oh, no, I'll just get my sewing basket and go back to the kitchen. I have some hemming and other handwork to do."

Both Paul and Liz protested as she crossed the room and picked up the large basket that sat on the floor beside the rocking chair. Clint was more agreeable. "Good idea. I'll go with you. These two don't need me anymore. They're at least discussing the problem now." He took her arm and walked with her out of the room.

Elyse hadn't anticipated this turn of events. She didn't want to spend time with Clint . . . with Senator Sterling. Her anger welled as she remembered what he'd done. If he'd honestly thought she was the one his brother was interested in, then why hadn't he simply told her who he was and asked the questions that bothered him?

Deception was a frightening thing, and she wanted nothing to do with anyone who practiced it.

Clint set the basket beside the chair he held for Elyse, and she sat down and rummaged in it to find her needle, thread and the peach-and-cream ruffled doll dress she was working on. Clint took the chair beside her, and for a moment neither spoke as she threaded her needle and he sipped at his hot coffee.

"I would have come to see you tonight even if Paul hadn't asked me to intercede for him," Clint finally said. "I'd have come sooner, but I was on the East Coast. I had no intention of leaving things the way they were between us on Sunday."

"I'm sure you didn't. It's difficult to get information from a person if that person's not speaking to you."

He sighed. "Elyse, don't. You have every right to be furious with me, but I'm trying my best to apologize. What I did was wrong, and I can only plead temporary insanity, but when I heard that Paul was being seen with still another woman I just assumed—"

He broke off and drained his coffee cup. "I've told you about his problem with women, and I had no reason to think this one was any different. Another spate of publicity like last time, and both our careers could be in trouble. Paul still has to pass his bar exam, and I'm running for reelection. In both cases moral character is important."

Damn him, he was stirring up feelings she didn't want stirred up. Why didn't he just leave her alone? Even if she forgave him—and in the interest of family harmony she'd have to if Paul and Liz got back together—it was not only pointless but dangerous to have tender feelings for him. He wasn't interested in her as anything but a possible sister-in-law—and maybe another voter.

The needle slipped and jabbed her fingers, and she winced. "You didn't tell Liz and Paul we'd met before, did you?"

"No. If you think Liz shouldn't know, then I won't tell her, but I'd really prefer to have everything out in the open now." The corners of his mouth turned up in a small grin. "As you know, I'm not good at intrigue."

In spite of her efforts not to, she couldn't help smiling with him. "You're probably right, but if things go wrong this time we'll both be to blame." She glanced down and gasped. "Oh, darn!"

"What's the matter?" Clint's grin was gone, replaced by a look of concern.

Elyse held up her hand to expose one finger with blood smeared on the tip. "I pricked my finger, and it bled on the delicate material. I'm not at all sure I can get the stain out."

He reached out and took her hand, and guided it to his mouth. "Poor little finger," he said softly, and gently licked it before placing it against his lips.

Elyse felt the tingle all the way to her toes, with emphasis on several extremely intimate places in between. Good heavens, she'd never dreamed that a finger could be an erogenous zone!

Before she could gather her scattered wits and pull away, he carefully folded her fingers into her palm and nestled the loose fist in his big one. "Such little hands to be so talented," he murmured. "They not only fashion exquisite dolls, they soothe a small daughter's fears and hurts. I'll bet they could drive a man mad."

The tingle turned into pinprick flames, and Elyse was in imminent danger of melting. No man had ever affected her this way before with just a touch and a few huskily spoken words. She had an overwhelming urge to find out just what her hands *could* do to him.

Her gaze was drawn irresistibly to his thigh resting so close to her own. If she moved her leg just a little, it would brush against the fine wool trousers that encased his firm leg.

She felt a gentle tug on her arm as he pulled her toward him, then the hot flush of embarrassment as her face flamed. He was seducing her—and without even half trying.

She jerked her hand from his and jumped up, scattering thread and fabric on the floor. "Go away, Clint," she rasped. "I don't want you here. Either go back into the other room with Paul and Liz or go home, but stay away from me. I'll try to get along with you for Liz's sake, but keep your hands off me."

He rose, too, and stood behind her. "I'm not sure I can," he said simply. "Turn around, Elyse."

His tone had a hypnotic effect, and she turned as if she had no choice in the matter. Again they were so close they were almost touching.

"I'm going to take your hand again," he said. "I won't make a pass, so please don't pull away."

As he spoke he reached down for her hand. His own was warm and strong and sent electric sparks up her arm. He brought it up between them and tucked it inside the expensive coat of his dark blue suit on the left side of his chest and held it there. She could feel his heart pounding.

"You see what you do to me?" It seemed to her the pounding speeded up beneath her palm. "I couldn't fake that, and there's no reason I'd want to. It's not pleasant for a man to be aroused by a woman who has nothing but contempt for him. If I could turn off my feelings, I would."

She looked up at him, and there was a painful brooding expression on his thoroughly masculine face. "Last weekend when we were together I was nearly torn apart with guilt because I thought you were the woman my brother was interested in, and I couldn't control the tender, protective feelings you inspired in me. The need to see you, hear your voice, keep you close.''

He continued to hold her hand against his chest as he slid his other arm around her waist and carefully drew her to him. ''I could have found out all I needed to know in just a few hours, but I couldn't bring myself to break the tenuous connection I had with you. I told myself you couldn't be as sweet and loving as you seemed to be, therefore I had to keep seeing you until I'd unveiled the kind of avaricious schemer Paul usually attracts. I couldn't admit you were a godsend for my brother—exactly the kind of woman he needed—because then I'd have to step out of the picture and give you to him.''

As he talked, Elyse found her head drawn to his shoulder, and she snuggled her face against the side of his neck. His heart jumped under her hand, and his arm tightened around her waist, but he continued to speak.

''By the time we left the zoo in Sacramento on Sunday, I was convinced you were everything you seemed to be, and I knew I had to stay away from you and give Paul my blessing. Then, when we stopped for lunch and I questioned you about your dates, you told me you didn't have many and there was no special man in your life. I thought you were lying. You had to be, because in my great wisdom I knew you were going out with Paul.''

He turned his head and kissed her exposed cheek. ''It never once occurred to me I might have been investigating the wrong woman all along. I didn't even consider the idea I might have made a mistake.'' His tone was self-deprecating. ''God, I didn't realize I'd started believing my own campaign publicity. The relief I felt when Paul introduced your sister as the woman he loved was almost overwhelming.''

His lips brushing her cheek released shivers down her spine, and she moved her head to rub her face in the soft wool that covered his broad shoulder. He smelled of fabric and soap and a fresh, woodsy shaving lotion.

When she spoke, her question had nothing to do with his long involved explanation and took them both by surprise. "Have you ever been married, Clint?"

She felt him relax slightly, and there was a trace of amusement in his voice as he answered. "No, never."

She pondered that for a moment. "I was going to be married once. The date was set, the invitations mailed and my white satin dress hanging in the closet wrapped in protective covering."

Clint waited a moment for her to go on. When she didn't he asked, "What happened?"

She took a deep breath, then let it out. "Three days before the wedding he collapsed and died of a heart attack. Two weeks later I found out I was pregnant."

She felt his hand stroking through her hair. "I'm sorry," he whispered against her ear, and compassion vibrated in his tone.

"So am I, but I have Janey, and she makes life beautiful."

For a few minutes they stood in silence, savoring their closeness. Then she asked another question. "Were you ever in love?"

Elyse was surprised at her boldness. She didn't usually ask such personal questions, but never before had the answers been so important to her. Neither had she ever volunteered information about her aborted wedding.

Clint didn't seem to mind. There was no resentment in his voice when he answered. "Yes, once."

"Did—did you lose her?"

"Yes, but not by death. She went away." He didn't explain further.

She turned her head again and trailed kisses along his jaw. "That must have been terribly painful for you."

He leaned into her lips, encouraging her to continue. "It was, but eventually I learned to live with the pain, and then it became more bearable."

With the slightest turn of both their heads their mouths met and clung. She moved her arms to encircle his neck, and he put both arms around her waist but didn't attempt to deepen the kiss. It was warm and tender and a little moist, and Elyse was lost in its sweetness.

She'd dreamed of an embrace like this—one of deep caring laced with, but not overcome by, passion.

Clint's hands stayed at her waist until one slid down her hip to push her against him. It was then that she realized it was determination, not disinclination, that was holding him back. He was urgently aroused, and she was rapidly becoming so.

They broke the kiss by mutual consent, but he continued to hold her. When their breathing had returned to normal, he said, "I haven't had dinner yet. Let's go find someplace to eat. Liz and Paul will be here with Janey."

Elyse wanted to go with him, and her first inclination was to say yes, but then her common sense resurfaced. He was a nice man, but he was way out of her league, and she was already becoming too fond of him. Her feelings were heightening too fast. Better to end things now. She wasn't sure she could survive a second heartbreak.

Reluctantly she took her arms from around his neck and stood back, breaking his hold on her. "Thank you, but I've already eaten," she said, "and I have an early appointment tomorrow with a customer who wants a custom-designed doll, so I'm going to bed."

He looked disappointed but didn't argue. "Perhaps it's just as well," he said, instead.

He tipped her pointed chin up with his finger and kissed her lightly on the lips. "Good night, little doll. I'll call you." He turned and walked away from her. "I can see myself out," he called over his shoulder.

Clint sat in the all-night chain restaurant on Main Street, just down the steep hill and around the corner from the Haley home, and contemplated the club sandwich the waitress had brought him. He hadn't realized it would be so huge. It nearly covered the platter-sized plate, and the remaining space was piled with thick french fries. If he ate all that, he'd have trouble sleeping.

Not that it mattered. He wasn't going to get much sleep anyway; he was still too worked up from his kitchen encounter with Elyse. He was high on the feel and the scent and the taste of her, and his loins ached with the need for more.

He shifted, trying to get comfortable. Damn, she'd really unhinged him, and it was his own fault. He should have apologized and kept his hands off her. He was too old to be playing with fire.

He bit into one of the sandwich quarters. Actually, to be truthful, he'd have to admit the time spent with Elyse in his arms was worth all the frustration he was feeling. She was a special lady, and he believed her now when she said she didn't date often. She'd been skittish, uneasy with him until he'd understood and taken things step by step.

When she'd finally relaxed, her response had been all he'd ever hoped for and more. She was shy but not afraid; willing, but only within the bounds of her moral standard; and generous enough to give as well as take.

Elyse Haley was a threat to his hard-won serenity. For the first time since Dinah had left, he'd met a woman who could get under the protective armor he'd so carefully constructed and stir his emotions. He didn't want that, couldn't chance it.

He'd been too badly scarred the last time. He was no longer capable of true love. Dinah had done real emotional damage, and in the end he'd do the same thing to Elyse. She'd already had one tragic love affair; he wasn't going to doom her to another.

It was five days before Elyse heard from Clint again. Five days of listening for the phone to ring, of watching the street in front of the house for a cream Cadillac, of rushing to the door when the bell rang, then trying to pretend she didn't care when it wasn't him.

By Monday she'd finally accepted the fact that he wasn't going to call. That's the way she'd wanted it, so why mope around and feel depressed? Senator Clinton Sterling was too old, too sophisticated, too rich and too powerful to be interested in a woman with an illegitimate daughter.

She washed off the breakfast dishes at the kitchen sink and stacked them in the dishwasher. A smile curved her mouth as she picked up the bowl with the soft-boiled egg stains. At least Liz was happy again and making a valiant effort to lose a few of the pounds she'd put on over the past couple of years.

Liz and Paul had arrived at a compromise Wednesday night. She'd agree to date him again if he would

forget about marriage—at least for the time being.
They'd been out together several times since, and after
they'd left Saturday night, Liz hadn't come home until
Sunday evening.

It wasn't an ideal situation. They were crazy in love
and Elyse was sure that neither of them would be content with this arrangement for long, but it bought them
time to consider both the problems and the joys of an
unconventional pairing. She wished them happiness.

Janey was in nursery school and Elyse was busy in her
attic workshop when the phone rang. She was pouring
slip into head molds and didn't interrupt her work but
waited until she was finished to answer.

"Good morning," said the baritone voice at the other
end.

It was Clint, and a flash of heat left Elyse feeling
weak.

She swallowed. "Good morning, Clint." Good, her
voice not only worked, but it was smooth and cool.

"Am I interrupting anything?"

"I'm molding doll heads." She wanted him to know
she had other things to do besides sit around waiting for
him to call.

"Sorry, I won't keep you but a minute," he said. "I'm
taking part in a panel discussion at CSUS Thursday
night at seven, and there's a reception afterward. Will
you go with me?"

California State University Sacramento. The school
she'd attended for two years before she'd had to drop
out to take on the more important role of mother. It
would be fun to go back, but... "Oh, Clint, I don't—"

"Please come," he interrupted. "You'd be doing me
a big favor. It's been a long time since I was in my teens

and early twenties, and I'm not sure I'll know how to talk to these kids.'' He chuckled. ''You're just the right age to translate for me.''

She felt let down. He wanted her along because she could be of use to him. ''I only had two years of college, Clint. I don't speak the language, either. You'd better find somebody—''

''You'll do just fine, and I don't want anybody else.'' He was serious now. ''This is a community services thing, and it's being held in the student union building. There's a snack bar there. I'll pick you up a little early and we can have a sandwich or something first.''

His tone told her he wasn't going to accept any excuses. ''Well, all right,'' she said, ''but there's no need for you to drive all the way from your office in Sacramento to Placerville to get me. I can meet you on the first floor of the student union.''

Clint hesitated. ''But then you'd have to drive all the way back up there alone after dark.''

Elyse was buoyed by his protectiveness toward her. ''Oh, come now, Clint,'' she teased, ''I'm a big girl. I've been known to stay out after dark before. I'll be on campus by six-thirty. Is that early enough?''

''Well, okay, but I'll drive behind you all the way home.'' He paused for a moment, then lowered his voice to a murmur. ''Elyse?''

''Yes?'' She sounded breathless.

''I've missed you. It's going to be a long time until Thursday. Don't let me down, please.''

She gripped the phone to keep her hand from shaking. ''I won't. I promise.''

Thursday did indeed take forever to arrive. Then when it did the day sped by and left her rushing to get ready.

What did a woman wear when being escorted to a forum by a state senator? Should she dress like a college girl, since she'd be on campus, or like a politically sophisticated businesswoman, which she definitely wasn't? In the end she decided to go as Mary Elyse Haley, mother, doll maker and novice senatorial date.

She chose a blue-and-white-striped cotton dress with a full skirt, long full sleeves, and white collar, cuffs and belt. It was prim, but pretty and stylish.

She spotted Clint as soon as she walked through the door of the student union building. He was talking to a tall thin balding man, but his gaze meshed with hers and he motioned her to come and join them.

He watched her as she crossed the room, then took her arm when she stopped beside him and smiled down at her. "Thank you for coming," he murmured before turning his attention to the other man. "Elyse, I'd like you to meet Dr. Grant Lowell, who's head of the political science department. Grant, this is Elyse Haley."

They shook hands, and Elyse said, "I remember you, Dr. Lowell. I was a student here about four years ago."

The three of them exchanged small talk for a few minutes before Clint and Elyse were able to break away and head for the coffee shop. He pressed Elyse's arm against him as they moved across the room. "You look like one of your own dolls," he told her, and his voice was soft with admiration. "I'm afraid you're going to prove to be a major distraction."

Elyse's doubts clutched at her. "Oh, Clint, I'm sorry. Should I have worn something else?" She looked around to see what the other women in the building were wearing.

"Honey, you distract me just by being in the same room. It wouldn't matter what you wore, but tonight you look especially appealing. I'd give anything to have you alone for a few minutes." His tone was low and seductive, and she shivered.

Chapter Four

Clint and Elyse had almost reached the student union coffee shop, when a young man in jeans and a sweatshirt stopped them. "Excuse me, but aren't you Senator Sterling?"

Clint nodded and put out his hand. "Yes, I am."

They shook hands, and the other man identified himself as a constituent and launched into a rambling discussion of a bill coming up in the legislature that he wanted passed. Clint tried several times to interrupt, but the enthusiastic student was determined to present his argument before he was stopped.

When he finally wound down, Clint thanked him for presenting his opinion and promised to weigh it before voting. The man walked away, and Clint looked at his watch and groaned. "I'm sorry, but I can't very well brush off a voter just before an election, and now I'm not going to have time to eat." He reached into his pocket and pulled out his wallet. "Here, you go have something and join us later upstairs.

He extracted some bills and offered them to her, but she shook her head. "No, that's all right. I'm not very hungry—I had a late lunch. I'd rather stay with you."

He put his arm around her waist and hugged her to his side before releasing her. "I'm glad," he said as they headed for the open staircase in the middle of the room. "I promise we'll have dinner when this is over."

There were three state senators sitting at the table in the front of the comfortably filled room. Each senator had a bill pending in the legislature and was there to discuss it. Elyse had known from news reports that there was a gun-control bill up for consideration, but she hadn't realized that her senator, Clint Sterling, had written it.

Gun control was a highly controversial subject, and although Clint repeatedly stated the legislation was aimed at handguns, the so-called Saturday night specials, and wouldn't interfere with the hunters or antique gun collectors, the questions and comments became loud and threatening and finally had to be cut off so the last speaker could make his presentation.

Clint handled himself with politeness and poise, but Elyse was shaken. This wasn't just polite haggling, and a couple of the men had gotten ugly. Was Clint in actual physical danger? There were a lot of crazies running around loose. The thought struck something akin to terror in her.

Afterward refreshments were served in another room, and soft music was played on a portable stereo. The senator from the Bay area was alone, but the one from Sacramento was accompanied by his wife, a pretty woman in her early thirties.

At first Clint kept Elyse by his side, but he was so besieged by people wanting to talk to him that eventually she wandered away and he didn't seem to notice. She stopped by the refreshment table, placed a few hors d'oeuvres on a small plate and found a corner where she could watch without being obvious.

She was joined a short time later by the wife of the senator from Sacramento, a tall willowy blonde named Reba Ogden, with the bearing of a model and an instinct for survival in the political jungle.

"You look lonely and a little frightened," Reba said with a sympathetic smile. "Is this your first date with a politician running for office?"

Elyse returned the smile nervously. "Is it that obvious?"

"Only to a seasoned veteran like me. Clint's a nice guy. Have you known him long?"

Elyse was a political innocent. All she knew about state politics was what she occasionally read in the headlines or saw in a quick news story on television. She hadn't even recognized Clint, and he represented her district, so she was uneasy about answering questions about her association with him. One thing she did know, and that was that simple statements could be twisted all out of proportion.

"Only a couple of weeks," she answered, being deliberately vague. "We're not dating. He's a...um... friend of the family."

"Oh, then you're a volunteer?"

Elyse hadn't the faintest idea what Reba was talking about. "Volunteer?"

The other woman laughed. "No, I can see you're not," she said dryly. "I was talking about a campaign volunteer. People who help out during elections."

Elyse felt the warm flush of embarrassment. "Oh, I guess you can see how naive I am," she said in a small voice. "I'm not even interested in politics. I'd be way out of my element in Clint's life."

Reba eyed her warily. "In that case you'd better stop looking at him with your heart in those big beautiful eyes, or everyone's going to know how you feel about him."

There was kindness in her tone, but her words scorched Elyse with humiliation, and in an involuntary reflex she squeezed her eyes shut and put her hand to her mouth. "I...I don't know what you mean... I wasn't..."

She felt the older woman touch her arm. "Hey, I didn't mean to upset you. Oh, God, you're even younger than I thought. Come on, let's get out of here. I'm sorry. I only meant to warn you." She took Elyse's arm and hurried her toward the door.

They found a comfortable lounge in the area at the top of the stairway, and Elyse dropped down on the sofa, her face still flaming with embarrassment.

Reba sat beside her. "Look," she said, "I'm really sorry. I'm used to senators' wives and girlfriends who are veterans of the wars, so to speak. I didn't realize you were so sensitive. If you're going to be seen with Clinton Sterling you'll have to toughen up a little."

Reba's no-nonsense but caring tone calmed Elyse a little, and she took a deep breath and tried to relax. "I'm not going to be seen with Clint, Mrs. Ogden—"

"Reba," the other insisted.

"All right, Reba. Clint really is just a friend. You see, his brother and my sister are dating, but there's nothing between Clint and me. He just brought me tonight because he figured I was the right age to translate in case he didn't understand the current college slang.''

Reba grunted. "I'm sorry to hear that. Clint needs a woman of his own, preferably a wife. I suppose you've heard about Dinah.''

Elyse blinked. "Dinah?''

"Dinah Jefferson... Oh, damn! Me and my big mouth.'' Reba held up her hand in a dismissive gesture. "Never mind. We'd better be getting back. Those men of ours will be wondering what happened to us.''

"Clint's not...''

"*Your man.*'' Reba finished the sentence for her. "So you've said, but methinks the lady doth protest too much. Clint may be a tad shy when it comes to marriage vows, but he's not a monk, so don't tell me he thinks of you as a little sister. He may be reticent, but he's not blind.''

They returned to the rapidly clearing room, and Clint excused himself from the cluster of students around him and hurried toward them. "So you're the one who stole my girl,'' he said to Reba as he tucked Elyse's hand in the crook of his arm. "I was afraid she'd run off with one of these lecherous male students.''

The warmth from his touch wafted all the way up her arm as Reba laughed. "She's just spent the past twenty minutes trying to convince me she's not your girl.''

Clint looked down at Elyse, and there was amusement in his green eyes. "In that case I'll have to think of a way to convince her.''

"Do that,'' Reba said, then turned away to join her husband.

Clint glanced at the refreshment table. "Did you get something to eat?''

"Uh-hum,'' she said. "Did you?''

"No. We'll stop somewhere on the way home and have dinner." He glanced at his watch and frowned. "I hope it's not too late."

Elyse had a thought. "If an omelet, hash browns and muffins is enough for you, I could fix them at home."

He looked pleased. "Are you sure you don't mind?"

"Actually, I'd prefer it. We've been surrounded by people all evening. I'd like to have you alone for a change."

The words were hardly out before she blushed a deep red.

Clint's eyes darkened with pleasure, and he pressed her arm against his side. "Keep talking like that," he murmured huskily, "and I'm going to kiss you right here in front of all these people."

Their gazes held, and she knew her heart was once more in her eyes for him to see. She looked down, and in doing so inadvertently brushed her cheek against his sleeve.

"Come on," he said raggedly, "let's go."

Without saying goodbye to anybody he turned and guided her out of the room.

The lobby of the main floor was brightly lit, as was the parking lot. Clint walked Elyse to her elderly Ford Mustang and saw her safely inside. "Drive carefully," he said through the open window. "I'll be right behind you."

Traffic on the freeway was light, and it took less than forty-five minutes to get to Placerville. Elyse drove her car into the driveway, leaving Clint to park at the curb, then met him at the front porch. She handed him the key, and he unlocked the door and pushed it open.

The hallway was dark, but a light shone from the family room at the end. Clint shut the door and took

Elyse into his arms. "I've been wanting to do this ever since you walked into the student union building," he whispered huskily as his face lowered to hers.

He covered her mouth with his, and her palms slid up his arms and shoulders before linking around his neck. His arms tightened around her, and the tip of his tongue slowly outlined her lips until they parted slightly. But instead of pursuing his advantage, he placed tiny kisses at either side of her mouth, then trailed more down the side of her throat, lingering just above her white collar.

Elyse shivered, and her fingers stroked through his thick black hair as she tilted her head to give him easier access. The darkness that surrounded them offered an intimate privacy and she melted against him, willing him to continue the sweet seduction with his mouth, his hands, which caressed the small of her back and his long hard body, which fit so hungrily against hers.

"There were times tonight," he murmured as he lifted his head and rubbed his face in her hair, "when I'd gladly have given up my seat in the Senate to be a private citizen again—to be able to kiss my lovely lady in the middle of a crowded room without having to worry about exposing her to unpleasant gossip. I didn't even dare hold your hand, and my fingers itched to touch you."

His soft-spoken words left her giddy with happiness. "Really?" she asked, a touch of wonder in her tone.

"You mean you didn't feel it?" He sounded disappointed. "It seemed to me we were generating enough electricity to set off sparks."

"Oh, I felt it," she hastened to reassure him, "but I didn't know if you did. You seemed so comfortable and at ease. I was afraid it was one-sided."

He kissed the top of her head. "Well, now you know better, don't you?"

She tipped her face up to him. "Yes, and I'm awfully glad."

He groaned and hugged her closer. "Oh, God, sweetheart, you're such a temptation. I think we'd better go fix those omelets before we get sidetracked any further."

Just then Liz's voice called from the family room. "Elyse, is that you?"

Simultaneously the light went on in the hall and Liz appeared in the doorway. Elyse tried to pull away from Clint, but he held her fast.

"Oh, sorry," Liz said, and turned away.

"That's okay," Clint called after her. "We need a chaperon. Stay and have a bite to eat with us."

Elyse cooked the omelet, Clint fried the hash browns and Liz baked the muffins, while Elyse and Clint told Liz about their evening at the college.

"I knew gun control was a controversial subject, but I hadn't realized it was quite so explosive," Elyse said, and again felt the quiver of fear that had attacked her earlier. "The cords actually stood out on that one man's neck he was so mad—and his language..." She left that to Liz's imagination.

Clint reached over and took Elyse's hand. "I'm sorry. I shouldn't have invited you along. I forgot that you aren't used to that sort of thing."

She squeezed his fingers. "Oh, no, I'm glad you took me, but are you sure you're safe? A couple of those men seemed pretty violent."

She saw Clint and Liz exchange a look before he answered. "People like that are mostly talk. They blow off a lot of steam, and you can be sure they're not going to vote for me, but they're relatively harmless.''

The qualifying "mostly" and "relatively" were noted by Elyse, but she didn't pursue the subject. She didn't want Clint thinking of her as Liz's little sister who had to be protected from life's harsher realities.

Clint adroitly changed the subject. "How's the teaching going, Liz? I imagine most of the students are afflicted with spring fever.''

Liz made a face. "Aren't they always? It lasts all year long, but from now to the end of the term I'll be lucky if they just study enough to pass their exams.''

Clint chuckled. "How true. Do you like teaching?''

"I love it," Liz said. "I think I was born to be a teacher. It's such a challenge, and so rewarding when I can get a student excited about learning. I've had young people who started high school as marginal students and graduated four years later in the top ten percent of their class.'' She shook her head. "Obviously I can't take all the credit for that, but somewhere along the line they were touched with a thirst for knowledge. It's exhilarating to think I had a small part in it.''

"I'm sure your part was a large one," Clint said. "I only wish Paul had gotten a teacher like you. He thinks studying's a waste of time. Thank God he's exceptionally bright, or he'd never have gotten through law school. I'm not sure he's ever going to settle down and pass the bar.''

A look of indignation crossed Liz's face. "Paul is much more serious than you give him credit for, Senator. He's been studying hard for that exam. I've been helping him when I can, and he's making a lot of progress.''

Clint's eyes widened with surprise. "I didn't know that. We don't see a lot of each other, but up until a few months ago he wasn't doing much of anything but goofing off. If he's studying now, then it's got to be your good influence."

Liz blushed. "I've never known him as anything but a responsible adult. He told me about the woman he'd been seeing who caused such a furor when they broke up. He's really been trying to do the right thing since then. Give him a little credit, Clint. He's so anxious to please you."

"I'll be happy to," Clint answered, "just as soon as he shows me he's earned it." His expression softened. "You're a special lady, Liz, just as he said you were. I hope he can convince you to marry him."

Liz's earlier blush deepened. "He can't," she said curtly, and pushed back her chair. "If you'll excuse me, I have an early parent conference in the morning, so I'm going to bed."

Clint stood. "Liz—" he began, but she was already out of the room. "Damn." he muttered as he sat down again. "I didn't mean to upset her."

"It's not that," Elyse assured him as he once more took her hand. "This is something she'll have to work out for herself. She loves Paul very much, but she has this deep-seated prejudice about marrying a man so much younger. She's convinced he's merely infatuated with the novelty of dating an older woman and that before long a younger one will come along and capture his fancy."

Clint frowned. "Ordinarily, I couldn't assure her that she's wrong. Paul has never been attracted to one girl for long. He likes playing the field. On the other hand, he's never before asked a woman to marry him. I don't think he'd do that unless he knew he loved her and wanted to settle down."

His thumb traced small circles in Elyse's palm. "Liz is probably wise to be apprehensive. Not because of the age difference, but because of the difference in their personalities. Maybe she's not sure she wants to marry an overgrown boy in the hope that he'll eventually grow up and accept the responsibilities of a man."

Elyse's fingers curled over Clint's adventurous thumb in an effort to halt the restless message its scrawlings were sending to the rest of her body. "As Liz said, she's never seen that side of Paul. Neither of us has. He's always been dependable, attentive and loving with her. I think it was love at first sight for both of them."

"I hope so," Clint said as he raised her hand to his mouth. "Liz is the best thing that ever happened to my brother." He planted tiny kisses on each of her fingers. "And you," he said softly, "are the sweetest thing that ever happened to me."

He turned her hand over and kissed her palm, then held it to his cleanly shaven cheek. "Soft warm hands, soft warm lips, I can't get enough of the touch of either one."

He leaned closer and brushed her lips with his own. His miniseduction was taking her breath away. She smiled and tenderly nibbled at his chin, while she brought her other hand up to stroke his other cheek. He made a growling sound and leaned against her caressing fingers. "If I don't leave right now," he said unsteadily, "you'll have to throw me out to get rid of me."

The idea of throwing him out was preposterous, and the thought of him staying was an intriguing fantasy that stirred desires Elyse thought had died with Jerry. She knew herself to be a highly sensuous woman, and Clint was sparking sensations she had kept banked for five years. She wasn't sure she could control them if they burst into flame, and Clint Sterling could definitely inflame her.

He didn't give her a vote, but once more brushed his lips against hers, then pushed his chair back to stand. "Thank you for going with me tonight," he said, "and for feeding me. A friend of mine gave me two tickets to the Sacramento Symphony concert for Sunday afternoon. If you'll go with me I swear on my honor that I'll buy you dinner afterward. No more excuses or evasions." He paused. "Will there be any problem getting a baby-sitter for Janey?"

She would have gone with him no matter where he proposed to take her, and his concern for her daughter touched her deeply. "I'd love to. Thank you. I'm partial to classical music...even without the inducement of dinner," she added facetiously. "Baby-sitters are no problem. Liz has several students who are mature, well trained and happy to earn the extra money."

He put his arm around her waist and led her up the hall to the door with him. "The concert starts at three. I'll pick you up at noon for brunch."

He put both arms around her and cradled her close. "Good night, angel," he murmured, and captured her mouth with his own. This time there was no hesitation and no playfulness. It was the kiss of a man hungry for the woman in his arms and not too sure how much longer his carefully leashed control would hold.

Stopping the kiss with obvious effort, he turned and walked out the door, leaving Elyse slumped against the wall, her heart pounding and her body fully awakened and throbbing.

It wasn't until later, when she was snuggled between the cool cotton sheets in her antique brass bed, that Reba Ogden's words, spoken earlier that evening, returned to gnaw at her. *I suppose you've heard about Dinah—Dinah Jefferson?*

Who was Dinah Jefferson, and where did she fit into Clint's life?

Clint moved restlessly in his bed. He felt like a teenager who'd gotten all worked up and then been frustrated when the girl responsible had said no. Only he was a mature man, and it was his own fault he was frustrated. He hadn't even asked the question.

He turned onto his other side in the king-size bed and punched his pillow. If it was anyone else, he'd be tempted to take her to bed a few times and get her out of his system, but he couldn't do that with Elyse. She was nothing like the women he usually dated.

Damn. How had he ever allowed himself to get involved with a woman almost half his age and vulnerable as a child? He had a gut feeling he could seduce her without half trying, and that knowledge was driving him crazy. She was so open and guileless about her feelings. If she'd made an effort to hide the yearning that flared in her expressive brown eyes when she looked at him, it wasn't working.

Elyse was a walking time bomb. A passionate woman who had sublimated and denied that passion far too long. He could capture her with a touch, melt her with a kiss—and if he didn't stop it, he was going to lose every shred of control and ravage her.

With a shuddering sigh he sat up and swung his legs over the side of the bed. He ran his hands through his hair, then buried his face in them. The problem was, he didn't want to stop. He was addicted not only to the touching and the kissing, but to the husky resonance of her voice, the fresh clean scent of her fragrance and the unconsciously seductive way she walked, like a dancer expressing herself through motion.

She was a powerful temptation, and he wanted her worse than he'd ever wanted any woman before...except Dinah.

And there was the nerve center of the dilemma. If Dinah ever came back to him, he wouldn't need Elyse or any other woman.

The concert on Sunday was conducted by Carter Nice and played in Sacramento's impressive Community Theater. It was the last performance of the season, and the house was sold out. By the time Clint found a parking space in the busy downtown area surrounding the convention center, which housed the theater, the performance was about to begin.

Their seats were in the orchestra section near the stage and Elyse was surprised to discover that Senator and Mrs. William Ogden had the ones next to them.

"Bill, Reba, I didn't know we'd run into you here," Clint said as he shook hands with the senator and kissed Reba on the cheek. "I believe you met Elyse the other night at the college."

Bill Ogden took Elyse's hand and Reba nodded. "Yeah, she's the one who's not your girl," she said with a wink at Elyse.

Clint grinned. "I'm working on it," he said as the lights dimmed and Carter Nice strode onto the stage. He took his place on the podium amid appreciative applause, and Clint and Elyse settled into their thickly cushioned seats. The baton was lowered, and the opening strains of Beethoven's *Eroica* captured the audience.

Clint reached for Elyse's hand and held it while the magic of the music surrounded them. She turned her head to watch him. Even in the near dark he was a commanding figure. This afternoon he'd worn a dark suit with a pink shirt and maroon-and-pink-striped tie, and he looked dashing. His black hair was cut short and curled naturally on top, and his fair complexion, unusual with raven hair, made his green eyes seem even more intense.

Elyse had worn her new Easter dress, a softly feminine turquoise silk that had evoked a low whistle of approval from Clint, and she had to admit they made an attractive pair.

At intermission the two couples returned to the plush lobby for champagne, and while Clint and Bill stood in line to be served, Reba looked at Elyse and raised one eyebrow. "So what are you translating for Clint this afternoon?" she asked with an impish twinkle in her blue eyes.

Elyse grinned. "Not a darn thing. I'm just enjoying his company."

"Good," Reba said. "Then we can forget all that nonsense about just being friends?"

Elyse's grin receded. "Not really, Reba. Clint's very sweet and attentive, but he hasn't said his feelings go beyond that."

"You mean he hasn't taken you to bed." It was a flat statement.

Elyse felt the color rush to her face. "Reba!"

The other woman frowned. "Sorry, I forgot you're little more than a child..."

"I'm not a child," Elyse replied indignantly. "I'm twenty-four years old, and I have a four-year-old daughter."

Reba blinked. "A daughter? Then you've been married?"

Elyse wished she'd never brought the subject up, but now that she had she wasn't going to be evasive. "No. My fiancé died of a heart attack before I knew I was pregnant."

"Oh, God," Reba sympathized, "that's awful. So it seems you and Clint have more in common than I thought."

Elyse blinked in confusion. "I beg your pardon."

Reba sighed. "He still hasn't told you about Dinah Jefferson, has he?"

Dinah again. Elyse decided it was time she found out just who this mysterious Dinah was. "No, he hasn't," she said, "but I'd appreciate it greatly if you would."

Before Reba could say anything, Clint and Bill returned with their drinks, and a few minutes later the lights dimmed and they made their way back to their seats.

When the concert was over the two couples decided to go to the Ogdens' house in the exclusive Willhagen area on the eastern outskirts of Sacramento for drinks, then later they would join Clint and Elyse for dinner at The Firehouse, a gourmet restaurant in a restored nineteenth-century firehouse in Old Sacramento.

Elyse was impressed with Reba and Bill's luxurious home and said so. "Doesn't the governor live in this area?" she asked.

Bill, a tall, prematurely gray-haired man in his late forties, responded. "Yes, just a few blocks over. Since we no longer have an official governor's mansion, the governor and his wife bought out here when they moved to Sacramento. Talk about security! We all feel safer with the measures that have been taken to protect them.'' He walked to the bar in the den, which they had just entered. ''Now, what's everyone drinking?''

Elyse asked for a screwdriver, and when it and Clint's Scotch on the rocks were poured, Clint led her over to the soft leather couch that faced the fireplace and sat down beside her. Putting his arm around her, he turned her gently until her back was against his chest and his arm circled her waist.

She loved to have him cuddle her like that, but she was uncomfortable doing it in front of the other couple and stiffened in protest. His arm tightened around her. ''It's all right, honey. The Ogdens are long-time friends. They won't gossip about us.''

He looked at Bill and Reba. ''Elyse has a small daughter and a sister who teaches high school in Placerville, and she doesn't want publicity.''

''Relax, Elyse, you're safe here,'' Reba said. ''We're all aware of that particular problem.'' She laughed. ''One time shortly after we were married Bill and I had a humdinger of a quarrel at the race track during the state fair. I'm afraid we got a little loud and I stalked off, furious with him over something I can't even remember now. Well, for the next six months we spent most of our time denying that we were getting a divorce. If it had been John and Jane Doe nobody would have paid the slightest attention, but since it was Senator and Mrs. Ogden the whole state knew about it.''

They all laughed, and Elyse leaned her head against Clint's shoulder and let herself be absorbed in his embrace.

Outwardly he was cool and circumspect. They were sitting so close that their thighs pressed naturally together and his hand rested on her ribs, but since his hand was large and she was small, the length of his thumb nestled beneath her breast, and all her attention seemed breathlessly focused on the two points of contact.

If her back hadn't been snuggled against Clint's chest she wouldn't have known his heartbeat had accelerated and his breathing had become as irregular as her own. He rubbed his cheek in her mass of auburn curls and unobtrusively caressed the underside of her throbbing breast with his thumb. Yet somehow he managed to keep up a lively conversation with their hosts.

Elyse, on the other hand, kept losing the battle to pay attention to what was being said. She was too aware of this kindly man who could so easily crumble all her carefully built defenses. The faint scent of his cologne and the light tickle of his fresh clean breath on her cheek heightened her urge to stroke the thigh that rested so tantalizingly near her own. That fabric that covered it would be soft and expensive, the flesh and muscle under it strong, hard and restless.

The clang of discordant bells snapped her out of her reverie, and Bill and Reba looked at each other and laughed. "You get the door while I get the phone," Reba said, and they both got up and left the room.

When they were out of sight Clint's hand slid up to cover Elyse's breast for one greedy moment before he turned her to face him. "Elyse," he breathed raggedly as his mouth covered hers and his arms crushed her to him.

Even as he devoured her she could sense his tight control and the effort it was costing him to hold back. One hand cupped her waiting breast while the other roamed lovingly over her thigh, but he made no move to pull up her skirt or reach inside her bodice.

For a moment they strained toward each other, then with a deep groan, Clint broke off the kiss and looked at her, his eyes glazed with desire. "We—we'd better slow down," he said unsteadily, "or I'm not going to be responsible for my behavior."

His confession only kindled the flames she was desperately trying to bank. Her arms tightened around his neck. "You don't hear me complaining, do you?" she murmured against his cheek.

He shook his head. "I've never heard you complain about anything. You're the easiest to please woman I've ever known, and I love being with you. You make me feel so...so good, so accepted."

She put her hands on either side of his head and examined his face. His expression was strained with suppressed passion, but his long straight nose, perfectly shaped mouth and high broad forehead were the features of a man with great strength and commitment.

She moistened her dry lips with the tip of her tongue and felt his fingers knead the soft flesh of her buttocks. "You have the most compelling eyes," she said. "They're like...like green fire that singes with a single glance. That's what you do to me. I can't believe you've ever been rejected."

She saw the leap of pain in the fire of those eyes before he closed his lids and buried his face in her shoulder.

A wave of despair swept over her as she held him close. "Oh, God, Clint, I'm sorry. I forgot..."

She had indeed forgotten until that moment his earlier confession that he had once loved a woman who'd left him.

Was that woman Dinah Jefferson?

Chapter Five

Excuse me. Would you two like to spend some time alone?'' Clint and Elyse jumped as one at the sound of Bill Ogden's amused voice.

"Hell, man, you might at least whistle or something,'' Clint grumbled good-naturedly as he straightened but kept a tight grip on Elyse.

"You wouldn't have heard me if I'd set off firecrackers,'' Bill continued happily. "How about a cold shower? Guaranteed to cool you off—''

He was interrupted by Reba's husky voice behind him. "Knock it off, love, or I'll see that you spend some time under that cold shower just to keep you from getting overconfident.'' She winked at Elyse, who by now was red with embarrassment.

Bill chuckled as he turned and put his arm around his stunningly beautiful wife. "Ah, my darling, life with you is anything but predictable, but I think we'd better divert these two until it's time to leave for dinner. Come on out to the garage with me, Clint. I want to show you the 1957 T-Bird I added to my collection of classic cars last week.''

"Gee, thanks, pal," Clint retorted with a sarcastic grin as he reluctantly tore himself away from Elyse and stood. "Just what I was hoping you'd suggest." He leaned down and kissed her flaming face. "Excuse me while I humor this idiot."

The two men ambled out of the room, and Reba grinned as she sat down on the couch with Elyse. "Sorry if Bill embarrassed you," she said. "He loves to tease. He's also happy to have something to tease Clint about. It's been far too long since Clint's shown enough interest in any one woman to be ragged about it." Her grin disappeared. "I hope you're serious about him, Elyse. If you're just stringing him along and intend to dump him later, I'm warning you. You'll have both Bill and me to contend with."

The menacing look Reba shot at her convinced Elyse that the other woman would be a dangerous adversary, but the knowledge was comforting rather than upsetting. These people cared enough about Clint to want to protect him from hurt. Elyse felt the same way.

"I'm not sure getting serious about Clint Sterling is wise," she said slowly. "He told me once he'd been in love with a woman who left him, and you've mentioned someone named Dinah several times. Are they by any chance the same person? And if so, why on earth did she walk out on him? She'll never find another man as kind and sweet and loving—"

"You're absolutely right," Reba interrupted with a sly chuckle. "Sounds like you belong on our team. He's all that and more, and Dinah was very much aware of it. To answer your first question, yes, Dinah Jefferson is the woman he loved, but the second question takes some explaining."

Reba reached for the drink she'd abandoned on the coffee table when she'd left to answer the phone, and sipped it. "Clint met Dinah when she went to work for one of the other senators as an administrative assistant. She, too, came from a family of politicians, only they lived back East somewhere.

"Clint was about thirty-two at the time and had recently been appointed to the Senate to serve out the term of his father, Senator Burton Sterling, who had resigned after suffering a disabling stroke. Clint was ready to settle down with a wife to raise a family, and he fell hard for Dinah."

Those last words rocked Elyse, even though she'd known they were coming. It was selfish, but she didn't like the idea of Clint's being deeply in love with any other woman.

"It's no wonder," Reba continued. "She was gorgeous. One of those tall, cool blondes with a body that fulfills every man's fantasy."

"You mean she looked a lot like you?"

Reba grinned and saluted Elyse with her raised glass. "Flattery will get you absolutely *anything*," she said, "but while I never managed to achieve that look of quiet elegance, Dinah was born with it. She was a lady all the way to her fingertips, and Clint was mesmerized. He couldn't have found a woman more perfectly suited to him if he'd had her hand-tailored. She was the consummate politician's wife. In fact, that's what she'd been until her husband was killed."

Elyse gasped. "She was married!"

"Not at the time she met Clint. She was a widow. Her husband had been an assemblyman in—Maryland, I think it was. Anyway, he was assassinated by a redneck with a gun who didn't like the way he'd voted on a bill."

"Oh, my God!" Elyse whispered, her horror reverberating in her tone. "How awful."

"Yes, it was." There was no levity in Reba now. "It's a terror all wives of public figures live with, and it never gets easier. I don't know how deeply it affected Dinah—she never talked about it—but her very silence on the subject would seem to indicate unresolved emotional stress. She was wild about Clint, though. No one ever doubted that."

"Then why did she leave him? If she loved him why didn't she marry him? I assume he asked her."

"Oh, yes, he asked her, and she even agreed to an engagement, but a couple of months later she packed up and left." Reba sighed, and pushed her silky hair back. "I can't give you any more details because I don't know them. Clint never discusses what happened. But I do know one thing. It damn near destroyed him."

Elyse closed her eyes as the pain rolled over her. Dear, sweet, considerate Clint. How could any woman do a thing like that to him? And why? It just didn't make sense. If Dinah loved him, how could she have wounded him so deeply?

Elyse sighed and settled back into the soft brown leather seat of Clint's car, watching the lit overhead signs appear and disappear as the car moved swiftly along Highway 50, headed for home.

It had been a wonderful day. Not only the concert, the company and the food, but just being with Clint had been stimulant enough to give her a natural high that promised to last indefinitely.

And Clint wasn't immune to her, either. Although there'd been no more embracing after he and Bill had come back from the garage, the magnetism that crackled between Elyse and him made it impossible not to touch. They'd held hands in the back seat of Bill's car on the way to the restaurant, under the table during dinner and again in the car on the way back to the Ogdens' home.

Now Clint glanced at her and murmured, "Tired?"

"No," she said softly. "Just happy."

He reached over and took her hand, then lifted it to his lips. "I hope you're as happy as I am," he said as he placed tiny kisses on her tingling palm. "You, my darling, are the perfect date. Beautiful, intelligent, charming and attentive. All the nice things you say make me feel about ten feet tall."

"I only say what I mean," she said.

He moved her hand down to rest on his thigh, then covered it with his own. She felt his muscles tighten under her palm, and she stroked her fingers lightly over the crisp wool of his trouser leg. He tensed even more, but squeezed her hand in encouragement.

She knew what she was inviting, and she knew she should stop, but when she made a tentative effort to slide her hand from beneath his he applied pressure to keep it there, and she couldn't refuse him. She didn't even want to. It had been so long since she'd experienced the dizzy excitement of arousal—and she'd never felt it so intensely.

Without speaking, Clint removed his hand from hers and gently caressed her thigh. Her leg twitched as a rush of quivering sensations collided in the most intimate recesses of her womanhood. She bit her lip to stifle a gasp, but couldn't keep her fingers from digging into his powerful flesh beneath her hand.

The car swerved slightly, and Clint groaned and removed his hand to grab the steering wheel. "I'm afraid," he said in a voice that was gravelly with frustration, "I need to keep my hands on the wheel and my attention on my driving, or I may run the car right off the road."

Elyse bowed her head. "I'm sorry," she muttered, embarrassed, and clutched both her hands in her lap.

"Sorry? Oh, please don't be sorry," Clint said. He reached for her hand again and once more put it on his leg. "Leave it there," he cautioned as she started to remove it. "I want you to touch me. I need your touch, Elyse. More than you can possibly know."

Again she couldn't bring herself to disappoint him, and her hand stayed firmly where he wanted it as she brushed her cheek against his arm. She was being unwise—there was no doubt about it. But she'd learned five years ago that nothing could be counted on to last forever. Why not be happy while she could and let the future take care of itself?

They drove for a while in silence, and as they approached the turnoff to Cameron Park, where Clint lived, it seemed to Elyse that he slowed down, as if debating the advisability of taking her to his house. If so, he decided against it, because he sped up just before they reached the exit and drove on toward Elyse's home in Placerville.

After a mile or two he spoke. "Did you enjoy the concert?"

She smiled at the memory. "Oh, yes, very much. I often watch the Symphony on television, but this is the first live concert I've heard. It was marvelous. The music just seemed to envelop me, and I got goose bumps every time the man at the timpani rolled those drums.''

Clint chuckled. "I know what you mean. How about dinner? Did you get enough to eat?"

She moaned and rubbed her stomach. "Did I! I may never need to eat again. This is the first time I've been to The Firehouse, but it won't be the last. The food was delicious. I could almost cut the prime rib with my fork."

He leaned over and kissed the top of her head where it lay against his arm. "If you were that impressed we'll do it again."

Elyse resisted the desire to stroke his leg, but let her hand rest lovingly against it. "I like your friends the Ogdens," she said dreamily. "Have you known them long?"

"I've known Bill ever since he was first elected to the Senate sixteen years ago. My dad was a senior senator then, and he sort of took Bill under his wing. Ten years later when I was appointed to fill out Dad's unexpired term, Bill did the same for me. I was best man when he married Reba five years ago."

Elyse was surprised. "Oh, they haven't been married long, then."

Clint turned off the freeway and into Placerville as he spoke. "Bill was married before and has two college-age daughters, but they live in Texas with their mother and her second husband. Reba was an actress doing television commercials in Los Angeles when Bill met her."

The car pulled into the driveway of the Haley home, and Clint turned off the motor and the lights, then reached for Elyse and took her in his arms. "Damn these bucket seats," he grumbled as his arms tightened around her waist in a vain effort to draw her closer.

She grinned as she silently cursed them, too. "I think they were designed as the modern-day chastity belt," she said, putting her arms around his neck. "There have been times when I've been grateful for them, but this isn't one of them."

His mouth closed over hers, and her response was immediate. This was what she'd been longing for all evening: his arms, strong and protective; his lips, firm, warm and ardent, and his scent, musky and masculine.

She ran her fingers through his clean ebony hair, and one of his hands moved up to fondle her breast, which was pressed against his chest. She tipped her head slightly to the side, and he nibbled at her lips in a series of short, intense kisses that had her clutching at his hair and straining to get closer.

It was Clint who finally ended the sweet torment, and he did it almost harshly. "Elyse!" The word was a cross between a moan and a cry as he pushed her away and turned from her to open the car door. "I'll walk you to the porch," he said as he got out of the car.

Landing off balance in her seat, Elyse sat watching him as he stood with his back to her for at least a minute before moving around to her side. She was glad for the delay. She, too, needed time to rouse herself from the daze his lovemaking had induced.

Why had he stopped? He must have known she'd have let him do anything he wanted to with her. Good Lord, what had happened to her celebrated self-control? Wasn't it the woman who was supposed to set the limits, stop things before they got out of hand? She flushed with shame. What must Clint think of her?

When he finally opened her door she scrambled out of the car without taking his helping hand. She took a series of deep breaths as they walked in the cool night air, and her senses calmed down a little.

When they got to the bottom of the steps she remembered the baby-sitter. She turned to Clint and spoke in a voice that faltered. "Um . . . would you mind taking the baby-sitter home? It's on your way. If I do it I'll have to wake Janey and take her with me."

His tone was once more friendly and gentle. "Of course I'll take her home. I don't want you and Janey driving around alone at night."

He walked up the steps with her, but inside the house all was quiet and deserted. Elyse looked at her watch. It was after eleven. "Liz must have gotten home before me," she said. "If you'll wait a minute I'll run up and check."

Upstairs Janey lay stretched out on her small bed clutching a disheveled Cabbage Patch doll. She was sound asleep. Elyse tiptoed in and kissed her daughter's forehead, then knocked softly on Liz's door. When there was no answer she peeked in to find Liz also asleep.

Downstairs she returned to the family room, where Clint stood waiting for her. He must have been watching the doorway, because when she walked through it their gazes collided. Elyse felt her bones start to melt. He looked so . . . so hungry.

He reached for her hand and squeezed it as she cleared her throat. "Both Liz and Janey are asleep," she said, and licked her suddenly dry lips. "Do . . . do you want a drink? Or I could make coffee. . . ."

He pulled lightly on her hand, bringing her closer without ever breaking eye contact. "You know what I want," he said in a husky whisper. "I want you. Now."

With a tiny cry of surrender she walked into his waiting arms.

They took up where they'd left off in the car, wrapped in a tight embrace, mouths locked together, straining to relieve some of the throbbing urgency that had been tormenting them for hours.

For the first time Clint allowed his hands to roam freely, and they slid tenderly over her back and shoulders, her breasts and her buttocks, leaving prickles of fire as they stopped, then moved restlessly on.

Elyse caressed his back, but his suit jacket was in the way. She reached between them and unfastened it so she could feel the flexing muscles beneath his pink shirt. He sighed deeply as her fingers gently massaged him, then moved provocatively up and down his spine. "I've wanted so badly to feel your hands on me," he murmured against her lips.

"It's my pleasure," she whispered back. "You have a strong, solid body, and touching it does the most indecent things to me."

He put both his hands on her bottom and pulled her against him, making her tingle with need. "I don't have to tell you what you do to me," he said, "and have been doing to me ever since we first met. There were times when I thought I'd go mad with frustration."

He was rigid with desire, and she shivered as he moved against her. She reveled in the knowledge that she could do this to him. The power it gave her was heady, but it also robbed her of her reason, her good sense and her ability to resist. She wanted him just as much as he wanted her, and his masculine need overwhelmed her as her body prepared itself for his possession.

He kissed her again, roughly this time, then broke off abruptly and nibbled at her earlobe. "Where's your bedroom?" he asked in a voice gravelly with yearning.

"Upstairs," she answered in a dazed tone.

"Are you protected?"

She blinked and tried to understand the question even as a cold chill swept her. "Protected?"

"Have you taken precautions, or do you want me to?"

Protected? Precautions? My God, *she could get pregnant*! How could she have been so careless—*again*?

She straightened in his arms and pulled back. "No. No, I'm not protected. Oh, Clint, I didn't even think!" The fire that had built in her died as the cold splash of reality and past mistakes drenched it.

Clint was still caught in the urgency of desire and didn't seem to notice her distress. "It's all right," he said, and tried to lead her toward the doorway. "I'm prepared."

Prepared. It sounded so cold. So rehearsed. Was he always "prepared" just in case a desirable woman crossed his path, or had sex simply been the last item in the agenda he'd planned for today? Symphony, dinner, bed. All nice and neat.

She knew she was being unreasonable, but her mind was in turmoil and she had no control over her thoughts. Shock that she could act so irresponsibly, guilt over her earlier unplanned pregnancy and the last remnants of arousal had jumbled her reason and left her depleted and unresponsive.

She felt a tug at her waist. "Elyse, come on. I told you I'd take care of it." Clint was frowning, and there was impatience in his tone.

She pulled back. "Clint, I . . . I can't."

She felt him tense. "You what?"

"I can't. I'm sorry, but—"

"What do you mean, you can't?" The impatience was gone, and his voice was cold.

He didn't understand. How could he? She didn't understand herself. "I just can't," she said disconsolately.

He dropped his arm from around her and stepped away. "I see." His words seemed frozen. "Then why did you let things go so far?"

"Oh, Clint, please—" she cried, desperate to explain, but unable to gather her thoughts into any semblance of order.

"I told you what I wanted," he said, without waiting for her to finish. "You could have refused then."

She could see the rage building in him and hear the disgust in his tone as he continued. "I wouldn't have pushed you into something you didn't want, so why in hell did you wait so long to say no?"

"It's not like that—"

"Never mind," he grated, and turned away from her. "I don't want to hear any excuses."

He stomped out of the room and slammed the front door behind him before she could pull herself together to follow him.

Elyse didn't go to bed. Instead she sat huddled in a ball in a corner of the sofa, alternately wailing and sobbing quietly. Thank heaven the bedrooms were on the second floor in this sturdily built house and she could grieve without being heard by the sleeping occupants.

How could she have mishandled everything so badly? It had been such a joyful day, and by the time they'd gotten home she'd wanted to make love just as badly as Clint had. Probably more, because she knew now that she was in love with him.

Another spurt of weeping shook her. It didn't seem possible that she could have gotten so carried away that she'd forgotten to take proper precautions. No one knew better than she the misery of being an unwed mother. Maybe it was different in the city, but in a small town like Placerville she'd endured the prejudices that had crept into the attitudes of her friends and neighbors.

Not that anyone had actually been unkind. They'd all known that she'd intended to marry soon, but still there had been the covert glances, the whispers and the rather smug pity that were almost worse than outright hostility.

And Janey. It was even worse for Janey. While several of her friends didn't live with their fathers, they at least had them and could see them now and then. Janey had never had a father, and as she grew older she would be more and more aware of that lack. It wasn't something that could be, or even should be, concealed, and it would set her apart.

If only Elyse could have pulled herself together and explained all this to Clint. But how could she, when for a moment she'd been so totally undone she'd even blamed him for being unwilling to proceed without caution!

Again hot tears poured down her cheeks. At that stage of arousal most men would have been too aware of their own needs to give a thought to the consequences, but Clint had managed to remain responsible and mature. No wonder he'd been so outraged—and she'd been too immature and tongue-tied to explain.

By four in the morning, Elyse's head was throbbing, her stomach was queasy and she was totally exhausted. She rose, wincing as cramped muscles protested, and dragged herself upstairs, where she fell into bed without even undressing.

Elyse slept until Janey woke her at eight-thirty on Monday morning, and as soon as she'd showered and dressed she telephoned Clint at his office in the Capitol Building in Sacramento. She knew the next move was up to her, and she was anxious to straighten things out, but she was told he was in a committee meeting and would be unavailable until midafternoon. That night she called his house, but he hadn't returned home. The housekeeper asked if she'd like to leave her name and a message, but she said no.

On Tuesday she spent a restless night and phoned the house shortly after daybreak, but he'd already left. She waited until nine, then called the office again and found that the Senate was in session and Senator Sterling was on the floor.

Elyse's nerves were strung tight, and it was almost impossible for her to concentrate on anything but her desperate need to contact Clint to try to make amends. She didn't expect him to ask to see her again, but she couldn't let him continue to think she'd been deliberately teasing him.

She waited until after eleven that night to ring the house again, but nobody answered.

Once more she got little sleep, and on Wednesday morning when she dialed his office for the third time in as many days her hands trembled so much that she had to hang up and start over again. When she asked for Senator Sterling the receptionist requested her name and telephone number. Elyse hung up quickly, but now it wasn't just her hands that were trembling.

She realized she would be the object of a security investigation if she called the office again. Anyone calling for a public figure three days in a row and requesting information of his whereabouts without identifying herself was suspect.

What was she going to do? She couldn't keep trying to reach him without identifying herself, but she didn't want to leave a message for him to call her. If she did it would be up to him to decide whether he wanted to talk to her. She couldn't let him make that decision. If she could find him and he'd allow it, she'd apologize in person. If he didn't want that she'd do it on the phone, but it was her responsibility, not his.

Things couldn't go on this way. She was a nervous wreck. She couldn't sleep, she had no appetite and she was getting jumpy and shrewish. She was even impatient with Janey, and although she hadn't told Liz about the quarrel with Clint, her sister had been eyeing her warily.

She had to take some type of action.

It wasn't until Liz came home from school and started getting ready for her date with Paul that the solution occurred to Elyse. Paul Sterling, Clint's brother. Maybe he could intervene on her behalf.

Fortunately Liz had been delayed by a visit from the worried mother of one of her problem students and was still dressing when Paul arrived. Elyse greeted him and they went into the family room to wait.

When the amenities were done with and they were seated in comfortable chairs she got right to the point. "Paul, I have a problem and I need your help."

Paul looked puzzled. "Sure, what do you want me to do?"

Elyse's smile was bittersweet. How much like Clint he was. He didn't ask what, where or why, just how he could help.

She clenched her hands and began quietly. "Clint and I had a...a disagreement. It was my fault entirely. He misunderstood...uh...something I did, but under the circumstances anyone would have."

It was hard going. She couldn't tell Paul what she'd done to Clint, and she wouldn't let him think his brother was in any way wrong. "He...he left before I could explain. Actually, I...I didn't seem to be explaining at all."

Paul leaned forward and spoke. "Take it easy, Elyse. You don't have to go into the reason. Just tell me what you want me to do."

His blue eyes were soft with compassion and there was a gentleness in his voice that was just like Clint's. Her sister would make a big mistake if she didn't marry him as quickly as possible. Paul loved Liz just as surely as Elyse had messed up any chance of Clint's ever loving her.

She felt tears gathering and quickly blinked them back. "I can't find him, Paul," she blurted. "I want to apologize, explain and tell him how sorry I am, but I can't seem to connect with him. I've phoned his home and his office so many times that I suspect they're thinking I'm some kind of nut, but he's never there."

"Clint's in Los Angeles, Elyse," Paul said. "I don't know where he was before, but he caught an early flight to L.A. this morning and will be gone for at least a couple of days."

"Oh." She felt a slight sense of relief. At least now she knew he wasn't in town, so she'd wait before trying to contact him again.

Paul spoke once more. "Are you saying he hasn't bothered to call you back?"

Elyse shook her head. "No, it's not that. I didn't leave my name or a message. I don't want to put him in the position of having to call me."

She saw Paul's look of bewilderment and hurried on. "I know it sounds silly, but it's important to me. I was wondering if there was some way you could find out the next time he planned to spend a day or evening at home and let me know." Her voice rose. "I've got to talk to him. I can't let him go on thinking—" She broke off and ran her fingers through her already disheveled curls. "Oh, Paul, I don't know what to do." There was anguish in her tone.

Paul jumped from his chair and went over to hunker down in front of her. "Hey, come on, it can't be that bad," he murmured as he clasped her hands between his. "I'm sure big brother hasn't been avoiding you. He's just busy. I can never get through to him, either. In an election year like this he's hardly ever home or in his office, but if you want me to track him down for you, I will."

Elyse managed a watery smile. "Oh, please. I'm going crazy. I promise not to bother him, but I have to make him understand."

"Tell you what I'll do. I've got an in with the family housekeeper. She likes to remind me she used to change my diapers." He grimaced and made Elyse giggle. "I'll ask her to call me the first time Clint comes home early and hasn't made plans to go out again. Then I'll call you. How's that?"

She breathed a little sigh. "Oh, Paul, you're an angel."

He made a face. "It's obvious you haven't been listening to Clint's analysis of my character. *Angel* is definitely not one of his adjectives."

"Then he doesn't know you as well as I do," she said gently. "You won't mention this to Liz, will you? She doesn't know about it."

Paul grinned. "Don't underestimate her, sweetie. She's complained that you've been on edge lately. But I won't say anything." He stood and offered her his hand. "Come on now. Pull yourself together. I hear Liz coming downstairs."

It was two days before she heard from Paul again. Meanwhile she'd managed to calm down sufficiently to stop snapping at everybody and her hands were again steady enough to paint faces on her doll heads.

Although Liz often spent the weekends with Paul in his Sacramento apartment, on this Friday night in early May she had to chaperon the senior ball and Paul was immersed in his studies as the time for the bar exams drew near.

Elyse was loading the dinner dishes in the dishwasher, when the phone rang. She picked it up in the kitchen. It was Paul. "Elyse, Alice, Clint's housekeeper, just called. She says he got back from L.A. late this afternoon and is now home and plans to stay there all night. He even referred all his calls to his answering service so he wouldn't be bothered. Good luck, sweetie, and don't worry. The poor idiot adores you."

Elyse wished she was as sure of that as Paul seemed to be, but she wasn't going to think about her doubts. She'd been making plans while she waited, and now she dialed Janey's favorite baby-sitter and was assured that the girl would be at the house within half an hour.

Next she went upstairs and told Liz, who was dressing for the dance, that she was going out and not to worry if she wasn't home by the time Liz returned. Her sister looked curious but managed to refrain from asking questions when it was obvious Elyse didn't want to answer.

By the time she got to her own room she was having second thoughts but she refused to let them sway her. She marched resolutely to the closet and pulled out a small red overnight case and opened it on her bed.

Again her hands shook as she began to pack; lacy underwear, a gossamer nightgown and peignoir in a delicate shade of lemon, matching satin slippers, toilet articles.

When she finished she quickly stripped off her clothes and stepped into the shower.

Elyse had just finished dressing in cream pleated slacks and a matching lightweight oversize sweater, when she heard the doorbell ring and Liz admit the baby-sitter. She picked up her purse and the small suitcase and walked out of the room.

Liz's eyes widened as she saw Elyse coming down the stairs with the overnight bag, and when Elyse reached the bottom Liz said, "I assume you aren't planning to come home tonight?" It was part question, part statement.

Elyse faltered. "I...I don't know. I hope not, but..."

Liz reached out and stroked her sister's cheek with her hand. "Be careful, baby. Don't let yourself be hurt."

The love in Liz's expression brought a lump to Elyse's throat and tears brimmed in her eyes. "I'll try not to," she said through a swallowed sob, "but I've found that nothing is free in this life. If you want something badly enough you have to go out and get it. So wish me luck."

The two women embraced, then Elyse called Janey, kissed her goodbye and hurried out of the house.

Chapter Six

Clint leaned back in the leather recliner and closed his eyes. God, but he was tired. Not only had work accelerated at the Capitol, but the last few weeks of the campaign were always hectic, even though his nearest rival was well behind him in the polls.

If only he could sleep once he finally did get to bed, it would help. He was used to long hours and late-night meetings, but he wasn't getting any younger. He could no longer function as efficiently as he used to without adequate rest. He hadn't slept worth a damn since Elyse...

He opened his eyes and swallowed the rest of the drink he held in his hand. No, he wasn't going to think about Elyse. He was lucky he'd found out about her problem before he'd gotten any more deeply involved emotionally. Not that he'd been in any danger of falling in love with her. But she had gotten under his skin. She'd apparently also short-circuited his judgment, because he never would have believed she was the type to tease a man and then indignantly withdraw when he was half-crazy with desire.

He shivered as the memory tore through him, then stood and took his empty glass to the kitchen. Four years ago when Dinah had left him he'd sworn he'd never again agonize or lose sleep over a woman. He wasn't about to break that vow now.

He ran water in the glass, then turned it upside down in the sink. Who did he think he was kidding? He'd already broken it. He'd been running himself ragged all week trying to escape the touch, the taste and the feel of Elyse. She'd imprinted herself on his libido.

He turned out the kitchen light and headed across the mammoth great room—the heart of the rambling ranch house, with its Douglas fir cathedral ceiling and its stone fireplace. The house faced west and was constructed with two separate wings extending from either side of the great room. The rooms opened onto the patio, swimming pool and gardens at the rear.

Clint continued to the bedroom wing and the master bedroom suite. It was only nine o'clock, but Alice and Grover had left after dinner to drive up to Lake Tahoe with friends for a vacation weekend of gambling and shows at the casinos, so he was alone. He might as well take a shower and go to bed early. It was quiet, and just maybe he would be able to sleep.

He stood for a long time under the hot stinging spray, letting it massage his aching muscles and relax his tense nerves. When he finally turned it off and walked nude into the bedroom, he heard the dogs barking and the doorbell ringing.

Damn! Who could that be? No one knew he was back from Los Angeles.

He debated ignoring the sound, but it wasn't likely anyone would make the trip all the way out here at this time of night unless it was important. He grabbed a pair of jeans from the dresser drawer and pulled them on as he headed toward the front door.

It had taken Elyse a long time to find the Sterling home in the sprawling area of Cameron Park. The lots were measured in acres here, instead of feet, and the large affluent homes were set well off the roads at the ends of long narrow lanes. Stands of shade trees and flowering bushes afforded a maximum of privacy.

Finally she'd stopped at a gas station and asked for directions. The helpful attendant had drawn her a map, and she'd started her quest over again. When she finally found the large ranch house, she discovered it was built on the bank of a small stream and she had to park in a private parking area and walk across a bridge to reach the front door.

To make matters worse there were only two dim lamps illuminating the shrubbery near the porch steps. The rest of the house as well as the grounds were dark except for widely placed streetlights on the main road.

At that point she'd been tempted to give up and turn back; it didn't look as if there were anybody home. But Paul had insisted Clint would be there. She couldn't leave without making sure.

She'd reached for the small piece of luggage on the seat beside her, but hadn't immediately picked it up, torn between her innate distaste for appearing uninvited on a man's doorstep, overnight case in hand, and her need to convince Clint she was ready to make love if he wanted to.

Now she'd been standing on his porch for the past several minutes, her finger pressed to the doorbell. So far all she'd managed to raise were several fierce-sounding dogs who were apparently contained somewhere on the other side of the house. Anyone in there couldn't help but hear the racket.

She took her finger off the button, but the dogs continued to bark. Now what was she going to do? Undoubtedly Paul had been misinformed. There didn't seem to be anybody home, not even the housekeeper he'd mentioned.

She turned around and looked back toward the main road. There weren't any cars going by. It was dark, spooky and deserted, and those dogs were sure to tear down whatever was holding them any minute.

She shivered, resisting the urge to run back to the car and escape. With a last surge of determination she stabbed at the doorbell again and held it down.

Just then a light went on inside the house, and seconds later the whole outside front of the house and grounds was lit. Elyse jumped and pulled her finger away as the massive carved wooden door opened and Clint, wearing only faded jeans, stood blinking at her. "Elyse. What are you doing here? Is something wrong?" He pulled the door wide and stood back. "Come in."

She stared, caught totally off balance by the large expanse of bare muscular chest. She'd never seen him less than fully dressed, and the sight was intoxicating.

Now that she had his undivided attention she wasn't sure she was doing the right thing, after all. He didn't look very pleased to see her. His features were stiff with surprise, and she was sure she saw annoyance there, too.

As she hesitated on the porch he reached out to take her arm and pull her gently but firmly into the wide foyer. "Elyse, are you all right? Come in, for heaven's sake."

He shut the door and his gaze roamed over her, stopping when it came to the suitcase in her hand.

A hot wave of shyness and humiliation swept over her, and she ducked her head in hopes he wouldn't notice her flaming face. It was then she noted he was barefoot, and her startled glance flew upward to his disheveled hair.

He looked as if she'd gotten him out of bed.

Dear Lord, had she interrupted something? Her eyes widened with distress. Did he have a woman here? Surely he wouldn't be going to bed alone this early.

A strangled moan forced its way past her throat, and she wished the floor would open up and swallow her. "I . . . I'm sorry," she wailed. "I should have called. I didn't think—" She turned and raced to the door, desperate to get away.

Clint caught her easily. "Hey, wait a minute. Where are you going? What in hell is the matter with you?" He whirled her around and held her by the shoulders. "Now calm down and tell me why you're here." Again his gaze was drawn to her overnight bag as he took her arm and urged her forward. "Let me take that," he said, and removed the case from her hand.

Elyse dug in her heels and refused to move. "Are you alone?" she asked hesitantly.

"Yes, of course I'm alone. Who else did you think would be here?" There was a tinge of impatience in his tone.

"I . . . well, nobody," she stammered. "But you . . ." She couldn't seem to lift her gaze from his chest.

His glance followed hers, and he seemed to realize for the first time his state of undress. He frowned, and his grip tightened on her arm. "For God's sake, Elyse, I'm not going to attack you, but if it'll make you feel safer I'll get fully dressed."

"No, please, it's not that." Oh, why on earth had she ever come here late at night, unannounced and uninvited? "I thought you might have . . . uh . . . company."

She saw as well as heard his sharp intake of breath. "You mean you thought I was entertaining a woman in my bed." It was a statement, not a question. "I'm sorry to disappoint you, but you caught me in the shower, *alone*." He sounded not only bitter but hurt.

She felt the sharp pain of remorse. Why couldn't she make herself understood? She'd never had this problem before. Actually, she'd always been good at communicating with people, so why now that it was so important was she tongue-tied and slow-witted? If only she dared put her arms around him and nuzzle her face in his bare chest. If she could tell him how much she loved him . . . But that would just make him uncomfortable and complicate matters even more.

She took a deep breath and prayed for strength. "Clint, that wasn't what I meant at all."

She was amazed to find her voice was strong and clear. "I came here tonight because I've been trying to reach you by telephone all week, but I always just missed you. Paul told me you were planning to be at home all evening, so I hurried over, but I got lost, and then it looked like no one was home, and it was dark—"

She stopped abruptly and put her hands over her mouth. She was rambling again. Good Lord, would she ever be able to talk to this man without sounding like an idiot?

His hold on her arm loosened and his voice softened. "Why did you want to reach me?"

She tipped her head back and looked straight into his dark green eyes. "I want to apologize for the way I behaved Sunday and to explain what happened."

She saw the flash of pain before he blinked it away. "That's not necessary. I was out of line. You had every right to say no. I only wish you'd said it sooner."

She could no longer resist the need to touch him, and she put her hand on his bare shoulder. The feel of his warm damp flesh sent tingles up her arm. "Please, Clint, just listen to me. It won't take long, and then I'll leave."

For a moment his shoulder seemed to settle against her palm, but then he carefully but firmly moved away from it and led her into the room beyond. It was huge—the largest room she'd ever seen in a private home—and featured a mammoth stone fireplace, that thrust right through the high, beamed ceiling.

They walked across the thick beige carpet to an oversized chair and ottoman upholstered in a tightly woven Indian design in shades of turquoise, beige and brown. "Sit down and wait for me," he said. "I'll put some clothes on and be right back." His eyes searched her face. "It won't do any good to try to run away. You need a key to unlock the door."

He set the suitcase down beside her and walked across the room to disappear through an archway on the south wall.

Elyse sank into the soft, thickly padded chair and curled her feet under her. She had a fleeting impression of the luxurious surroundings, but was too upset to really notice.

Trembling with tension, she leaned her head back and closed her eyes in an effort to calm down as Clint had suggested. She took deep breaths and forced her muscles to relax one by one while she tried to clear her turbulent mind.

Clint sprinted to the bedroom and pawed through a drawer in search of a shirt. His heart was racing and his mind was mired in confusion. What was Elyse doing standing on his doorstep at nine-thirty at night? Coming here was the last thing he'd expected from her.

He grabbed a navy polo shirt and pulled it over his head. Why was she so upset? He'd never known her to lose her composure before. Of course he hadn't known her long, and every time he'd thought he had her figured out he'd discovered he was wrong, so he might as well admit he didn't really know her at all. Still, something was bothering her. He couldn't have misread the panic he'd seen on her face and heard in her tone.

He looked in the mirror and grimaced. No wonder she thought he'd been interrupted in the middle of a hot-and-heavy session with a woman. He'd been toweling his hair dry when he heard the doorbell, and it was standing up in all directions.

He picked up a comb and started to smooth it down. Dammit, he was almost as unstrung as Elyse. He hadn't believed his eyes when he'd seen her standing there, holding an overnight bag and looking as if she expected him to slam the door in her face.

He laid the comb on the dresser. *Drop it, Sterling,* he mentally castigated himself. He wasn't going to give her a second chance to manipulate him. He'd known all along this relationship was going nowhere, so now was the time to put an end to it. He'd listen to her apology, assure her she was forgiven and send her away.

He rummaged in the closet for his house slippers and put them on. He'd remind her that soon they'd probably be related by marriage since his brother and her sister were lovers, so they'd always be friends.

He ran his fingers through his newly combed hair. *If only she hadn't brought along that suitcase. Did it mean she intended to spend the night? If so, did he have the strength to refuse?*

The carpeting was so thick Elyse didn't hear Clint returning until he appeared in the archway and headed toward the wet bar in one corner of the room. "Sorry for the delay," he said. "Is brandy okay for you, or do you prefer something else?"

"I don't want anything to drink, thank you," she said, and straightened up in the chair.

He took a bottle from the cabinet and poured its contents into two snifters. "I think you'd better. This brandy will settle your nerves."

He picked up the glasses and walked across the room to hand her one, then took the matching chair on the other side of the fireplace. "So you had trouble finding the house? It's rather hidden."

Elyse took a swallow of her drink and was grateful for the smoothness with which it slid down her throat. It was obvious he was trying to make this easier for her, but his thoughtfulness made things even harder.

"I don't want to make small talk, Clint. I want to make you understand I wasn't teasing Sunday night."

She saw his look of skepticism. "I know that's hard for you to believe after the way I acted, but I really did want to make love with you. I was just as eager as you were until . . ."

She paused and took another sip of brandy. She'd played this scene so often in her mind and had known exactly what she was going to say, but now her mind was blank and she had no idea how to proceed. "Maybe it'll help if I tell you about Jerry."

Clint frowned. "Elyse, I don't—"

"Please, let me do this my way," she pleaded. "Jerry and I were high school sweethearts, and after graduation we enrolled at Sacramento State. We'd intended to get married after we'd gotten our degrees, but during our sophomore year we decided we couldn't wait any longer. Jerry gave me a ring and we announced our engagement. We were going to be married during the Christmas holidays, but we were both too impatient to wait that long to... to make love.

Elyse was acutely uncomfortable. She'd never before discussed the intimate side of her relationship with Jerry, not even with Liz. It was private and personal, and not to be shared with anybody.

She lowered her eyes and concentrated on the crystal snifter she was clasping with both hands. "The first time..." She paused and cleared her throat. "The first time we were both... overeager... and it wasn't until afterward that we remembered we should have been more... careful."

Her voice broke, and for a moment she couldn't go on. She and Jerry had been so naive, and in their innocence they'd botched the whole thing. Unfortunately the damage had been done.

"Elyse, don't." Clint set his glass down and leaned forward. "I'm beginning to get the picture. It's not necessary to continue."

She swallowed and looked at him. "Yes, it is, Clint. I don't want any more misunderstandings between us. I've got to say it all."

He nodded and sat back again while she swallowed more of the brandy. "After that we always used protection, and in the excitement of planning the wedding I forgot about that first oversight. When I finally realized that my...cycle...had been interrupted I thought it was just the tension from all that was happening. It wasn't until two weeks after Jerry died that I found out I was ten weeks pregnant."

Elyse slumped back, exhausted from the effort of remembering and telling.

Clint gripped the arms of the chair to keep himself from jumping up and going to her. *Stay away from her,* a voice in his mind warned. *If you take her in your arms you'll never be able to send her away.*

"Elyse, I can imagine what you must have gone through," he said softly. "I'm sorry—"

She gestured for silence. "I'm not finished."

"It's not necessary—"

"I have to." She finished her drink and put the glass on the floor. "On Sunday I was so afraid you were going to leave again with just a quick kiss, and then when you took me in your arms and said you wanted me, I...I just went up in smoke."

She buried her face in her hands, but continued speaking. "Oh, God, Clint, I was going to make the same mistake again!" Her anguish was heavy in her tone. "I would have blithely gone to you without even thinking of contraception. I would have risked the same situation all over again because I'm too irresponsible to have good sense."

A sob shook her, and Clint was out of the chair and had her in his arms before he had time to debate the advisability of his action. "Sweetheart, oh, sweetheart, no.

You're not irresponsible, and you wouldn't have gotten pregnant. I wouldn't have let that happen.''

He picked her up and sat down in the chair with her on his lap.

She snuggled into his embrace and let the tears come. ''That's no excuse,'' she said brokenly. ''I should be responsible for my own body, my own actions. When you mentioned precautions and I realized what I'd almost done, I was so shocked and appalled that I just went cold all over.''

Her arms around his neck tightened, and she rubbed her tearstained cheek against his throat. ''I still wanted to make love with you, but I couldn't. I...just couldn't.''

Clint held her close and rocked gently from side to side. The depression that had gnawed at him all week lifted, and he felt light and happy.

He'd been right about Elyse. She wasn't the type to tease and torment. She'd been going through a hell of self-condemnation because she wanted him so badly that she'd momentarily forgotten the consequences.

''My poor little doll,'' he murmured against her ear. ''I'm surprised you'd want to apologize after the way I behaved, the things I said. I'm so sorry. I don't know if you can understand, but I was wanting you so badly, and had been for the whole hour it took us to get home. When you wrenched yourself away from me and said no after you'd been so responsive, so apparently willing, I guess I just went a little berserk.'' He chuckled mirthlessly. ''I spent the rest of the night pacing the floor and damning you to hell.''

She burrowed her face against his shoulder. ''I'm sorry.'' Her voice was thick with regret.

''Hush, now,'' he said. ''We've established the fact that we're both sorry. There's no need to belabor the point. I've forgiven you and I hope you've forgiven me, so let's forget it.''

They sat quietly in the chair, wrapped in each other's arms for a long time, until finally Elyse worked up enough nerve to bring up the most important subject of all.

She kissed the side of his neck. ''Clint.''

He rubbed his cheek in her abundant hair. ''Uh-huh?''

''I came prepared to spend the night if you want me to, and I'm fully protected.'' There, it was out, and she held her breath as she waited for his reaction.

It was a while in coming. He just sat there quietly, and she could feel his heart beating against her breast. Why didn't he say something? She'd expected him either to pick her up and carry her off to the bedroom or to dump her on the floor and tell her to go home—either of which would have been preferable to no reaction at all!

Her nerves were almost at the screaming point, when he finally spoke. ''Elyse, I'm flattered and sorely tempted, but I think we should take advantage of the cooling-off period we've been given and think about where our relationship is going before we get any more deeply involved.''

Her heart sank. What cooling-off period? She'd been in a hot misery of frustration all week, and there was sure nothing cool about her feelings right now.

''You're young and exquisitely beautiful,'' he continued. ''Someday the right man will come along and you'll marry. I'm pushing forty and I like my life the way it is. I'm not looking for a wife, and I don't have time for a love affair. Between now and the general election in November I'll hardly have time to eat and sleep. The life of a politician is a merry-go-round, but it's what I've chosen. I'd like to be governor of California by the time I'm fifty, and to achieve that I'll have to be totally committed to it.''

He caressed her back tenderly. "I'm only human, and you're exceedingly desirable. If you still want to stay I'm not going to send you away, but you're almost sure to be hurt even though I'd never deliberately make you unhappy."

Elyse felt as though she'd been kicked. Gently, but kicked all the same. Clint didn't want her! He'd told her as politely as possible, but the message was clear. He wanted her to go home tonight and to stay the hell out of his life in the future.

Again she felt the familiar despair of humiliation. She'd thrown herself at him and been firmly rejected! Now what did she do? How could she face him, let alone talk to him?

Carefully she sat up and slid off his lap. She stood with her back to him and straightened her clothes. "You're probably right," she said, tightening her stomach muscles to make her voice stronger. "It wasn't a good idea. I guess I got carried away with my apology. I tend to go overboard at times."

She reached down and picked up her suitcase, then started toward the foyer. "If you'll just unlock the door so I can get out, I'll be on my way."

Dammit, she was babbling again. Why couldn't she just shut up and make a dignified exit?

Clint was right behind her. "Elyse..." He sounded odd, too.

She quickened her pace, then stopped at the front door. Clint took a key from his pocket and turned it in the lock, then reached for the luggage she held. "Here, I'll carry this for you," he said as he opened the door.

"It's not necessary for you to come to the car with me," she protested.

He took her arm and helped her down the stairs and onto the bridge. "I want to," he said, and continued to hold her arm protectively.

They crossed the bridge and walked the few feet to where her car was parked. Clint opened the door and tossed the overnight bag across the seat to the passenger side.

Elyse stood back and waited for him to get out of the way so she could slide in. There was a light pole in the parking area, and she could see the ripple of his back and shoulder muscles as he handled the luggage. How she loved those muscles, and the man they belonged to.

He backed out of the car and turned to her. His eyes searched her face and his own looked grim. She hoped he wouldn't touch her. If he did she'd cry, and she badly wanted to preserve at least a show of poise.

Her gaze locked with his, and she was surprised to see a dark shadow of agony in his eyes. She felt herself drawn magnetically toward him just before his arms went around her and brought her hard against his long lean body. Her mouth opened, and his covered it in a kiss that destroyed her will and left her defenseless and vulnerable to the hurt he'd promised her.

When at last he tore his lips from hers it was with a shuddering groan. "Oh, my darling," he whispered huskily. "If you leave I don't think I can stand it."

She didn't try to speak—her relief was too profound—but she put her hands behind his head and pushed it down to place slow, moist kisses on either side of his mouth. "I don't think I could, either," she whispered just before their lips met again.

He scooped her up in his arms and carried her back across the bridge and into the house.

He didn't put her down until they got to the bedroom, a large masculine room done in earth tones and furnished with dark, heavy, solid wood furnishings, beautiful and expensive. The outside wall was covered with woven drapes in shades of sea foam, cinnamon and camel, and indirect lighting gave a soft dusky glow of intimacy to the area.

Clint walked to the bed, then lowered Elyse to her feet but kept her in the circle of his embrace. He looked down at her, and the anguish that had shadowed his eyes was replaced with tenderness. "How do you manage to shoot my self-control and good intentions all to hell?" he asked with amusement.

"Just lucky, I guess," she retorted breathlessly, touching her lips to his. "Are...are you sure this is what you want?"

She couldn't bear it if he was just accommodating her.

For an answer he lifted her slightly and ground her to him. He was hard with unbridled desire, and she shivered with pleasure as he thrust against her. "Do you have any doubt?" he whispered shakily into her ear.

"No." She hid her face in his shoulder. "Just tell me what you want me to do."

She'd never made love with a man who was experienced before, and she wanted so much to please him.

He seemed to understand as he nibbled at her neck. "You're doing just fine. Does this sweater unbutton somewhere?" He stood her back on her feet.

"No, it's loose," she said, and held up her arms so he could pull it over her head.

Her breasts were firm and high, and she hadn't worn a bra. His gaze fastened on them, and they seemed to swell and grow tight. With a quivering sigh he reached out and touched them. They fit perfectly in his palms, and he leaned down and kissed first one tingling nipple, then the other.

She clutched his shoulders and moaned as his tongue caressed the acutely sensitive tips.

He let go of her for a moment as he stripped his own shirt off, then took her in his arms again. "Now, you do that to me," he instructed.

It was a novel idea, and she lowered her head and touched her lips to first one and then the other of the large nipples on his flat chest. To her surprise they hardened, just as hers had. "I didn't know that was a sensual area for a man," she said, and licked at one of the tips.

"It feels good," he said unsteadily. "Anyplace you touch me is erotic."

She moved her head to the other side and sucked gently. A soft purr slid from his throat, and he searched at her waist until he found and unfastened the tab and the zipper at the side of her slacks. They were pleated and roomy, and when they'd slid effortlessly to the floor, she stepped out of them.

His hands roamed over her bare flesh until they encountered the skimpy bikini panties. He dispensed with them, too, then pressed her against him and shivered. "You feel the way I knew you would," he murmured, "soft and smooth and incredibly exciting."

She had been caressing his back, and just rubbing the firm skin and feeling the solid muscles contract caused an itch deep in her body that made her squirm.

Working her fingers under the waistband of his belt-less jeans, she slid them around to the front. He drew in a deep, shuddering breath, and his own fingers clenched her firm, round buttocks. She pulled at the heavy snap, but it didn't give and she pulled again, each time inadvertently brushing her fist against the hardness beneath. He clenched his jaw and tensed, but didn't interfere.

On the third try the snap flew apart, but the zipper remained locked. An attack of shyness overcame her. What should she do now? She'd expected the zipper to open along with the snap.

She looked up and saw the strained expression on his face, but he managed a wicked grin. "Well, go ahead and finish the job."

She knew she was blushing, and ducked her head as she tried to get ahold of the tiny zipper pull with the tips of her fingers without touching the distended jeans beneath it. Unfortunately she was so flustered that her hand slipped.

Clint groaned and covered her hand with his, tightening her hold on him. "Good Lord, Elyse," he muttered. "My endurance isn't unlimited. You'd better let me do that." He removed her tingling hand and quickly pulled off his pants.

He wasn't wearing briefs, and he was magnificent in the buff. There wasn't an ounce of spare flesh on him. He was firm and smooth and only slightly hairy. Elyse had never been turned on by furry chests and long thick hair on arms and legs, and Clint was just right.

She knew he'd caught her staring, but she didn't care. Then she realized he was staring just as intently at her. When their gazes met she went eagerly into his arms, and he enfolded her in an ardent embrace. "You're so exquisite I'm almost afraid to touch you," he murmured.

"You're beautiful, too," she said with a touch of awe. "Like a rare and perfect sculpture."

He reached down and threw back the bedcovers, then tumbled her onto the sheet and followed her down. "Aren't you going to turn off the lights?" she asked.

"Not unless you want me to. I want to look at you."

He began to caress her lightly. "I want to see your flawless body and watch your expression as I do this...and this...and this."

She moaned with pleasure and smiled with delight as his hands did fantastic things to her. Then his lips followed his hands, sucking and nibbling until she was writhing with sensations she'd never experienced before.

She arched toward him, and he moved to lie against her side with one leg thrown over hers and the hardness of his desire pressed alongside her hip.

His breathing was labored and his heart was pounding. She knew he was having difficulty holding back, but he continued the unhurried fondling that was driving her wild with the need for still more. As if reading her mind, his fingers stroked lower and lower, until she cried out with desperation and her hips started rocking in the rhythm of passion.

Only then did he move over her and join their two bodies as one to continue the throbbing tempo. Elyse clasped her legs around his thrusting hips and dug her fingernails into his shoulders as she opened her mouth to meet his.

The rapidly escalating fervor exploded into a kaleidoscope of swirling sensations that were almost too exhilarating to endure.

Chapter Seven

Clint woke without an alarm just as he did every morning at seven o'clock; but this morning was different. This morning there was a soft, warm woman snuggled in his arms, and he didn't have to open his eyes to remember it was Elyse.

He smiled as he looked down at her, sleeping soundly with her head on his shoulder. They'd made love three times during the long night, and every time had been incendiary. Now she fit so perfectly against him, her face relaxed into the innocent look of a child.

He moved his hand lightly over the indentation of her waist, the curve of her hip. Her body was definitely not that of a child, and if he didn't get out of bed and away from her he wouldn't be able to resist waking her. Besides, his arm and shoulder tingled from lack of circulation where she lay on them.

Carefully he disentangled himself from her and slid out of bed. She didn't move, and he walked to the closet and put on his maroon thigh-length robe.

A glance at the bed reminded him of the delights that lay under the thin sheet that covered her, and he forced himself to look away. He needed his wits about him, and remembering her satiny, responsive body wasn't the way to keep them.

He pulled the drapes away from the sliding door in the glass wall and opened it. The fresh clean scent of pine wafted on the cool spring air, and the water in the pool sparkled as light danced across it. It was a beautiful morning, but for some reason the very brightness of it depressed him.

Clint leaned against the doorjamb and looked out over the gardens, a riot of color from daffodils, tulips, hyacinths, primroses and pansies, but he couldn't keep his mind on the yellows, red, purples and greens. Instead he focused on the night just past.

It had been fantastic, but was it worth the price he must surely pay?

The lovemaking had been. He wasn't sure it had ever been that good before, even with Dinah. The first time had been an exercise in restraint. He'd been determined not to hurt Elyse, or rush her, even though he'd been on the ragged edge from the time he'd picked her up and carried her to the bedroom, but when his self-control shattered she'd been with him all the way.

The next two times were sheer magic, with neither of them holding back.

Ah, yes, good sex was important, and maybe it was enough. Maybe that's what love was all about, after all, the intimate giving and receiving. The sharing of pleasure too intense to be denied.

Clint shifted from one foot to the other. He knew men who would give up everything for a woman who could bring them the ecstasy Elyse had so freely given him. But would it last? Or, more likely, would it be tamed by repeated exposure until it could no longer carry a relationship...a marriage...?

He knew he must either stop seeing Elyse or marry her. Before last night he'd had a choice; now he didn't. She loved him. She'd told him so. Not with words, but with her body. She was sweet and honest and one of the most morally upright women he'd ever met. She would never come to a man the way she'd come to him unless she were truly in love with him. He'd understood that, but he'd taken her, anyway, because he'd felt he had to have her.

Now if he wanted to keep his self-respect and protect Elyse from losing hers, he'd have to marry her. She'd come to him freely with love and trust, and he'd accepted what she'd been willing to give. If he walked away from her now she'd feel betrayed and humiliated. He couldn't do that to her.

Maybe he did love her, after all. Not the deeply passionate way he'd loved Dinah, but Elyse was precious to him. He wouldn't hurt her so brutally.

Elyse opened her eyes and felt a moment of panic. Where was she? There was nothing familiar about this room.

Then her gaze fastened on Clint, wearing a robe that exposed most of his strong muscular legs and standing in the open doorway with his back to her. The memory of the night returned, and she snuggled under the sheet with a little purr of contentment.

Never in her wildest dreams had she imagined that making love could be such an incredible experience! It had been good with Jerry, but with Clint it had been...awesome.

She was disappointed he'd gotten out of bed before she was awake. She wondered what it would be like to wake up in the mornings with him in bed beside her.

She rolled over, and he turned around. For just a moment there was a closed, strained look on his face, but then he smiled at her. "Good morning. Did I wake you? I didn't mean to."

She smiled back and shook her head. "No, you didn't, but what are you doing up and about so early?"

He walked over and bent down to kiss her. "I wake up at the same time every day. It's an automatic reflex from years of early rising. I rarely sleep past seven o'clock."

He took off his robe and climbed into bed beside her. "Come here and give me a proper kiss," he said as he took her in his arms.

She complied immediately, and he rolled her onto her back and lay partially across her as he ravaged her willing mouth. "Did I wear you out last night?" he murmured as he moved from her lips to her throat. "I couldn't seem to get enough of you. Every time I thought I was finally appeased you'd touch me, and I was ready to go again." He raised his head and grinned at her. "You're going to make an old man of me before I'm forty."

She reached up and stroked her fingers through his tousled hair. "I might as well have been a virgin," she said, and there was a touch of wonder in her tone. "I've never experienced anything like last night. I didn't know that making love could be so beautiful, so...so soul searing."

She ran one finger across his cheek and touched his lips. "Oh, Clint, I love you so."

She'd hoped he'd be pleased, but the look that flashed in his eyes wasn't pleasure; it was almost certainly remorse.

With a blink of his eyelids it was gone, replaced by a melting softness. "Since we seem to have such a great thing going for us, I guess we ought to get married."

He kissed her again, but a chill replaced the warm glow that had been burning brightly inside her. *Seem. Guess. Ought.* Hardly the words of a man impatient to make her his bride!

He must have felt her withdrawal, because he looked at her questioningly. "What's the matter? Don't you want to marry me?"

"That depends," she said. "Are you saying that you *guess* we should get married because after last night you feel we *ought* to? You don't owe me anything, Clint."

His frown deepened. "That's nonsense. It was just a poor choice of words." He rolled off her and sat up. "Proposing marriage isn't something I've had a lot of practice at. Besides, it's hard for me to think, let alone talk, when you're lying beneath me with no clothes on."

Was she being overly sensitive? She hadn't expected him to ask her to marry him at all, so why was she quibbling over semantics? Words were easily garbled, but it was also possible he'd inadvertently said what he felt, instead of what she wanted to hear.

She wanted to marry Clint more than she'd ever wanted anything, but not if he felt trapped into it. After all, she'd seduced him and then made the mistake of telling him she loved him. Did he feel guilty? Did he think he'd taken advantage of her because she was younger and relatively inexperienced?

Was he still carrying a torch for Dinah?

Elyse sat up, too, and pulled the sheet over her breasts. Clint was sitting beside her, with the same sheet covering his lap. He was so definitely male, and she wanted to throw herself into his arms and tell him yes, of course, she'd marry him, and to hell with the consequences.

She could make him happy. She'd love him and cherish him and give him children of his own. But could she share him with the ghost of another woman? Would his first love always stand between them?

She had to know, and there was only one way to find out.

She turned her head to look at him. "Clint, I think you'd better tell me about Dinah Jefferson."

Clint stared. "Who told you about Dinah?" His tone was grim.

She opened her mouth to answer, but he didn't give her a chance. "Never mind. I know it wasn't Paul. That only leaves Reba Ogden."

"It doesn't matter who told me, except for the fact that it wasn't you. Had you expected to keep her a secret?"

She almost wished the knowledge had been kept from her. She'd have married Clint with no reservations, and maybe by the time she found out he'd have forgotten all about his other love.

"No, I suppose not," he said, "but that's been over for a long time. I haven't seen or heard from Dinah in four years. She has nothing to do with you and me."

"I hope you're right," Elyse said, "but surely you can understand why I'm skeptical. Just last night you told me you weren't looking for a wife and had no time for an affair. Now, after I've seduced you against your better judgment, you say it *seems* we *ought* to get married.''

Clint ran his hand through his hair. ''You didn't seduce me, and I didn't mean what you're implying.''

He looked so upset and bewildered she couldn't resist the urge to reassure. She moved her legs and twisted around so that she was kneeling before him on the mattress, her hands on his bare shoulders. ''Of course I seduced you, darling. That's exactly what I came here to do, but I wasn't trying to trap you into marriage.'' She leaned forward and touched his lips with hers. ''I just wanted to apologize and convince you I wasn't teasing when I pulled away from you on Sunday.''

The strain disappeared from his face and was replaced by a much warmer expression. ''Look at you,'' he said softly as he reached out and cupped her naked breasts. ''How can you say you're not a tease when you set my blood to boiling every time I look at you?''

Her glance flew downward, and for the first time she was aware that she'd totally dislodged the sheet when she changed position. Her eyes opened wide, but he smiled and pulled her into his arms and cuddled her against him. ''You tease me and seduce me and keep me in such a state of arousal that I can't think of anything but how intensely I need you.''

He took one of her hands and moved it to his lap. ''You see what you do to me.'' His words ended in a strangled moan of gratification as her fingers explored his pulsating hardness. ''Even after a night like the one we just spent, you can make me stand up and beg for more without even touching me.''

His arms tightened around her, and he buried his face in her shoulder. ''My God, Elyse, what man wouldn't want to marry such a woman and keep her with him always?''

Elyse knew there was a flaw in his logic somewhere, but she was in no shape to analyze it as he readjusted their positions so she was lying on her back with his feverish body covering hers.

This time there were no preliminaries. They didn't need them and couldn't slow down enough to enjoy them as they made love with a frenzied excitement that exploded in a molten convulsion of erotic fireworks.

It was nearly noon when Elyse woke for the second time, and again Clint was gone from the bed. But a few minutes later the bathroom door opened and he stepped out wearing nothing but a navy towel wrapped around his hips.

"Good, you're awake," he said as he walked across the room and sat down on the side of the bed.

He leaned over and kissed her thoroughly, then sat up before she could get her arms around him to hold him. "Enough of that," he said with a grin. "Do you realize we could starve to death if we don't take strong disciplinary measures and get out of bed?"

She grinned back. "Just like a man," she grumbled playfully. "Always thinking of your stomach."

He reached under the sheet and caressed her intimately. "It's not my stomach that's been uppermost in my mind for the past fifteen hours," he said, and reluctantly withdrew his hand.

He stood and went to the walk-in closet. "I'll fix breakfast while you shower and dress," he called to her, "and you'd better be out of that bed by the time I get my clothes gathered up, or I'll climb back in with you and you won't get another chance to eat until dinner."

Elyse laughed and moved stiffly to comply. "Promises, promises," she shouted, darting into the still steamy bathroom.

As she stood under the shower the warm, invigorating spray refreshed her mind as well as her body, and with the fog of passion cleared away she knew what had bothered her about Clint's argument in favor of marriage. It was all based on lovemaking rather than love.

She could almost hear his derisive snort if she dared say such a thing to him, but the truth was there even if the words sounded silly.

Clint wanted her in his bed. She'd even agree that he probably needed her in the strictly physical sense. She needed him that way, too, and there was nothing wrong with that. It was good and beautiful and even necessary in a marriage, but it was only a part of the vital elements.

Sex without love was always an emotional risk, Elyse knew, and it was no basis on which to build a life. Clint had never mentioned love. He liked her, he enjoyed being with her, he even felt protective of her, but was that enough?

It might be. Possibly in time he'd grow to love her the way she wanted him to.

But not if he still loved another woman.

With a heavy heart she turned off the water and stepped out of the shower stall.

Back in the bedroom she discovered that Clint had brought her overnight case and laid it on a luggage stand. She opened it and put on clean underwear, then dressed again in her cream slacks and lightweight sweater. She brushed her teeth, and applied a rosy shade of lipstick, the only makeup she usually wore in the daytime.

In the kitchen Clint prepared the coffee maker and plugged it in. He knew the discussion about Dinah hadn't been ended, only postponed. Not that he'd deliberately initiated that last interlude in bed with Elyse in order to distract her. He just plain lost his ability to reason every time he touched her.

He hadn't expected the subject of Dinah Jefferson to come up. He never talked about her or discussed his feelings, and he'd just assumed that everyone had forgotten about their relationship. It was nobody's business but his.

He got the bacon out of the refrigerator. No, that wasn't quite true, he thought. If other people were still gossiping about the breakup of his engagement to Dinah, then he owed it to Elyse to tell her the truth before she heard garbled versions of it from others.

What had she been told? Reba loved to gossip, but she usually got her facts straight, and she never knowingly distorted them. If Reba were Elyse's only source, then she had only the bare facts.

Clint grimaced. He tried never to think about that painful occasion, and he'd refused to discuss it. It was going to be difficult to try to explain it to Elyse, but maybe it was for the best. Possibly bringing it out and examining it, reliving it in the telling, would help to defuse it and lay it to rest once and for all.

He put the rack with the bacon in the microwave, then leaned against the wall and closed his eyes. It might, but he doubted it. Did he really want Elyse badly enough to put himself through the emotional carnage of a replay of that year with Dinah?

Elyse found her way to the great room, then followed the mouth-watering aroma of bacon and toast to the kitchen in the other wing. Clint, wearing jeans and a tan open-necked polo shirt, was busy at the stove.

He looked up and smiled. "You're just in time," he said. "How do you like your eggs?"

"Scrambled," she answered promptly, heading for the coffee maker on the tile counter.

"Good. I never quite mastered the art of turning fried eggs over. They always break and wind up scrambled, anyway." He cracked several eggs in a bowl and began to whip them.

Elyse poured coffee into the two bright mugs that had been set out and carried them to the heavy round oak kitchen table. She put one on each of the quilted turquoise-and-brown place mats and sat down. Clint appeared immediately with a warm ironstone plate piled high with bacon, eggs and toast and set it in front of her.

Elyse eyed it with dismay. "Clint, I can't eat all that."

"Of course you can," he replied. "You can wash it down with orange juice." He left and returned with a full pitcher and two juice glasses. "We've got to keep your energy level high." He grinned suggestively as he brought his own plate and sat down beside her.

He seemed in good spirits. Was he happy she'd hadn't said yes to his proposal, or did he think she had said yes by sleeping with him again?

She didn't press the point while they were eating, and afterward he was the one who brought it up.

They took their mugs of fresh coffee into the great room and sat down together on the king-size leather sofa. Clint put his mug on the highly polished free-form redwood burl coffee table and turned to look at her. "I've had time to think, Elyse, and I've decided that you're right. You are entitled to know about my relationship with Dinah Jefferson."

Elyse caught her breath, and the liquid swayed in her cup as her hand jerked. She hadn't expected him to agree so readily, and now that he had she wasn't at all sure she wanted to know, after all. There were times when ignorance really was bliss.

She sighed and put her mug down, too. Unfortunately this wasn't one of those times.

She tried to relax, but even her jaw was tense as she spoke. "Please understand, Clint. You don't have to tell me anything. I'm not prying into your private life. It's only if you want me to share that life that I have to know, and then only because I feel strongly that it has a bearing on the present. On my well-being as well as yours."

He leaned over and kissed her gently. "It's a painful subject and I won't deny that I prefer not to discuss it, but I don't want you listening to a lot of garbage from people who don't know what they're talking about."

He settled himself rather stiffly on the couch. "I met Dinah Jefferson almost six years ago when she came to work at the Capitol. She was a widow. Her husband, a congressman in Maryland, had been assassinated three years before. She was with him at the time, and he died in her arms."

Elyse gasped. "Oh, how awful."

Clint nodded. "Yes. They'd been married only four years and were very much in love. Dinah suffered a breakdown and spent almost a year in a hospital, but by the time I met her she seemed to have adjusted to the grief and shock. She enjoyed her position as an administrative assistant to one of the other senators and was very good at it."

He paused, and Elyse murmured, "Reba said she was beautiful."

Clint's gaze seemed to drift without focusing. "Yes, she was. Tall and slender as a model, with thick golden hair and wide blue eyes."

Elyse glanced down at her own generous curves and wished she was ten pounds lighter, although she knew her weight was normal for her height. With her unruly auburn hair and ordinary brown eyes, she was surprised Clint had even looked twice at her. She wished she'd never brought the subject of Dinah up.

"I was attracted to her," Clint continued, "and so were all the other unattached men who worked in the Capitol, but, although we all tried to date her, she refused to go out with any of the public officials. I persisted, and finally she told me she'd never again get involved with a man who was in a dangerous occupation, that she couldn't survive losing another loved one in such a shocking manner. I tried to reason with her, but she was adamant, so I retreated and vowed to forget about her."

He shrugged. "It was easy to say, but impossible to do. That fall one of the senators' wives talked me into buying two tickets for a charity fashion show and dinner dance. I decided I had nothing to lose by asking Dinah to go with me, and to my surprise she agreed."

He shifted restlessly. "After that we saw a lot of each other, and by Christmas we were in love. I was sure she'd finally come to terms with her husband's tragic death and realized that a politician is no more likely to be killed than a man in any other profession."

Clint got to his feet and stood in front of the fireplace. "I asked her to marry me, but she refused. She said it was too soon, she was too recently widowed, we didn't know each other well enough. This was all nonsense, but I could see the idea of marriage to me still upset her, so I didn't push it.

"For months we were almost inseparable, but still she refused to talk about a final commitment. At last I lost patience and we quarreled." He ran his fingers through his hair and turned away. "It was a very...difficult...time. I was stubborn and she was unyielding."

His tone had become harsh with emotion. "After two weeks I realized that...I...I..."

Clint turned suddenly, and his face was white and twisted with anguish. "Dammit, Elyse, there's no way I can put this delicately," he grated. "I found out I couldn't live without her and was getting ready to go to her and tell her so, when she came to me."

He jammed his hands into his pockets and began to pace. Elyse was numb with misery. She wanted to stop him, but she didn't seem to be able to move or utter a sound.

When he spoke again it was as if he'd forgotten she was there. "Dinah told me she loved me, that she couldn't lose me, and she'd agree to announcing our engagement if I'd give her a little more time before setting a wedding date. I'd have done anything, anything at all, just to have her back."

Elyse had an almost uncontrollable urge to put her hands over her ears. She didn't want to hear anymore. "Clint, don't, please—"

He continued as if he hadn't heard her, and she was sure he hadn't. "We made the announcement, attended the prenuptial parties and started planning the wedding. Everything, that is, but the date. Dinah still refused to set one.

"For several more months she kept me in a purgatory of uncertainty. I wanted her, needed her for my wife, but she was content to go on as we were, seeing each other when we could, grabbing a couple of hours here, a day there, sometimes a whole weekend. I felt I'd been put on hold, and I resented it more and more as time passed."

The more he talked the more impassioned his voice became, and Elyse realized he was actually feeling the frustration all over again. Once more she tried to stop him, but he'd retreated into the past where she couldn't reach him.

"I tried to understand and be patient, but eventually I reached the end of my endurance and blew up. I said things I didn't mean, made accusations that weren't true. I yelled . . . she cried—"

His voice broke and he turned away again, but Elyse was on her feet and stumbling toward him. She wrapped her arms around his waist and pressed herself against his back, her cheek against his shoulder. "Oh, Clint, don't do this to yourself," she wailed. "It's not necessary. You've told me more than enough already."

He turned in her arms and clasped her to him, and she realized he was trembling. This dredging up of old wounds had been a monstrous strain. She never should have asked it of him.

They stood holding each other for several minutes until the trembling slowed and then stopped and his breathing became less labored.

He kissed the top of her head where his face had been resting. "I need a drink," he said. "How about you?"

She nodded, not sure she could speak, and he let go of her and walked over to the bar.

As he had last night, he poured brandy into two snifters and brought one to her. "Come sit on the couch with me," he said, and put his arm around her waist.

They sat down close together, and Clint leaned his head back and closed his eyes. "I didn't mean to get so...so emotional," he said. "Forgive me."

Elyse knew what she had to do, but she clutched eagerly at any excuse to put if off for a little while. She swallowed some of the brandy. "I'm the one who should ask forgiveness. I shouldn't have put you through that. I'm so sorry."

He took her hand and held it. "I don't want your sympathy, Elyse. I just want you to try to understand why I still find it difficult to talk about the experience."

Difficult was a classic understatement, Elyse thought. Recounting his affair with Dinah had nearly torn him apart.

He drained his brandy and placed the snifter on the thickly carpeted floor. "After the quarrel," Clint began, picking up his story again, "when we'd finally calmed down and could discuss things rationally, Dinah begged me to agree to our just living together. She still couldn't bring herself to marry another politician—"

"Clint, no," Elyse interrupted. "You don't need to tell me anymore."

"Yes, I do." He sounded weary but determined. "I want you to know everything, just the way it happened."

She wanted to protest, but knew it would do no good. Besides, maybe talking it out to the bitter end would help him.

"A live-in lover wasn't what I wanted. I needed a respectable marriage with a wife and children and a lifetime commitment. I told her so, and she said that was the one thing she couldn't give me. She knew she was being unreasonable, but she honestly couldn't help it. She'd been so traumatized by the political assassination of her husband that she'd been psychologically damaged."

He sat up straight, but kept her hand in his. "I even offered to give up my career and go back to practicing law, but she wouldn't hear of it. We'd reached an impasse, and there was nowhere else to go.

"She gave me back the diamond I'd given her, and I took it with only a nominal protest. By then I was used up, emotionally battered. I'd run out of arguments. Nothing I said could counteract the terror she felt that I'd be killed, too, and she'd have to go through the whole damn ordeal all over again. I knew she had no control over her fear, but I also knew I could no longer beg and still keep my self-respect."

The volume of his voice had gotten lower until he was almost whispering. "She left and I never saw or heard from her again."

He'd loosened his hold on her hand, and she pulled it gently from his. It was time to bring this to a close. She couldn't bear to watch him suffer.

"You're still in love with her, aren't you?" she said gently.

He just stared ahead and didn't answer. His silence was all the confirmation she needed, and she stood and walked to the bedroom, where she gathered up her purse and overnight case.

When she got back to the great room he was still sitting where she'd left him. He looked so alone and lonely, and she hated Dinah Jefferson with a passion that was frightening. She hoped Dinah had hurt herself every bit as much as she'd hurt Clint.

Elyse walked over to the couch and touched him on the shoulder. "Clint, are you all right?"

"Yes," he said, then looked up and saw that she carried her purse and bag. "You're leaving?" He blinked with surprise.

"Yes," she said unsteadily.

"Please don't."

She knelt in front of him and put her hands on either side of his pinched face. "I have to." Her voice quivered. "Much as I love you, I can't marry you when you're in love with another woman."

He ran a finger across her trembling lips. "That was a long time ago."

She closed her eyes to blink back the tears that welled in them. "I guess for some of us love really is forever."

She reached up and kissed him tenderly. "Do you want me to call Paul to come and be with you?"

He shook his head. "No, if you won't stay I'd rather be alone for a while. Will you still be my friend?"

She felt a lone tear roll slowly down her cheek. "Of course. We'll even be related if Liz and Paul decide to get married."

Another tear fell, and then another, and she got hastily to her feet. Clint rose, too, and reached for her bag, but she was quicker. "No, please don't come to the car with me."

He nodded, then reached into his pocket and handed her a key. "You'll need it to open the door," he said. "Take it with you, and feel free to use it anytime."

She took it and hurried away, hoping she'd be gone before the sobs that were choking her escaped.

Chapter Eight

For days Elyse determinedly battled the depression that drifted like a fog into the recesses of her mind. She told herself she didn't have time for despair—she had a daughter to care for, a business to run, a life to live. But the fog settled in and left her days gray and her nights black without the hope of stars.

She recognized grief. She'd experienced its cloying debility before and was well acquainted with its capacity to undermine and disable. For Janey's sake as well as her own she couldn't let that happen.

When she'd come home on Saturday morning with tears still streaming down her face, Liz had taken her in her arms, and the whole story of her glorious conquest and her agonizing rejection had come pouring out. Her sister had held her and comforted her and encouraged her to cry until there were no tears left.

When Paul had arrived a few hours later, Elyse had been able to give him a coherent account of what had happened between her and Clint. She'd asked Paul to stop in to see his brother that evening and make sure he really was all right. She knew Paul had done as she asked, but though she'd seen him briefly since, they hadn't discussed what had taken place between the brothers.

Meanwhile she worked hard to dispel her gloom and the constant ache of sorrow that accompanied it. She sketched the design for a new doll, Little Red Riding Hood, and the wolf that was a companion piece. A tame, nonthreatening wolf that would never frighten a child or make an adult uneasy. There was enough misery in the world already.

She and Janey spent one day on the road, taking replacement stock to the two outlets that sold her dolls on consignment: a toy store in Sacramento and another in Berkeley. In the evenings she and Liz relaxed in the family room while she sewed the intricate costumes that made her dolls so appealing and Liz prepared lessons for her classes the following day. Elyse carefully avoided the subject of Clint, and Liz didn't press her.

On Friday, just one week after she'd won then lost Clint all within a few hours, Paul and Liz tried to get Elyse to bring Janey and spend the weekend in San Francisco with them. "You need to get away," Liz argued, "and there's a lot to do with a small child in the city. Remember the fabulous zoo? The beach front? And Golden Gate Park is a great place for an active little girl to run around and let off steam. Say you'll come, honey. It'll do you both good."

Elyse sighed and shook her head. "It's sweet of you to ask us, but you two don't need a moody sister and a four-year-old child around. You have too little time to yourselves as it is. Go ahead and have fun. Janey and I will be fine. Maybe we'll drive up to Pollock Pines after church on Sunday and have a picnic at Jenkinson Lake.''

They argued, but Elyse wouldn't be persuaded.

The next two days were lonely ones for Elyse, and to make matters worse she inadvertently caught Clint's latest political advertisement on television. She'd been carefully avoiding the station she knew carried his messages, but on Saturday she was making a costume pattern for the Little Red Riding Hood doll while Janey watched cartoons. Elyse was absorbed in what she was doing and didn't notice when the program ended and her daughter wandered out of the room without turning off the set.

Suddenly without warning a familiar baritone voice captured her attention. "Hello, I'm State Senator Clinton Sterling, and I'd like to tell you about the ease with which handguns can be bought in our state.''

Elyse dropped the scissors as her head jerked up and she turned in the direction of the screen. There was Clint, looking right at her with those extraordinary green eyes.

The muscles in her stomach knotted, and for a moment she had trouble breathing. He was sitting at a desk with a view of Capitol Park through the picture window behind him. The ad had apparently been filmed at his office.

He was dressed in a gray business suit with a crisp white shirt and maroon tie, and he looked like a movie star portraying a senator. Real-life politicians just weren't that handsome, but she knew for a fact that this one not only had almost perfect facial features but was flawless over every inch of his six-foot body.

She had a wholly irrational desire to reach out and touch him there on the screen, and had actually raised her hand before she caught herself and lowered it again. The picture blurred, and she blinked away the mist in her eyes that had made her vision fuzzy. He looked happy and relaxed and self-assured.

She felt a sharp stab of disappointment. He obviously hadn't been much affected by their breakup. It was several moments before she realized the message would have been taped well before their quarrel. By then Clint's image had disappeared and the newscaster was telling about a bank robbery.

When Elyse reached down to pick up her scissors she noticed her hands were shaking.

Paul and Liz arrived home Sunday evening positively beaming, and before they said a word Liz held out her left hand to show Elyse the glittering diamond ring on the fourth finger. Elyse threw her arms around her sister and squealed. "You're getting married!"

Liz nodded, too overcome to speak, and Elyse released her and hugged Paul. "Oh, I'm so happy for you."

He hugged her back. "So am I," he said, and his voice was thick with emotion.

Elyse again put her arm around Liz as they headed for the back of the house. "I want to hear all about it," she babbled excitedly. "You two go on into the family room. I'll get that bottle of champagne we've been saving for a special occasion. Nothing could be more special than this."

When they were settled in the living room with the good crystal stemware glasses filled with bubbling wine, Elyse prodded, "Now tell me everything. When is this big event going to take place?"

Liz laughed. "Actually, it's going to be a very small event. Neither of us wants a big wedding, so we're going to Lake Tahoe next weekend."

Elyse was truly delighted for her sister, but it was a bittersweet happiness mixed with might-have-beens. If she'd taken Clint's proposal at face value and accepted it, she'd be planning a wedding now, too. Or maybe she'd already be his wife.

Had she made a dreadful mistake? Could she have made Clint forget about Dinah Jefferson? Wouldn't almost anything have been better than the wretchedness she'd been feeling ever since she'd walked out on him?

Elyse forced a wide smile and looked at Paul, who was sitting on the sofa with Liz wrapped tightly in his arms. "How did you finally get her to say yes?" she asked.

Paul looked down at Liz and his expression sobered. "Actually, Elyse, I didn't do anything new or spectacular. It was you who made up her mind for her."

Elyse gasped. "Me?"

Liz looked up at Paul and frowned, but he ignored her obvious warning. "Liz has seen you go through two heartbreaking experiences, first when your fiancé died, and now with my brother and his stubborn insistence on clinging to the past—"

"No, Paul," Elyse half rose from her chair as she interrupted. "It's not Clint's fault he can't forget Dinah."

"The hell it's not," Paul said, and slammed his champagne glass down on the table. "Dinah was a beautiful woman, both physically and spiritually. I liked her—everybody who knew her did—and no one felt sorrier for Clint than I when she walked out on him. It shattered him. I can accept that and even understand it, but dammit, it's been four years. He can't grieve forever. She's not worth it.''

Elyse dropped back into the chair. "But . . . but you said you liked her," she said in a puzzled tone.

Paul sighed. "I did like her, but the truth is she just didn't love Clint enough."

Elyse grimaced. "How can you say that?"

"Easy. She knew how crazy he was about her. If she'd loved him as much as she insisted she did, she wouldn't have let anything come between them."

Elyse relaxed a little. That thought had occurred to her, too, but she'd pushed it aside, unwilling to judge the woman Clint loved so deeply.

Paul continued. "I realize that seeing her husband gunned down was an extremely traumatic experience, but it had been several years and she'd spent part of them in therapy. She should have come to terms with his death."

Liz was trying to shush Paul, but Elyse put up her hand. "No, Liz, it's all right. I want to hear what he has to say."

She looked again at Paul. "You're an intelligent man. Surely you'll agree that some people are stronger emotionally than others."

"Sure, but Dinah was a strong woman. She wasn't still grieving for her husband. She was afraid of the remote possibility that since Clint was a politician he might someday be the target of another assassin." Paul snorted. "Hell, the chances were a lot better that he'd be hit by a car or drown while swimming. She was manufacturing problems that didn't exist."

It was Liz who spoke next. "Look, you two," she said as she sat up a little straighter in Paul's arms, "you aren't doing Clint any favor by trying to analyze his feelings or Dinah's. That's something only the two people involved can know for sure. But, Elyse, Paul's right when he said you were partly responsible for my decision to marry him. I finally woke up to the fact that none of us knows what the future holds, so we'd better make the most of the present.''

She snorted self-deprecatingly. ''In a sense I've been guilty of the same sin as Dinah Jefferson, the sin of letting myself be paralyzed by an unreasonable fear of something that will probably never happen. I was afraid Paul might someday fall in love with a younger woman. In effect, I haven't trusted him to know his own mind.''

She turned and kissed him tenderly on the mouth. ''That's insulting, darling, and I'm truly sorry.''

She turned again to look at Elyse. ''After watching you wander around all week like the ghost of your usual joyful self, I decided to live my life in the present and let the future take care of itself. Paul and I might have to work a little harder to make our marriage a success, but if every couple did that the divorce rate surely would be lower.''

Liz looked away and toyed with her glass during a few moments of silence, then spoke again, still not looking directly at her sister. ''We have a favor to ask of you, Elyse.''

Elyse was puzzled by Liz's apparent evasiveness. ''Surely you know I'll do anything I can for you.''

Liz sighed. ''I hope so. We want you and Clint to go to the lake with us and be our witness.''

Elyse gasped and shook her head, but Liz continued. ''I know it's asking a lot of you, but you're all the family I've got, and I want you at my wedding.''

Elyse felt as though she'd been punched. ''Oh, Liz—''

"No, now wait, hear me out. Clint is the only member of Paul's family who's available on such short notice, and we both want loved ones with us at such a special time."

"I can't. I just can't." Elyse could hear the note of panic in her voice.

Liz got up and crossed the floor to kneel in front of her. "Look, honey, I don't want to add to your unhappiness, but Clint is going to be my brother-in-law from now on. You can't avoid him completely."

She took Elyse's cold hands between her warm ones. "Please do this for me. You're not only my baby sister, but you're practically my daughter as well. I raised you. I was as much of a mother to you as Mom was before she died, and afterward you were my total responsibility. You're my sister, my daughter and my best friend all rolled into one package, and I can't envision getting married without you present."

Elyse's body shook with silent sobs as love for her sister welled in her. She slid off her chair and put her arms around Liz while they knelt together on the floor and wept with nostalgia for the past, joy and sadness for the present and hope for the future. Paul sat quietly on the sofa, but his eyes were also misty.

After a while Liz asked for a handkerchief, which Paul handed her. Then she put her hand under Elyse's chin and lifted her face. She wiped her sister's streaming eyes and put the linen cloth to her nose. "Now blow," she ordered.

Elyse giggled. "Yes, Mama," she said, and blew.

The tension was broken, and both women got up off the floor and went back to their seats.

Elyse swiped at her wet cheeks with the backs of her hands and smiled. "So what time are we leaving for the lake Sunday morning?"

Paul answered while Liz dried her own eyes and face. "We thought if we left here by eight we could have breakfast when we got up there. That will give us plenty of time to get a license, find a wedding chapel that meets with our approval and take care of any other arrangements you ladies feel are indispensable."

"Have you talked to Clint?" Elyse asked apprehensively.

"No," Paul said. "We haven't seen him yet. I'm hoping to catch up with him tonight to make arrangements for Liz and me to get together with him tomorrow. He's been out of town, but I think he was due back today."

So Clint had been gone. He'd probably been too busy to give her a thought. Elyse wished she'd had something to do this past week that would have taken her mind off him.

"What makes you so sure he'll be willing to go if I'm along?" she asked.

Paul looked surprised. "He'll jump at the chance. Maybe he doesn't love you, Elyse, although I'm far from convinced of that, but you're very special to him. He wouldn't have asked you to marry him if you weren't. He's as miserable as you are with this situation."

Elyse made circles with her finger on the arm of the chair. "Yes, I guess he does care for me in his own way. He asked if I'd be his friend."

Paul ran his hand over his hair. "The man's an idiot," he snapped. "But why don't you give it a try? He's bound to come to his senses before long."

Elyse shook her head sadly. "No, I'm not going to hang around hoping for something that will never happen. Liz is right, though. If we're going to be related it would be awkward if I constantly tried to avoid him."

On Monday Paul and Liz spent the evening with Clint and reported back to Elyse that he was delighted about their marriage plans and had even cancelled another engagement so as to be free to go to Lake Tahoe with them on Saturday. Elyse was torn between her desire to see Clint and dread of the pain it would cause her.

After school on Tuesday Liz and Elyse left Janey with her favorite baby-sitter and drove into Sacramento to shop for wedding clothes. Liz chose an oyster linen suit with a midcalf-length full skirt and a mauve silk blouse, while Elyse, after a diligent search, found a linen coat dress in a matching shade of mauve. It buttoned off center to the left with big black buttons and featured a gently flaring skirt and short sleeves.

Afterward they met Paul for dinner at the Bull Market, an elegant restaurant in downtown Sacramento. As they lingered over dessert and coffee Paul made a suggestion. "Elyse, you've never seen my apartment." He looked at his watch. "It's early yet—only eight-thirty. Why don't we take a run over there? After all, it's where Liz and I will be living, at least for a while, and it's only a few blocks away."

"That's a good idea," Liz exclaimed enthusiastically before Elyse could answer. "Besides, last time I was there I left the only bottle of my favorite perfume behind and I'd like to get it."

Paul lived in one of the high-rise apartment buildings on Capitol Mall, with a view of the state capitol to the east and the Sacramento River to the west. They parked in the underground lot and took the elevator to the twelfth floor. Paul unlocked the door and stood aside to let Liz and Elyse enter.

Walking into the small entryway, Elyse noticed there was a light on in the room beyond. She covered the few steps to the arched doorway and gasped.

Coming toward her from across the luxurious living room was Clint!

He was wearing a dark business suit, and he stopped directly in front of her. His gaze roamed slowly over her, then returned to her face. "Hello, sweetheart," he said softly.

The floor seemed to rock under her feet, but she quickly regained her composure. "Clint," she said with only a hint of a quiver. "Paul and Liz didn't tell me you'd be here." She looked around, but the entryway was empty. "Where are they?"

"They've left," he said, then hurried to add when he saw her dismay, "but you're not being held prisoner. I'll take you home anytime you want me to. I hope you'll stay and listen to what I have to say though."

I'll kill that sneaky matchmaking sister of mine! Elyse thought as rage and humiliation warred for dominance. *First she insists Clint and I go to Tahoe with them, and now she's lured us here to talk. How can Liz be so insensitive? He must be just as uncomfortable as I am.*

Elyse was determined to be friendly but distant—and to get out of there as quickly as possible.

She stepped around him and walked over to the wall of windows. "So how are you, Clint? I understand you've been out of town." Good, her voice sounded firm and a little detached.

"I've been thoroughly miserable," he said from directly behind her, "and tearing around all over the state, making speeches in favor of gun control, didn't help. I was too sick—''

Startled, she turned and found herself standing chest to chest with him. ''Oh, Clint, I didn't realize you'd been ill. Paul didn't tell me.''

Her tone was anything but cool and detached. Now that she thought about it, he did look pale and drawn, but she'd been too shocked at finding him here to notice.

His arms went around her then and pulled her against him. Dimly she remembered she mustn't let him do that, but it felt so good that she couldn't resist. She buried her face in his shoulder and he rubbed his cheek in her hair. ''Not in the physical sense,'' he said. ''I was going to say I was sick with remorse. When you walked out of my house nine days ago you took all my hard won peace of mind and left only desolation and pain.''

She raised her head and looked at him, her face mirroring her surprise. ''I find that hard to believe,'' she said.

He lowered his head and kissed the tip of her nose, sending pinpricks down her spine. ''Why? Don't you know how much I've come to depend on your warmth? The sweetness of your smile? The tenderness of your touch?''

His arms tightened to draw her even closer. ''No,'' he said sadly, ''of course you don't. I never bothered to tell you, did I? I wouldn't even admit it to myself.

''I was so sure I'd never love again, so anxious not to. I'd had about all the punishment I could take in the name of love. I was too smart ever to let myself be that vulnerable a second time.''

He nuzzled the side of her throat. ''I was so busy protecting myself from love that I didn't even notice when quietly and without fanfare, you stole my patched-up heart."

Elyse melted against him, but her mind screamed at her to wait, to find out what he was talking about before she surrendered to her rampant desire to believe everything he said without question.

Just what did he want of her? If he still yearned for Dinah, then why did he miss Elyse when she refused to continue their relationship? Was she just a warm body to him, or did he really care for her?

It took all her willpower, but she pushed him away and stepped back. "I don't understand, Clint. If you wanted to talk to me, why didn't you come to see me, or call and ask me to meet you somewhere? Why this elaborate deception to get me here?"

Clint sighed and shoved his hands into his pockets. "I was terrified you'd refuse to see or listen to me. That's why I enlisted Paul and Liz's help in arranging a meeting with you. I was desperate."

She couldn't misunderstand the earnest plea in his words. Her gaze searched his worried face. "I thought we'd said everything there was to say on Sunday."

He shook his head. "We didn't even touch on the subject of you and me on Sunday," he said. "Elyse, you're one of the most empathetic women I've ever known. You must have understood how difficult it was for me to dredge up all those painful memories. It took me a long time to put them behind me and get on with my life, and bringing them up and examining them again was a harrowing experience. It left me literally wiped out."

Her heart constricted as she remembered how totally spent he'd looked after telling her the story of his love for Dinah Jefferson. Elyse felt she'd already caused him so much anguish. She didn't want to torture him any further, but there didn't seem to be any way to avoid it.

"Of course I understood, Clint. That's why I left. I'd already put you through enough. I wasn't going to make you admit you're still in love with Dinah."

He took her arm, and together they walked to the sofa and sat down before he spoke again. "But that's what we have to talk about," he said gently, "and we would have done it sooner if I hadn't had to go out of town on that speaking tour. I didn't call because this is something that has to be done in person. Also I needed time to get my thoughts in order."

"And now you have?" she asked, and wished for the thousandth time she'd never broached the subject of Dinah Jefferson in the first place.

"Yes," he said soberly. "And I discovered it wasn't the memory of Dinah that was tormenting me. It was the fact that I'd lost you."

Elyse jerked her head back to look at him. "Me?"

Placing one finger under her chin, he closed her still open mouth. "Yes, you. Why did you think I asked you to marry me?"

"Because you felt guilty about making love with me," she answered honestly.

He closed his eyes for a moment. "I did feel a little guilty because I hadn't been able to wait until I got my feelings sorted out before I took you to bed, but it had nothing to do with Dinah. At least, not with any nonsense about being disloyal to her, or hoping she'd come back. My concern was that I might not be able to love again, at least not in the way you deserve to be loved."

Elyse held her breath as she waited for him to continue.

"I discovered during this past week that my fears were unfounded. What I feel for you has got to be love—it's too strong not to be. I'm happy when you're happy, and miserable when you're upset. I worry about you when you're away from me, and I feel whole only when you're with me. I admire your fine mind and your artistic talent, and such a small everyday thing as the touch of your hand in mine brightens my life. I experience an ecstasy beyond words when we make love, and all of those feelings together add up to love, my darling. They make a strong sure bond for building a marriage."

He put his arms around her then and lifted her face so she looked directly at him. "Say you'll marry me, Elyse. I want you, I need you, I love you. I want to be Janey's father, I'd like to adopt her, and I promise to love her as my own."

Tears shimmered in Elyse's eyes, and she trembled with the overpowering emotions of love, joy and exuberance that racked her slender body. It would be all right; everything would work out. Clint loved her, and oh, God, how she loved him."

She put her arms around his neck and kissed the pulse beating below his jaw. "Of course I'll marry you." Her voice quavered. "I can't even imagine a life without you."

She turned her head and their lips met. It was a cautious kiss, hungry but restrained as they each fought for self-control. Clint's hand roamed over her almost roughly, as if the need to touch every part of her was more than he could resist.

Elyse put her arms under his suit jacket and pulled his shirt out of his trousers so she could caress his bare back, and he shivered as her fingers kneaded his flexing muscles. One of his hands cupped her breast while the other dropped to her thigh and worked its way under her skirt. Throbbing with need, Elyse dipped her fingers below the waistband of his trousers.

Clint tensed and clutched at her bare thigh. "Have mercy, love," he groaned. "Don't keep me waiting any longer."

"Who's resisting?" she murmured, squirming impatiently. "Does this apartment have a bedroom?"

His mouth turned up at the corners in a small grin. "Does it matter?"

She nibbled at his bottom lip. "Not at all. I'll make love with you anyplace."

His arms tightened spasmodically. "Keep talking like that and we'll wind up right here on the floor." He released her, then stood and took her hand to lead her down the hall to a bedroom.

He flicked a wall switch, and a brass lamp on a cherrywood table beside a matching bed provided soft illumination for the blue-and-white room. Clint removed his jacket and tossed it onto a chair, then turned back to Elyse. "Now let's get you out of those clothes," he said, and reached for her zipper.

He undressed her quickly, but when she reached for his shirt buttons he caught her hand and moved it to his lips, instead. "You'd better let me do that myself," he said, and kissed her palm. "I'd never survive those seductive little fingers touching and stroking and probing me into insanity."

He stripped his clothes off while she turned back the covers, and they tumbled into bed together. Rolling over so that his body partially covered her, Clint lowered his mouth to hers. Elyse wrapped her arms around his neck and parted her lips to his seeking tongue.

"Oh, how I've missed you," he murmured as his hand caressed her firm round breast. "You've built a fire in me that can't be quenched."

"I try," she whispered as she ran her fingernails across his shoulders. She shuddered as his hand slid down to her stomach while his mouth moved to tease her breast.

Slowly she played her fingertips down his spine until they settled in the hollow at the base. His breathing was raspy. "If you try any harder I'm going to be incinerated," Clint warned as her palms rubbed his firm hard buttocks.

He shifted downward and laid his cheek against her abdomen. Elyse felt a rush of liquid warmth deep inside her and clutched at his hair as he planted moist kisses around her navel, then veered lower.

"Clint, no," she moaned, wriggling with a combination of intense pleasure and apprehension. "I've never—"

He raised up, repositioning his face to the soft space between her breasts. "It's all right, love," he reassured her. "I won't do anything you don't want me to do."

She kissed the top of his head. "It's just that I...I've never...never..."

"I'm glad," he said softly. "When you're ready I want to be the first and only."

His fingers stroked the soft curly hair that protected her most intimate recesses. She gasped and arched against his hand as she clutched his shoulders. "Clint!" she cried, and dug her heels into the back of his thighs as his fingers probed deeper. "Please. Now!"

With a tortured growl of surrender he moved over her and plunged swiftly into her moist heat, locking her in a fierce embrace that made them truly a part of each other as together they touched the stars.

Chapter Nine

Clint and Elyse were jubilant as they drove to Placerville early that morning. When they told Liz of their marriage plans, she hugged them both and steadfastly refused to apologize for her part in the deception that had brought them together the night before. "Why don't we make it a double wedding at Tahoe next weekend?" she asked.

Elyse looked at Clint, expecting him to agree, and was surprised to see him hesitate. "I don't think that's a good idea, Liz," he said slowly. "With the election coming up early next month I have a schedule that hardly leaves me time to breathe. I have appointments that start at six in the morning and go on into the night."

He put his arm around Elyse and hugged her to his side. "When I marry your beautiful little sister I want to take her away someplace where we can have at least a month of uninterrupted honeymoon."

He leaned down and kissed Elyse on the nose, then winked at Liz. "If I knew she was home waiting for me now, I'd lose the election for sure. It's difficult to run for office from the bedroom."

Elyse laughed and punched him and vowed not to let him see her disappointment. She was being silly. After all, what difference did a few weeks make?

It was late in the afternoon on Wednesday before she saw him again. He picked her up to take her to his house for dinner, where he introduced her to Alice and Grover Irwin, who served him as housekeeper and handyman. But when he made the introductions, he didn't mention that he and Elyse were engaged. She liked the elderly couple, who treated Clint more as a son than an employer, and she wondered why he hadn't told them he was going to be married.

"We're having a visitor after dinner," Clint told her as they sipped sherry while waiting for the meal to be served."

Elyse felt a stab of dismay. She'd assumed they'd be spending the evening alone, preferably in bed, but she flashed a determined smile. "Oh, how nice," she said brightly.

"Like hell it is," Clint muttered, "but it'll be up to you how long he stays."

"Me?"

He grinned. "Yeah, so rush it a little, will you? We have better things to do than visit."

Just then Alice announced that dinner was ready, and Clint teasingly refused to discuss the subject further.

They were finishing coffee and cherry pie in the great room, when the doorbell rang and Alice escorted a well-dressed middle-aged man in to join them. Clint rose and extended his hand. "Harold—good to see you. I really appreciate your coming here like this."

Harold shifted the leather briefcase he carried and shook hands with Clint. "Happy to do it, Senator," he said with a smile.

Clint introduced Harold to Elyse, then said, "Harold owns Gaylord's Jewelry Store in Sacramento, and I've asked him to bring a selection of rings for you to look at."

Elyse stared as the jeweler set his case on the coffee table and opened it. Everyone was familiar with Gaylord's but few could afford to shop there. She watched as he uncovered a velvet tray of diamond rings. They were gorgeous, and although there were no price tags in evidence, she knew the rings must be monstrously expensive.

"I . . . I don't know what to say." She moved closer to Clint, and he took her hand.

"Don't say anything." There was a note of humor in his tone. "Just look them over and see if there's one you like."

"I like them all!"

"Ah, now there's a lady after my own heart," Harold said with a chuckle.

Clint laughed. "I'm afraid my checking account isn't quite *that* healthy."

"Oh, I didn't mean—"

He squeezed her hand. "I know you didn't, love. I only wish I could shower you with jewels, but at the current market price we'll have to work up to that a few at a time."

Clint picked up a ring with an oval-shaped diamond that was almost obscenely large and had several rows of smaller diamonds around it. "How about this one?"

She shook her head, refusing even to consider it. "If I wore that one I wouldn't be able to raise my hand," she teased.

Elyse had never yearned for jewels. On her list of priorities they were near the bottom. She hadn't had a ring when she was engaged to Jerry; they couldn't afford it. They'd chosen a plain gold band to be married with, and had the wedding taken place, she would have cherished it as much as if it had been encrusted with diamonds.

Clint could afford the engagement gift, but it wasn't the size of the jewel that would make it precious to her; it was what it symbolized: the promise of love and commitment.

As she fingered the beautiful jewelry she remembered Clint had mentioned a diamond ring that Dinah had returned to him. She wondered what it looked like. She didn't want to inadvertently pick a similar one. Maybe she could...

She addressed her question to the jeweler. "Do engagement rings always have to be diamonds?"

"Not at all," he said, "although the diamond is traditional. Would you prefer to see some other gemstones?"

She looked questioningly at Clint. "Would you mind?"

"Whatever you want," he said, sounding perplexed. "Don't you like diamonds?"

"I've never had one, but they seem so...so cold, somehow."

Harold had removed another velvet tray from his briefcase, and he opened it to reveal a mixture of green, red, blue and amber jewels.

Elyse caught her breath. "Oh, they're exquisite!"

One ring in particular caught her eye. It was a solitary brilliant green gem that almost exactly matched the color of Clint's eyes. She picked it up and held it to the light. It seemed nearly alive in its warm sparkling beauty, and she knew this was the one she wanted.

She held it out to Harold. "Is this one terribly expensive?"

Clint answered. "As long as you don't want a whole tray full of them, cost is no object. Do you like that one?"

"I love it," she said simply. "It almost breathes."

The jeweller smiled. "That's a premier quality emerald. An excellent choice. Would you like to try it on?"

Wordlessly she slid the ring onto her fourth finger, left hand, and it fit as if it had been sized for her. It occurred to her that it wasn't a very practical ring—the stone was so large and prominently set that it would probably catch on everything—but all her life she'd been practical. This time she was going to take what she wanted, and to hell with the consequences.

As she pulled the ring off she realized she was doing the same thing by marrying Clint. Taking what she wanted, and to hell with the consequences. She'd deal with the future as it came along.

When the transaction was concluded, Harold left, and Clint held the ring. He put his arms around Elyse and kissed her, then took her left hand in his and slid the ring on her finger. "From this day forward, for better or for worse," he said.

She choked back tears of happiness as he gathered her close and held her.

When she was sure she could talk around the lump in her throat she pulled back to look at him and said, "I didn't know jewelers made house calls."

He chuckled. "Usually they don't, but we've done business with Harold for years. I explained that I didn't really have the time to bring you into the store, and also that we didn't want—"

He stopped talking and a look of chagrin crossed his face.

She waited for him to continue, but when he didn't she said, "Yes? We didn't want *what*?"

He didn't answer, but led her over to the couch where they sat down side by side. "Honey," he said, not looking directly at her. "Would you mind if we postponed announcing our engagement until after the election next month?"

Elyse was startled, but she managed to keep it from sounding in her voice. "I suppose not, if you think it's best. I know you said you didn't want to get married right away, but is there some reason we should keep our plans a secret?"

He nodded. "If we wait until the election is over and things settle down we can do it properly. You haven't met any of my family yet except Paul. I don't want them to learn about the woman who's going to be my wife through a hurried phone call or, worse, from the newspapers. Besides, we don't want to steal the spotlight from Liz and Paul. Next week, after they're married, I'll write to my parents and two sisters and tell them about us. Then we'll call and talk to them. We'll set a date for an engagement party and insist they all come home for it."

Everything he said made sense. Elyse could find no fault in it, and she told herself she was glad he was the type of man to be concerned about his family's feelings.

She cuddled against him and said, "That sounds fine. I'm really looking forward to meeting your parents."

He put his arms around her. "I knew you'd understand." He nibbled her earlobe. "There's just one more thing."

Elyse tensed in spite of her efforts not to. "Oh?"

"The ring," he said carefully. "When we're in public, could you wear it on your right hand? Otherwise it will cause a lot of speculation."

A cold wave of apprehension swept over her, and it was all she could do not to shiver. She pulled out of his embrace and moved away. "Clint, does this have anything to do with Janey?"

He looked genuinely surprised. "Janey?"

"Yes. Is the fact that I have an illegitimate child going to cause problems for you politically? Are you so anxious to postpone acknowledging us until later because we could damage your chances of getting reelected?"

She stood and started to move around the room. "If that's it, then we can forget the whole thing right now. I won't allow your career to be ruined because of me, but neither will I let my daughter and I be hidden in hopes that none of your constituents will notice us."

Clint sprang off the sofa and glared at her. "Sweet Lord, woman, is that what you think of me?" he bellowed. "Do you honestly believe I give a damn what people think about my private life? How can you say you love me and in the next breath accuse me of being such a creep?"

He clutched her by the upper arms, and his fingers were like claws digging into her flesh. She'd never seen him so furious. "I admit you haven't known me long," he said, and she could see the effort he was making to calm down, "but have I ever indicated in any way that I thought you were less than respectable? Or that I considered Janey a bastard and therefore unworthy to be my daughter?''

Elyse gaped at him, totally unable to respond in her astonishment at his use of those ugly words. "What have I done to give you such a low opinion of me?" he continued. "I love Janey almost as much as I love you, and it never even entered my mind that marrying you and adopting her might lose me a few votes. The scarlet *A* went out of vogue a long time ago, and I don't want the support of anyone who has a mind to bring it back."

He let go of her so suddenly she almost lost her balance as he strode across the room to pick up a telephone. The action released her stunned senses, and she hurried after him. "Clint, what are you going to do?"

She was trembling, and her knees threatened to buckle as she grabbed at the arm he was using to dial.

He jerked away from her and his features were stony. "I'm calling my parents to tell them about our engagement, and then I'm going to get in touch with the news media. By tomorrow you'll have all the publicity you could ever hope for."

Elyse felt sick as she jammed her hand on the dial. "No! Listen to me. I didn't mean—"

He put the phone back in the cradle, and suddenly all the rage drained out of him. He turned to look at her, and her heart melted at the hopelessness mirrored on his face. "I think you'd better decide just what you mean, Elyse," he said in a voice devoid of emotion. "First you indicated you wanted to make love, then pushed me away when I tried. Then you came to me and apologized, but when I asked you to marry me you said you couldn't until I told you about Dinah. I did that, and you said you wouldn't marry me because of what I'd told you, and walked out. Now you've agreed to marry me, but you accuse me of being a son of a bitch.''

He walked away from her and stood facing the fireplace. "I'm not going to put myself through much more of this. I don't pretend to be perfect, but I do try to be honorable. If you can't trust me, if you're always going to misunderstand my motives, I don't see much future for us.''

His words were like whips lashing at her. He was right. She'd never behaved so irrationally as she had since she'd met and fallen in love with Clint. Just minutes ago she'd analyzed his reasons for wanting to postpone announcing their engagement and found them sound. Seconds later she'd accused him of subterfuge. She was being childish, and she didn't blame him for pulling back, for wondering if he wanted to marry her after all.

The thought was more than she could bear, and she approached him slowly with her eyes downcast. She stopped in front of him and looked up into his white, weary face. "I'm sorry," she said brokenly. "You're right. I've been behaving like a spoiled child. I've thrown a tantrum every time things haven't gone just exactly the way I wanted them to, and I don't blame you for being disgusted with me.''

She looked down at the ring on her finger and discovered she was twisting it with the fingers of her other hand. "If you want the ring back I'll understand, but Clint—'' her voice broke, and she had to take a deep breath before she could go on "—don't ever think I don't love you.''

She laced her fingers together and looked into the unlit fireplace. "I guess it's because I love you so much that I panic when you show signs of being...less involved...than I am. Of having a life apart from me.''

He moved as if to protest, but she looked up and shook her head. "No, please, let me finish. That wasn't a complaint. You're older than I am, you've been an adult longer than I have and you have a much more complicated life than I do. It will take me a while to fit in. I don't want to smother you with my love."

She slowly slid the glittering emerald off her finger and held it out to him. "Here," she said, and again her voice broke. "Maybe we should think about this before we make a firm commitment."

There was a heavy pressure in her chest, and she found it difficult to breathe. *Could this be what it feels like when your heart breaks?*

Clint ignored her outstretched hand with the ring and took her in his arms. "I don't want the ring," he said in a gravelly tone. "I want you."

With a sob Elyse clutched the gem and put her arms around his neck as she snuggled against him. She tried to tell him with her pliable and willing body how sorry she was and how much she loved him, but although he held her close, the passion in him had died and could not, or would not, be rekindled.

A few minutes later he took her home.

Elyse didn't hear from Clint again until after eleven on the following night, Thursday, when the phone rang. "I'm sorry for calling so late, sweetheart," he said, "but I've been chasing my tail all day. How are you?"

Elyse's relief at hearing from him was all the greater because he didn't sound angry anymore. "It's all right, Clint, I was hoping you'd call. And I'm fine. A little tired. I didn't sleep much last night."

"Neither did I," he said, and there was a catch in his voice. "I'm sorry. I didn't mean to blow up the way I did."

"I'm sorry, too. I didn't mean to be so silly." Her voice softened. "I love you, Clint."

"I love you, too," he said tenderly. "I just got off the phone with my dad and mom. I told them I'd fallen in love with the sweetest, most beautiful lady in all of California and that we're going to be married very soon."

Elyse felt a stab of guilt. "Oh, Clint," she said, "I'm sorry you've done that. It wasn't necessary—really. I know you didn't want to tell them that way."

"I was being stubborn," he said grimly. "I didn't even think how it would sound to you when I asked that we postpone the announcement. My reticence had nothing whatsoever to do with Janey. I never think of her as anything but your beautiful and adorable daughter, who very soon will be mine, too. My parents were delighted, and they're anxious to meet the two of you."

But a few minutes later Clint frowned as he hung up. What he'd told Elyse wasn't exactly true. His parents had not been delighted. Especially when they'd found out Elyse had a child but had never been married.

His mother had seemed reserved, but his father had reacted as Clint had known he would. He'd fumed and blustered and predicted that marrying a woman with an illegitimate child would cost Clint his political career. It had turned into a shouting match between the two men until Grace Sterling had intervened in a three-way conversation and calmed them both down.

Clint was still furious with his dad, but he could understand his position. Burton Sterling had started his career in the 1930s, when having a child out of wedlock was considered moral turpitude and a man whose wife or daughter had done such a thing had little chance of being elected to public office. At age seventy-five he'd never been able to adjust his way of thinking to embrace the "new morality."

He wasn't vindictive. He wouldn't condemn Elyse. But neither would he be persuaded that she wasn't a detriment to Clint's career. Fortunately Clint's father was a gentleman of the old school, and he'd never intentionally let Elyse know he objected to his son marrying her.

Elyse didn't see Clint again until he and Paul came to pick up Elyse and Liz for the trip to Lake Tahoe early Saturday morning, Paul and Liz's wedding day. Both men looked smashing in their dark suits, and each whistled appreciatively as he caught sight of his lady.

Clint led Elyse into the doll shop, where they could have a little privacy, and clasped her in his arms as he ravaged her willing mouth. "It seems like three weeks instead of three days since I last saw you," he murmured, burrowing his lips into the side of her neck.

It had seemed that way to her, too, and she caressed his ear with her tongue as she told him so.

He shivered with pleasure and encouraged her by stroking the sides of her breasts. "I wish now that we were getting married today, too," he said. "I don't know what I was thinking of when I insisted on waiting. Would you consider making this a double wedding, after all?"

Her first inclination was to say yes, yes, yes! But she quickly stifled the impulse. He was male and she aroused him and he was impatient to take her to bed. She was just as impatient as he, but they'd make love tonight whether they got married this afternoon or not. There was no need to rush the vows, and he'd been emphatic about wanting to wait.

She'd let him set the date for both the announcement and the wedding, but not until after the election. He must never look back and wonder if he'd been coerced into a marriage he didn't really want.

"No, Clint," she said firmly. "I want our wedding day to be special and all ours. Also, I want Janey to be there, and I've already taken her to her grandparents to spend this weekend."

"Her grandparents? I didn't know she had any."

"Jerry's folks. They have an orchard in the apple hill area. They don't see Janey nearly as often as they'd like, and I wouldn't go back on my word to let them have her for the next two days."

He sighed. "Okay, you're right, we'll have a proper wedding later and let Janey be the flower girl. Come on, we'd better get started. Paul's going to be a nervous wreck if we don't get this show on the road soon."

Elyse grinned. "So's Liz. She's already repacked her overnight bag three times, and she nearly went into a tizzy over which nightgown to take. I finally had to remind her that it didn't matter since it would never get unpacked."

Clint laughed and took her hand. He brought it to his lips, then frowned. "Where's your ring?"

She flexed her naked fingers, then unbuttoned the top button on her coatdress and pulled out a thin gold chain with the ring attached. "It's right here, see?"

He glared at her. "Why in hell are you wearing it around your neck under your clothes? Dammit, Elyse, I didn't mean you had to hide it. I told you I'd call the newspapers if that's what you wanted."

Her nerves weren't in much better shape than Liz's, and she snapped back, "It's not what I want, but neither do I intend to let my friends think I'm accepting expensive jewelry from my 'good friend' the senator."

Clint was silent for a moment. Then he reached out and rebuttoned her dress. "All right," he said tightly. "I'm not going to argue with you today. But we'll discuss it later."

The wedding took place that afternoon in an elegant little white chapel tucked away in a grove of pine and spruce trees. Both Liz and Elyse wore floral headpieces constructed of baby orchids, and soft organ music wafted on the air as the minister read the age-old vows. The stars in Liz's eyes sparkled more brightly than the diamonds in the ring Paul slipped on her finger before he took his new wife in his arms and kissed her.

Elyse watched through a mist of happy tears and murmured a little prayer that her beloved sister would live happily ever after with her handsome young husband. Liz, who had given up her own youth to shoulder the burden of raising an adolescent sister, deserved the adoration that Paul made no attempt to hide when he looked at her. *Please, God, may their love last forever,* Elyse silently asked.

Later Clint and Elyse hosted an early wedding dinner in a small private dining room at Harrah's. Afterward Paul and Liz left for the family's summer home on the shore of the lake, and Clint and Elyse played the slot machines for a while, then went upstairs.

Clint ushered Elyse into the spacious room and closed the door, then took her in his arms. She was so soft and fragrant and cuddly, and it seemed he'd been waiting an eternity for this moment. Just thinking of her made him hot, and when he touched her he burned.

Dammit, why was he dragging his feet about this relationship? He'd grown used to loneliness until Elyse came into his life, but now it was intolerable. After Dinah he'd promised himself he'd never need a woman again, but he needed Elyse. Why had he hurt her by insisting they wait until later to marry—or even to announce their engagement? The reasons he'd given himself and her were valid, but they weren't good enough.

He kissed her long and lingeringly. "Have you been waiting as impatiently as I have for this?" he murmured against the side of her mouth.

"At least as impatiently," she replied, turning her head slightly to capture his lips once more.

It had been a week since they'd made love, and the fire that simmered in his groin made it difficult for him not to rush her. He pulled her skirt up until he could get his hand under it, then encountered panty hose where he'd hoped for bare flesh. "Are all these clothes necessary?" he muttered as he caressed her sheer-stocking-covered thighs.

"Only if we're going back downstairs," she answered between kisses.

"Over my dead body," he said firmly, and slid his hand up to her round little bottom. "We're going to bed." He crushed her up against him.

She started unfastening the knot in his tie. "Soon, I hope?" She rubbed slowly against him, and he clenched his teeth in an attempt to control his raging desire.

He gripped her errant derriere. "I'd thought we'd shower first." His voice betrayed his intolerable strain, "but—"

"Together?" Her breathing was jerky.

"Of course."

"Can I wash your... back?"

He bit back a groan as a vision of her coming at him with a washcloth in her talented little hands nearly did him in. "Honey," he grated fervently, "you can wash anything you want to."

They quickly removed their clothes and headed for the bathroom, but they made it only as far as the bed.

It was midnight before they got that shower, and by morning they had to do it all over again.

For the next ten days, Clint was so caught up in legislative sessions during the day and campaigning evenings and weekends that Elyse saw little of him until the election the first week in June. He called Elyse every day, though, and she watched his campaign ads on television. The few times they were together were hurried and frustrating, and she clearly understood why he'd wanted to postpone their engagement announcement until things settled down. She had a lot to learn about being a politician's wife.

When the votes were finally in and counted, Clint retained his Senate seat with a wide margin to spare. The party at his campaign headquarters on election night began early and went on until the wee hours of the morning; and Elyse had never seen anything like it. It was the first time she'd attended a major political event with Clint, and she attracted a lot of attention.

The crush was a little frightening, but Elyse smiled a lot and managed to answer questions without really saying anything. Paul and Liz were there, receiving congratulations and best wishes on their recent marriage, but Clint was the star of the show. Elyse was surprised by his public presence. He was skilled in projecting just the image he wanted. Tonight it had been confidence and, once it became obvious he'd won, gratitude and happiness.

In public he appeared to be gregarious. He talked with anyone who approached him, posed for pictures, allowed himself to be interviewed by the news media and supplied food and drinks for everyone—a contrast to the quiet, retiring man Elyse had come to know. She suspected that maintaining two different personalities must be a strain, and she vowed to do all she could to keep things running smoothly for him at home once they were married.

Immediately after the primaries, Paul and Liz left on a delayed honeymoon to Europe and Clint started campaigning for the general election. His opponent was a well-known and well-liked rancher in the district. The man's rugged good looks and down-home manner appealed to the other ranchers, farmers and small-business people who made up a large portion of the population, and Clint was worried.

It was a week before he brought up the subject of the engagement announcement party. Elyse had cooked dinner for him that Tuesday evening, and after they'd put Janey to bed they settled down on the couch in the family room.

Following a long, intimate kiss he snuggled her against him. "Honey, I talked to Mom today. She and Dad are coming home next week for a stopover before going on to the summer place at Tahoe. She says if you'd like, she'd be happy to help with plans for the announcement party, and she hopes you'll have it at the house."

Elyse had talked to the Sterlings on the phone once or twice, and they'd seemed friendly and polite. "I'm glad they're coming," she said. "I'm anxious to meet them, and I'll be forever grateful for your mother's help. Did you have a date in mind?"

They settled on a Saturday night in mid-July, three weeks away. Much later, when Clint was leaving, he turned to her. "Oh, I almost forgot. Bill Ogden stopped in my office today to invite us to a swimming party and barbecue at their house Sunday afternoon. Nothing elaborate, just a few couples. I told him I'd ask you and let him know tomorrow."

Elyse smiled. "Sure. Sounds like fun. I've been hoping we'd see the Ogdens again soon. Maybe Reba can give me pointers on how a senator's wife should behave."

Clint chuckled and put his hand inside her pink cotton robe to fondle her breast. "If you'd like to go back upstairs with me I'll be happy to show you how I want this senator's wife to behave."

"You're insatiable," she said with a grin. "Besides, you told me you have an early morning appointment."

He grimaced and removed his restless hand. "Ah, yes, my constituents. Can't get elected without them." He kissed her and left.

On Sunday Elyse dressed in white slacks and a tank top with a multicolored oversize shirt worn loose over it. Janey had gone home after church with the family of one of her friends from Sunday school, with plans to stay overnight.

Elyse leaned against the leather seat in Clint's car as the Cadillac streaked down the freeway. Clint held her hand against his denim-covered thigh, and music from the stereo system literally surrounded them.

She was happy and content. The world was bright and beautiful, and her ghosts had been laid to rest. Clint loved her, they were making plans for their engagement party and he had tentatively broached the possibility of an August wedding and a two-week honeymoon in Hawaii before the last hectic weeks of the campaign and the November election.

For now, she was eagerly looking forward to an afternoon of swimming and feasting with Bill and Reba Ogden and their guests—and she was pleased at the opportunity to meet more of Clint's friends from the legislature.

There were several luxury cars parked in front of the Ogdens' home when they drove up, and Elyse reached for the beach bag that contained her new black one-piece bathing suit, which exposed a great deal more than it hid. As they approached the house they heard music coming from the backyard, and Clint took her arm and led her down a flagstone path through a profusely blooming flower garden along the side of the house.

They heard voices as they got closer, and when they rounded the back corner of the building they stepped onto a wide, covered patio that ran the width of the house. The music was coming from speakers mounted under the overhang, and there were several casually clad men and women gathered in a cluster on the tiled area by the kidney-shaped swimming pool. Numerous round tables and chairs were strategically placed for informal dining, and Elyse noticed a bathhouse on the far side of the pool. The rest of the huge lot was covered with carpetlike green lawn, flowering bushes and massive old shade trees.

At first they moved toward the group unnoticed, but then Bill caught sight of them. "Clint," he called, starting in their direction. But he didn't look very welcoming. There was no smile, and if Elyse hadn't known better she'd have thought he was intent on heading them off.

"Hi," Clint said happily. "Sorry we're a little late."

The rest of the cluster of people turned almost as one and stared. The sound of happy voices stopped so abruptly that it left a total silence, broken only by the lilting melody of the string section of a symphony orchestra in the background.

Clint stopped and looked around, perplexed. It was Bill who finally spoke. "Clint, we have an unexpected...um...that is..."

Elyse had never seen anyone quite so flustered, and she knew this had to be out of character for the suave, unflappable Senator William Ogden. A cold feeling of dread blew across the back of her neck, and she blinked as a tall blond woman with sapphire eyes and beautifully chiseled features separated herself from the group and came toward them.

"Hello, Clint," she said in a throaty whisper that raised the goose bumps on Elyse's flesh.

She felt him jerk with surprise beside her, and the hand that held her arm clenched with such force that she almost cried out.

For a few interminable seconds he just stood there. When he spoke, it was in a voice dead with shock. "Hello, Dinah."

Chapter Ten

Clint's face had lost every trace of color, and his skin seemed to be stretched taut across the bones beneath. He and Dinah Jefferson, the woman who'd rejected his love and caused him such grief, looked at each other with gazes that seemed to devour each of them, yet melded them into one being.

There was a roar in Elyse's head that drowned out everything else, and for a moment she thought she was going to fall. Then an arm around her waist steadied her, and Reba's voice whispered in her ear. "Hang in there. Now smile and come with me."

Elyse hoped the grimace she made would be construed as a smile, and she moved with Reba, although she had to break Clint's unconsciously tight hold on her arm first.

Reba's strong arm was the only thing holding Elyse up as they walked toward the house. Reba slid the glass doors back and ushered her inside, but some imp in Elyse made her turn back in time to see Clint and Dinah come together in an embrace that spoke more eloquently than words ever could.

The pain that attacked her and held her prisoner was icy, and she wondered why hell was always referred to as hot.

Reba saw, too, and quickly tugged Elyse away from the door and down a hall to a room that was obviously an office. Still in shock, Elyse sank bonelessly down on the leather couch and let the world whirl around her.

She was roused a minute later by Reba, who put a small crystal glass half full of amber liquid in her hand. ''Here,'' she said. ''Drink this.''

Elyse was shaking so badly the liquor sloshed. She gripped the glass with both hands and raised it to her lips. The swallow she took was smooth and the liquor slid down her throat before she realized it was whiskey. She took another gulp, then set the glass down on the table in front of her. ''Was this your idea of a joke?'' she asked, still too shaken for anger.

''Good Lord, no!'' Reba replied. ''Please believe me. We had no idea Dinah was even in the country, let alone Sacramento. She showed up just minutes before you did. There was no time to get rid of her—or to warn Clint. She was surprised we had company and started to leave, but the others spotted her and insisted she stay.''

Reba took a sip of her own drink. ''Elyse, I'm almost certain she didn't know Clint was coming, and it's obvious he didn't know she was here.''

Yes, Clint hadn't known Dinah would be here. He certainly would never have brought Elyse if he had. She wondered how long it would take him to remember that she was with him now.

She picked up her glass of whiskey and took another swallow. It broke up some of the chilling coldness in her and calmed her a little. At least it made her head stop spinning so she could talk.

"Would you please call a cab for me?" she asked.

Reba looked startled. "I'll take you anywhere you want to go, but if you run away you're going to provide everyone here with enough juicy gossip to keep them weaving tales for years. You can bet that everyone noticed Dinah's not wearing a wedding ring. If you're serious about Clint you'd better be prepared to fight for him."

"Serious about him!" Elyse started to laugh, but there was no humor in it. "How can I be serious about him—" she stopped as the laughter again erupted "— when his true love...has just come back...to claim him?" She was gasping with hysterical mirth. Reba couldn't know how serious she was, or that she and Clint had been making plans to announce their engagement.

Reba grasped her by the shoulders and shook her. "Stop it, Elyse. Get a hold on yourself. You can't fall to pieces now."

Elyse took a deep breath and the hysteria subsided. "I'm sorry," she said, and ran her hand through her hair. "I don't seem to be handling this very well."

Reba hugged her. "You're doing just fine, love. A whole lot better than I would be if it were Bill." She finished her drink. "Why in hell did Dinah have to come back here?"

"Maybe she missed Clint as much as he missed her."

Reba turned her head to look at Elyse closely. "You've got it bad, haven't you?"

Elyse was too undone to attempt a lie; she just nodded.

Reba muttered an indelicate oath, and seconds later Clint's voice boomed down the hall, calling Elyse's name.

Elyse brought her feet up onto the couch in front of her and wrapped her arms around her legs as she buried her face in her knees. "Oh, God," she wailed.

Reba jumped up to head Clint off, but she was too late. The door opened and he walked in, looking distraught. "Reba, have you seen—"

His gaze moved to the couch. "Elyse!" He walked over to sit beside her. "Honey, don't," he said, and took her in his arms.

She didn't lift her head or change position, but sat stiffly in his embrace. Reba slipped quietly out of the room and closed the door.

"I've been looking all over for you." His voice was low and strained. "I couldn't find you anywhere. I was afraid..."

He didn't attempt to continue, but rocked her gently back and forth as she slowly began to relax and uncurl. She put her feet back on the floor and leaned against him. He was so strong and yet so tender. She could feel his heart beat against her cheek.

She closed her eyes and tried not to think. Outside she could hear the music—now an old Cole Porter tune— and the muffled sound of voices, punctuated by an occasional splash as someone dived into the pool.

Why had Dinah Jefferson come back? As far as Elyse knew she didn't have relatives in the area. Had she decided she wanted to marry Clint, after all? How did he feel about her reappearance? Shocked, obviously, but did he still love her? Want her?

Of course he did. He'd practically said as much when he'd told Elyse about their affair, but he'd been convinced that Dinah was lost to him forever. Elyse had known when she'd agreed to marry Clint that she wasn't the great love of his life, but she'd been willing to gamble that they could be happy together.

All that had been less than an hour ago. Now, in the blink of an eye, everything had changed. If she lost him she didn't think she could bear it, but neither could she marry him if he was in love with someone else.

Oh, God, why me? I've been through this once. I lost a man I loved five years ago. Isn't that enough? Am I fated to keep repeating the experience all the days of my life?

A sob tore through her, and Clint's arms tightened. "It's all right, honey," he said soothingly. "Everything will be all right. Do you want to leave?"

Yes, of course she wanted to leave. She wanted to run as far away as she could get and never have to face the facts of life and love and other women.

But Reba had effectively blocked that escape. She'd been right when she'd pointed out that leaving now would only cause Elyse more humiliation. At least if she stayed and brazened it out nobody would have to know about her hopes and dreams where Clint was concerned.

For the first time she was grateful that he had been reluctant to announce their engagement. She couldn't have gone through the experience of calling off another wedding. No woman should have to do that more than once in a lifetime.

She got a firm grip on her shattered emotions and pulled away from Clint. "No," she said, "we might as well stay, unless you'd prefer not to."

He looked surprised. "Whatever you want is all right with me."

She stood, praying her legs were steadier than they had been when she'd sat down. They were. "If you'll tell me where I can find a bathroom, I'll freshen up a little and then we'll join the others."

When she rejoined Clint she'd combed her hair and done what she could to hide the despair that ravaged her eyes. She forced a smile and took his arm. "I guess you'd better introduce me to Dinah," she said, and tugged him toward the patio.

Elyse recognized the other three couples as people she'd met at Clint's headquarters the night of the election, and she nodded and said hello as he led her through them to the stunning blonde in the elegantly tailored blue dress that exactly matched her eyes.

Dinah watched them as they approached. "Dinah," Clint said, "I'd like you to meet Elyse Haley. Elyse is my—"

"I'm his sister-in-law," Elyse broke in quickly. "His brother, Paul, married my sister, Liz, last month."

Clint's eyes narrowed, and a frown creased his forehead as Dinah smiled. "Oh, yes, I'd heard that Paul was married. I'm pleased to meet you, Elyse."

There was a husky timbre to her voice that was unaffected and incredibly sexy. Elyse wished she'd taken the easy way out and left. "Thank you." She hoped her own voice wouldn't waver. "I understand you've been gone for several years. Are you visiting, or are you back for good?"

Elyse's stomach was tied in knots, but she was going to get some information while she could still do it under the guise of an interested newcomer to the ranks. She had to know Dinah's plans.

"Well, I'm not sure." Dinah glanced at Clint before she continued. "I've taken a month's vacation from the

American Embassy in Paris, where I work. I've been...homesick...lately, and I decided to come back and reassess my priorities.''

Elyse felt Clint tense beside her, and for a moment she was afraid she was going to be sick. She'd learned one important thing about herself in the past few minutes. She was no match in the game of wits with Clint's former fiancée. She wasn't sophisticated or mature or tough enough to spar with this woman. If Dinah wanted Clint, Elyse was pretty sure that all Dinah had to do was beckon and he'd follow, but Elyse was damned if she was going to make it easy for the other woman.

She squeezed Clint's arm against her side and looked up at him with a smile. ''I distinctly remember your promising me a swim this afternoon,'' she said.

''You bet I did.'' He grinned down at her. ''And you promised to wear a new and risqué bathing suit.'' He took her hand. ''Last one in is a rotten egg.'' They ran to the bathhouse, leaving Dinah watching after them.

By the time they'd finished swimming Dinah was gone.

The tension eased after that, and Elyse made a determined effort to appear lighthearted and happy. Dinner was served, and afterward there was dancing on the patio and around the pool.

Clint seemed relaxed and held Elyse close, humming in her ear as they moved to the rhythm of the music. For a while she could almost forget that her future had just been destroyed, and enjoy being in his arms.

The tension between them returned when they got in the car and started home. For a while neither spoke. Elyse was tongue-tied. With the specter of Dinah hanging over her she wasn't up to small talk, but neither could she handle a full-fledged confrontation about the other woman. She needed time to get her scattered wits about her and think.

Clint apparently didn't feel the same way. He waded right into the subject. "Elyse, why did you interrupt when I was about to tell Dinah you're my fiancée?"

Elyse shivered. "I didn't want it announced that way. Actually, I didn't want it announced at all."

Clint turned his head to look at her. "Just what's that supposed to mean?" he growled.

"It means I don't intend to announce our engagement until I'm damn sure there's going to be a wedding," she snapped, unstrung by his harsh tone.

"Oh, for God's sake! Are you threatening to cancel our marriage plans just because one of my old girlfriends is back in town? If that's going to bother you, then you're in for a rough time, because I'm pushing forty and there have been a lot of women in my life."

Elyse gasped, unprepared for the attack. "I'm sure there have been," she said, fighting tears, "but none like Dinah, and we both know it. I can't compete with her. I won't even try."

"Your trust in me is a little overwhelming." His tone was thick with sarcasm. "Do you think I've just been marking time with you until something better came along?"

He was angry, and she had to admit he had good reason. "Oh, Clint," she said disconsolately, "I don't know. I mean, of course I know you haven't just been stringing me along, but you thought Dinah was lost to you forever. Now she's back. Why? What if she's decided she wants to marry you, after all? Will you still want me then?"

"What in hell do you think I am, a football to be kicked around between the two of you?" There was outrage in his tone. "Give me credit for just a little in-telligence and enough sense to know what I want. Di-nah made her choice four years ago and I accepted it. I haven't been waiting in the wings for her to change her mind and come back."

Oh, but you have, my darling, Elyse thought. *And now that she's come you're stuck with me.*

She reached over and put her hand on his leg. "I'm sorry," she said tremulously, "I'm acting jealous, and that's exactly what I am. It was bad enough when you didn't know where she was, but to have her show up just out of the blue and seemingly ready to take up where you left off—"

"She didn't say anything about taking up where we left off," he grated. "You're jumping to conclusions. She's just here for a visit."

Elyse removed her hand. For the first time she no-ticed they'd passed the turnoff for Cameron Ranch and were nearly to the Placerville exit. Their plans had been for her to spend the night at Clint's house since Janey wouldn't be home. Had he forgotten in all the turmoil? Or had he changed his mind? Had his encounter with Dinah made him unwilling or unable to make love with any other woman?

Or had Elyse's jealous reaction angered him too much? She couldn't blame him much if it had. She knew how badly she'd been shocked by the events of this af-ternoon, and it must be far worse for him. She should be using her advantage of proximity to show him how un-derstanding and loving she could be. Instead she was driving him farther away with unfair accusations.

It was no doubt just as well that he was taking her to her own home. If she stayed with him they were almost certain to have a blazing quarrel before morning.

The car stopped in front of her house, and Clint grunted as he unstrapped his seat belt. "Looks like the baby-sitter forgot to turn on the porch light. I'll talk to her about that when I take her home."

Elyse felt a wave of relief. He'd forgotten that Janey was spending the night with a friend. He hadn't brought her home because he was mad at her.

"There isn't any baby-sitter, Clint," she said as she unfastened her own seat belt. "Don't you remember? Janey's not home."

Clint swore and clenched the steering wheel. "You're spending the night at my house," he remembered indignantly. "For God's sake, why didn't you say something when I missed the turnoff?"

Elyse opened her door. "I figured if I had to remind you, it wasn't all that important," she said, equally indignant, and she got out of the car.

"Elyse! Dammit!" Clint got out and caught her by the arm as she came around the back. "You know better than that. I'm sorry. Now get back in the car and we'll go home."

She jerked her arm out of his grasp. "I am home, Clint, and this is where I'm going to stay."

She ran up the steps and unlocked the front door, then went inside, with Clint following right behind her. He flipped the switch to turn on both the outdoor and indoor lights as he pushed the door closed. They walked down the hall and into the family room, where Elyse lit a lamp.

She was standing with her back to him, when he came up behind her and put his arms around her. "Don't do this to me, Elyse," he said huskily. "I'm sorry. I know I'm being a jerk, but I feel as if I've been poleaxed somewhere along the way. My head is splitting, my nerves are raw and I can't think straight."

Her strong maternal instinct responded to his plea, and her urge to comfort took over. She turned in his embrace and put her arms around his neck, ashamed of herself for not being more patient with him, more sympathetic. She'd been thinking only of herself, her own feelings, and not even trying to understand what all this was doing to him.

"I love you, darling," she murmured, pulling his aching head down on her shoulder.

He sighed. "Then come home with me where we can relax and talk quietly. I'm about out on my feet."

She caressed his cheek with her lips. "Let's stay here tonight, then I can take you right upstairs and put you to bed."

His arms tightened around her. "I don't care where I spend the night as long as you're with me."

They walked upstairs with their arms around each other, and when they came to Elyse's room Clint sank wearily onto the side of the bed. Elyse went down the hall to the bathroom and returned almost immediately with two aspirin and a glass of water. "Here, take these. They'll help your headache."

He swallowed the pills while she knelt between his parted knees and removed his shoes. "Hey, you don't have to do that," he protested.

"I want to," she said as she pulled off his socks. "You look as if you could use some tender loving care tonight."

She rubbed her cheek against his thigh. "Now sit quietly and let me undress you."

He cupped her face in his hands and leaned down to kiss her. "Sweetheart, I could get addicted to your tender loving care," he said in a voice filled with gratitude, "and you can undress me anytime."

He slipped his arms around her shoulders and pulled her closer so that her head lay against his chest. She tugged his shirt out of his trousers and rubbed her palms over his bare back. "You feel awfully warm," she murmured against his heart. "Do you suppose you're running a temperature?"

He kissed the top of her head. "No, I probably got a touch of sunburn when we were swimming. Then, too, I'm always hot when you cuddle with me. Maybe you just haven't noticed before."

"I've noticed," she said, but she was also close enough to him now to know he wasn't urgently aroused. He really didn't feel well.

She sat back on her heels and unfastened the heavy button on his jeans, then stood and lifted his knit shirt over his head. He grinned as she pulled him to his feet and quickly unzipped his fly so she could push his jeans down over his slender hips to where he could step out of them.

Then she turned down the covers. "Okay, crawl in," she ordered when he just stood there.

"Aren't you forgetting something?" he asked quizzically, and looked down at his skimpy blue briefs.

She wrinkled her nose and smiled innocently. "We'll leave those on," she said. "Now lie down and behave yourself."

He didn't argue, and she smoothed the sheet and a lightweight blanket over him. He reached up and pulled her off balance so she tumbled down across his chest. "Don't I get to undress you?" he asked, and reached under her tank top to unfasten her bra.

She kissed him briefly and slid off the bed. "I'll do it this time and you can watch."

She slid off her top, taking the loose bra with it, then quickly unzipped her slacks and stepped out of them. Clint didn't take his eyes off her as she walked to the dresser and removed a creamy satin nightgown from one of the drawers.

As she put it on he raised up on his elbow. "Honey, I seem to have overstated my weariness. I'm tired, not dead."

Elyse stepped out of her panties and turned off the light before she got in beside him. "I know," she said as he reached for her and cuddled her against him. "But there's nothing in the house rules that says we have to make love every time we spend the night together. You've had a rough day and you don't feel well. Let's wait until morning, when we'll both be bright eyed and bushy tailed."

"I'm bushy tailed right now," he grumbled, but with a chuckle in his tone.

She kissed the firm male nipple that lay closest to her mouth. "You'll get over it," she teased.

"Not if you keep doing that," he murmured, nuzzling the moist spot where her hair covered her neck. "Oh, Elyse, I do love you." His voice was a tortured rasp. "Don't ever doubt that."

"I don't," she whispered and felt him begin to relax beside her.

No, she didn't doubt that he loved her; she knew he did. But did he love her the way a man should love a wife? Did she stand a chance now that Dinah had come back into his life to probe old wounds and rake up long-buried passions?

It was almost two o'clock in the morning when Clint got out of bed and headed down the hall toward the bathroom. He felt awful. His head was pounding, his throat was raspy and he ached in every joint. This was more than just a reaction to shock—he must have caught something. Several senators had been out with a viral influenza in the past few weeks.

He groaned at the thought and rummaged through the medicine cabinet until he found a bottle of extra strength aspirin. Swallowing a couple of them, he washed them down with cold water directly out of the faucet.

He was radiating heat and had no doubt he was running a temperature. Damn. He was going to have to get dressed and go home. He couldn't risk exposing Elyse, and through her Janey, to whatever was ailing him.

He went back to the bedroom and found the clothes Elyse had taken off him. His gaze was drawn to her as she lay on her side, illuminated by the light from the hall. She was sleeping so peacefully with her hand under her cheek—like a child dreaming of sugarplums. Her hair lay in disarray on the pillow around her delicate features, and he had an almost irresistible desire to climb back into bed and curl up around her. To bury his aching head in her soft shoulder and feel her cool hands on his hot skin.

He tore his gaze away from her and dressed before he could act on his urge. Hell, he was a grown man; he didn't need mothering.

He stepped into his soft leather loafers, then bent over and shook Elyse lightly. "Sweetheart, I'm sorry to wake you, but I have to leave."

She opened her eyes and looked sleepily at him. "Clint?"

He brushed a strand of hair off her cheek. "Sorry, love. Don't wake up. I just wanted you to know I have to go home."

Her eyes widened. "You're leaving? But why? Is something wrong?"

"Not really, but I'm not feeling well. I think I'm coming down with something, and I don't want you to get it."

She sat up, wide-awake. "If you're sick then come back to bed. Are you running a temperature? Let me get a thermometer."

She threw off the sheet and started to climb over the side, but he was in the way. "No, don't get up." He put the sheet back over her. "I've probably caught a flu bug, and I want to get out of here before I give it to you."

She put her hand against his forehead. "You're burning up." There was alarm in her tone. "You can't drive home like that. Please come back to bed. I never get sick."

Her palm felt so cool and comforting on his throbbing head that it took all his resolve not to lie down and let her fuss over him. "Neither do I," he said with all the determination he could muster. "But I got this, and I'm not going to expose you any more than I have already. We've got to think of Janey, too."

Elyse sighed and ran her fingers through his hair. "Yes, I guess you're right. But will you be okay? At least let me drive you home."

He smiled, liking her concern. "I'll be fine. Don't forget, Alice and Grover are there, and I'm perfectly capable of driving myself home."

He stood up, anxious to get away before he lost the battle with himself and took her in his arms. "I can't kiss you goodbye, but I'll call you tomorrow."

He turned and hurried out of the house.

The next day Clint's doctor diagnosed his illness as the viral influenza that had been prevalent for the past month or so in Sacramento, and he was confined to bed at home. He instructed Alice to call his parents in Palm Springs and tell them not to come up this weekend as planned, but to wait until he could be sure he wasn't contagious.

For the first couple of days he was too sick to care, but by the third day, Wednesday, he was feeling just enough better to be restless and irritable. He hated being stuck at home while work was piling up and his secretaries were cancelling appointments at his office.

Elyse called morning and night, but he adamantly refused to let her come to see him. She was sweet and understanding, but she left him with another ache, which he sure didn't need—the ache to have her in bed with him. Not that he could have done anything about it, but he'd had a taste of her tender loving care and he missed it.

There was something else that tormented his fever-induced dreams, but he tried not to think of it. Where was Dinah? Why had she come back and what did she want?

He'd been so thunderstruck when he'd glanced up to see her coming toward him by the Ogdens' pool that his entire nervous system seemed to short-circuit. She'd stood before him looking exactly as she had four years before, and he'd been too stunned to control his reaction. When she'd touched him he'd taken her in his arms as he'd longed to do for so long and hugged her to him with all the pent-up frustration he'd endured for an eternity.

If they spoke he didn't remember. The whole scene was hazy, like a slow-motion movie photographed through a mist. There was one thing that came back to him, though, and it didn't make sense.

Dinah hadn't seemed to fit in his embrace the way she used to.

Maybe that's when he'd remembered he was with Elyse and started looking for her. From there his memory was vivid enough; the panic when he'd realized that Elyse had witnessed the meeting with Dinah and was nowhere to be found, the guilt when he finally did find her, curled up in a ball and looking so crushed in the Ogdens' office.

Damn it to hell! Was he going to be placed in the intolerable position of having to choose between Elyse and Dinah?

It was midafternoon when the bedside phone rang, and the voice at the other end drove everything else from his mind. "Hello, Clint. This is Dinah."

By Friday morning Elyse had reached the end of her patience. It had been five days since Clint had fallen victim to that nasty virus, but he admitted he was feeling better now. He'd sounded much livelier on the phone when she'd talked to him at breakfast time—surely he wasn't still contagious. He was sweet to be concerned for her and Janey, but she'd waited long enough. She wanted to see him.

She looked at her watch. It was a quarter to eleven. Janey's nursery school class had gone into Sacramento on a field trip to Fairy-tale Town and wasn't due back until two. It would take only about twenty minutes to drive over to Cameron Park; she could go and have lunch with Clint and be back in plenty of time to pick Janey up.

She reached for the phone to call and let him know she was coming, but then drew back. He was still afraid of giving his illness to her and he'd tell her not to come. No, it would be better just to walk in unannounced. She knew he wouldn't send her away once she was there.

The red shorts and bandanna print shirt she was wearing were clean and nearly new, so she wouldn't need to change. She turned on the telephone answering machine, picked up her purse and rushed out of the house.

Eighteen minutes later, when Elyse drove into Clint's parking area, a shiny red Corvair was occupying one of the spaces. Was someone visiting him? No, that wasn't likely. He'd been very careful to keep people away. Maybe it was his doctor. She knew doctors didn't make house calls, but for a senator...who knows?

She got out of her poor old battered Mustang and hurried across the bridge and up the steps to the deck. The dogs, which she now knew as a German Shepherd-chow mix named Bear and a black Labrador called Pip, had set up their usual clamor, and within seconds after she'd rung the bell the door was opened by Alice Irwin, the housekeeper.

"Good morning, Alice," she said cheerfully. "I decided to come over and see for myself how the senator is feeling."

She'd stepped inside and walked past the housekeeper before she realized that the woman had paled visibly and there was a look akin to panic in her faded hazel eyes. "Alice...? Is something wrong?"

"N—no, Miss Haley. I—it's just that Senator Sterling doesn't want you to come here and take a chance on getting sick."

The sound of laughter floated toward them from the direction of the great room, and Elyse turned toward it. "Oh, my, am I interrupting something? Does Clint have visitors?"

She walked into the great room just as a man and woman came strolling out of the hallway that led to the bedrooms. They were holding hands and giggling like teenagers.

The man, dressed in maroon silk pajamas and a matching short robe, was Clint, and the woman, wearing an abbreviated pair of lavender shorts and matching halter top, was Dinah Jefferson!

Chapter Eleven

Clint and Dinah stood in the hallway, frozen in the position in which they'd been caught like children in the game of "statue." They still held hands, and their mouths still turned up, but in smiles that had now become grimaces. Elyse, too, was frozen, with dismay.

Surprisingly it was Elyse who recovered first. She felt no pain, but neither did she feel anything else. It was as if her emotions had been anesthetized, but her mind was sharp and she was in full control. Had she subconsciously been expecting something like this and prepared herself for it?

When she spoke her voice was steady, with no trace of a quiver. "It looks as if I've been tactless, blundering in where I'm neither wanted nor welcome."

Clint and Dinah both sprang to life and started talking at once, but Elyse held up her hand for silence and glanced at Clint. He managed to look both guilty and ashamed, and she wondered if he really felt either emotion. Probably not. She'd forgotten that politicians were consummate actors.

"It would have been kinder, Clint, if you'd simply told me that Dinah was staying with you."

"Elyse!" His voice had a strangled sound. "For God's sake, that's not true. She just—"

"I just got here a few minutes ago," Dinah broke in.

Elyse's gaze focused on Dinah's feet, which were bare. "Long enough to take off your shoes, I see. But, then, you're used to making yourself at home here, aren't you? I'm the one who's the interloper."

Clint covered the few steps between them and grasped her shoulders. "Elyse, stop this. Let me explain—"

"Take your hands off me, Clint." Her tone was still pleasant, but it was reinforced with steel.

His hands dropped to his sides. "Look," he said, obviously trying to regain his shattered composure. "Let's sit down and talk this over calmly."

She walked toward one of the big chairs. "But I am talking calmly. In fact, I seem to be the calmest one here."

She sat down and waited until Clint, who still looked pale and ill, took one of the other chairs, while Dinah settled on the sofa. Elyse was uncomfortably aware of her own shorts, and wished she had something to cover her legs. She felt . . . violated . . . every time Clint looked at her.

"Well, now, what are we going to talk over calmly?" She turned toward Dinah. "Would you like to tell me what you were doing in the bedroom with my fiancé?" She swung back to look at Clint. "Or are you going to explain why you were too ill to see me but are well enough to entertain another woman in your pajamas?"

It was Dinah who answered. "It's not Clint's fault. He told me not to come here, but I came, anyway."

Elyse smiled sadly, and wondered why she wasn't screaming. She wanted to rant and rage and throw things, but it was as if she'd been split into two personalities—one behaving like a lady while the other stood by helplessly urging her to stamp her feet and shout obscenities. "I can't speak for *your* actions," she said quietly, "but, you see, Clint knew how to manipulate me. He appealed to my responsibility as a mother to keep me away so he'd be free to make love with you—"

Clint jumped to his feet. "That's enough, dammit! I haven't been making love with Dinah."

Elyse cringed, and felt a crack in her emotional armor. Obviously she wasn't as detached as she'd thought. She sank back in the chair and closed her eyes. "You're right, we've all had enough," she said, and her voice wasn't quite so clear. "I guess we'd better get this over with as quickly as possible."

She stood and unfastened the gold chain that hung around her neck, pulling the emerald ring from its hiding place under her blouse. She laid it in the palm of her hand and held it out to him. "I guess I always knew I'd never wear this," she said sadly.

Clint jammed his hands into the pockets of his robe. "The ring is yours. I expect you to keep it and wear it."

Elyse turned her hand over and let the expensive jewel drop to the floor. "I can't be used and then paid off, Clint."

She stood and walked regally to the door, opened it, then shut it quietly behind her.

By the time she got back across the bridge and to the car her composure was rapidly disintegrating. She wasn't prepared to find Alice sitting quietly in the passenger seat. Elyse leaned down and looked through the open window, but before she could say anything Alice spoke. "Get in and drive down the road and around the corner. I need to talk to you."

Without saying a word Elyse did as she was told and stopped the car on the shoulder out of sight of the house.

She turned and looked at Alice. The housekeeper shifted uncomfortably. "I didn't mean to eavesdrop," she began, "but I couldn't help overhearing. I know it looks bad, but I think you should know that there's nothing...wrong...going on between Clint and Dinah Jefferson."

Elyse clutched the steering wheel and shook her head. "There isn't anything wrong about making love."

"There is if one of the people doing it is betraying someone else's trust. Clint wouldn't do that to you. I know what I'm talking about. Oh, I don't mean he's blameless—he should have let me turn her away when she first came on Wednesday. He wasn't feeling up to having company, and he couldn't have...uh..."

Alice's face was red, and Elyse was touched by the older woman's insistence on saying what she felt she must say, even though it was acutely embarrassing to her.

Elyse reached out and touched her arm. "Alice," she said softly, "it's very dear of you to want to spare me, but I'm not judging Clint. He's been in love with Dinah for a long time, and now that she's back—"

The housekeeper shook her head. "No, ma'am, you don't understand. I'm not covering up for him. I know that those two haven't been messin' around. I've been here all day every day this week, and it's true that Dinah was with him most of yesterday, but they were never alone long enough to—to—oh, shoot, he's not tusslin' her in bed or anywhere else.''

The poor woman was red all over and deeply mortified to be discussing such an intimate subject. Elyse knew she was telling the truth. If she hadn't felt it so strongly she would never have talked about it so openly. Elyse was sure that when her own emotions thawed she'd feel greatly relieved.

She patted Alice's arm. "I believe you, and thanks for telling me. I know it's been difficult, and it does make it easier for me, but it doesn't change anything. I couldn't hold him to a marriage he no longer wants.

Alice shrugged. "If he doesn't come after you he's a darn fool. That Dinah's a nice woman, but she's given him nothing but sorrow." She opened the door and got out of the car. "I'll walk back to the house." She shut the door and walked away before Elyse could say anything.

There were tears on Elyse's face when she got home, and soon afterward the numbness receded and the pain surged with delayed force. She was glad Janey was gone, because the sobs that shook her couldn't be held back.

She'd learned after Jerry's death to give vent to her crying spells, and eventually they'd hurried the healing. She wasn't sure why she'd been targeted to lose at the game of love a second time, but she'd better get all her tears spent now, because she had no intention of letting her young daughter see her cry.

Early the following morning Clint appeared on Elyse's doorstep.

She and Janey had just finished their breakfast, and since it was Saturday, neither was dressed. Elyse wore a cotton robe over her nightgown and Janey hadn't yet changed out of her Mickey Mouse pajamas. She jumped down from her chair and raced for the door when the bell rang.

She pulled aside the curtain that covered the glass panels and wiggled with excitement. "It's Clint! Hurry, Mommy, it's Clint. Hi, Clint."

Elyse wasn't altogether surprised. She'd known that Clint wouldn't just let her walk away from him like that. He was too caring a person to let her go without explanations and apologies and offers to make things right, but she cursed her traitorous heart for accelerating even as she slowed her steps. Her earlier protective shield of acceptance had crumbled, and she was vulnerable and defenseless.

Janey was knocking on the glass and waving at him as she called, "Come on, Mommy. Let Clint in."

Now Elyse had another burden to bear, which she'd been to upset to think about before. How could she tell her happy and loving child that her beloved Clint—hero, playmate and surrogate father—wouldn't be coming around anymore?

She reached the door and opened it, and Janey flew into Clint's arms. He held her tight and hugged her as she squealed with delight. "You want some breakfast?" she asked. "We got pancakes."

Clint looked over Janey's shoulder at Elyse, seeking permission. There was nothing she could do but give it, unless she wanted to deal with her daughter right then and there.

She nodded, and Clint said, "I'd love some pancakes. Is there coffee, too?"

The child bobbed her strawberry blond head up and down. "An' orange juice an' eggs an' you can sit next to me."

Elyse turned and led them down the hall to the kitchen.

Clint continued to devote all his attention to Janey while Elyse fixed his breakfast. When she'd finished she put it on the table in front of him and excused herself to go upstairs and dress, leaving them alone.

As she pulled on an old pair of jeans and a blue-and-white striped pullover shirt she noticed that her hands were shaking. So be it. She'd never claimed to be an automaton, and she still loved the man. It would take her a long time to get over that, but she wasn't going to dress up for him and pretend this was a social visit.

Why hadn't he given her more time to pull herself together? Last night she'd hardly slept, but neither could she think. She'd finally turned on the television and watched a couple of old movies, but when they'd ended she realized she hadn't the least idea what they were about.

Playing for time now, she made the beds in her room and Janey's. But eventually time ran out, and she had to go downstairs and face the situation—and Clint. She glanced at her ravaged face in the mirror and wondered why she'd been in such a hurry to grow up when she was younger.

She found Clint and Janey in the family room, sitting on the couch, watching cartoons on television. Janey was curled up on his lap, and Clint rested his chin on the top of her head. A sharp stab of anguish jolted Elyse. He did love Janey, and he would have been a marvelous father, both for her and for the children they would have had together.

She took a deep breath and looked away for a moment before she walked into the room. "Janey," she said, interrupting the child's concentration on *The ad-*

ventures of Alvin and the Chipmunks, "I laid your clothes out on your bed. You'd better run up and get dressed."

Janey huddled deeper in Clint's arms. "Aw, Mommy, we're watchin' the Chipmunks."

Clint straightened up and lifted her off his lap. "Do as your mother says, honey. You can finish watching the program on the set upstairs. Now scoot."

"Don't go till I get back, promise?" she asked.

"Cross my heart," he said, drawing an *X* on the left side of his chest. Then he gave her a playful shove in the right direction, and she laughed and scrambled out of the room.

Elyse turned off the set and sat down in the chair beside it. "All right, Clint, what do you want?"

Gone was the smile and the good humor he'd displayed for Janey. He looked even worse than she did. But of course, he'd been sick for a week, which would explain it. He slumped forward and put his elbows on his knees. "How can you even ask what I want? We have so much to talk about, to straighten out."

She bit back a groan. Why couldn't he just say "It's been nice knowin' ya" and leave? Was it really necessary to hash over the whole thing?

"No, we don't," she said firmly. "I'm not asking for explanations. I wish you'd been more truthful with me, but I've known all along how you felt about Dinah—"

"That's nothing short of miraculous," he snapped, "since it's a hell of a lot more than I've known. I wish you'd stop jumping to conclusions and let me tell you."

Elyse sank back in her chair and closed her eyes. "I'm sorry, but this is very painful for me. I'd hoped we wouldn't have to put ourselves through a long postmortem."

"There's no postmortem unless something dies," he said quietly, "and our engagement isn't dead. I haven't been committing adultery with Dinah."

She opened her eyes. "You can't commit adultery unless one of the partners is married. Are you telling me Dinah has a husband?"

"No, but I have a fiancée, and in my book that's every bit as binding as marriage. I wouldn't cheat on you, Elyse."

Oh, God, if he'd only go away and leave her alone. She couldn't take much more of this. It would be easier if he'd just let her think the worst of him.

"I know you wouldn't, Clint. I'm sorry if I implied that's what I thought."

His head jerked up. "You what? But you said—"

"I know what I said, and I'm telling you now that I know I was wrong. I didn't come to that conclusion by myself, though. Alice convinced me."

"Alice! What the hell does Alice know about it?"

The corners of Elyse's mouth quirked upward. "She knows that you weren't, and I quote, 'tusslin' Dinah in bed or anywhere else'."

Clint dropped his face in his hands and muttered an obscenity. "So much for privacy in my own home," he grunted sarcastically. "Would you mind telling me why you believed her and not me or Dinah?"

"Not at all. If you'd seen how embarrassed she was to be talking about it, you'd have believed her, too."

She told him about her conversation with his housekeeper and how it had come about. "She's kind and thoughtful, and I appreciate her trying to intervene. You have to admit you both looked guilty. How would you have felt if Jerry were still alive, and he had left me and you'd come over to find us coming out of my bedroom together, me dressed in a nightgown and negligee and him in shorts and nothing else?''

He looked at her, and when he spoke his tone was rough. "I'd have killed him first and asked questions later. When you put it that way, I'd say you behaved with remarkable restraint. Does this mean you'll take your ring back?''

She wasn't sure whether he sounded hopeful or apprehensive.

"No, Clint," she said sadly. "I know you're an honorable man, but while you may be able to control your actions, you can't be expected to control your feelings. You were honest when you proposed to me. You told me you were in love with Dinah. I agreed to marry you anyway because I loved you and I thought she was out of your life forever. But now she's come back, and everything's changed.''

He rubbed his hands across his face. "Elyse, when I asked you to marry me I told you I was in love with *you*. You asked about Dinah, and I said I *had been* in love with her years ago. I haven't been nursing an unrequited passion for the past four years. I'm not that self-destructive.''

She wanted to go to him and put her arms around him, but she couldn't. She didn't dare. If he held her, kissed her, she'd never be able to give him up.

She shifted far back in the chair and planted her feet firmly on the floor to hold herself there. "I know you didn't 'nurse' your love for Dinah after she left, but it was there all the same. I heard it in your voice and saw it on your face when you were telling me about her. Even so, I think we could have been happy if she'd stayed away, but now I'm no longer willing to take that chance. You're free, for God's sake, so why are you arguing?''

"I'm arguing because I didn't ask to be free. You're the one who's weaving romantic fantasies about me finally getting together with my lost love and wandering off into the sunset. She wasn't lost, dammit, and I didn't ask her to come back."

Elyse was taken by surprise. "You mean you knew where she was all along?"

Clint shook his head. "No, but I could have found out with very little effort."

Elyse's eyes widened. "Then why didn't you? Don't tell me you didn't want her, because you've already described quite graphically how broken up you were."

"That's true, I was. I went through hell, and frankly, I've had all I intend to put up with. No man with any smarts is going to give a woman a second chance to do that to him. I wasn't going to force her to marry me or, worse yet, seduce her into it. If she's changed her mind now, that's her problem."

Elyse was puzzled. Was he denying he was still in love with Dinah? If so, why didn't he just come right out and say it?

She decided to probe, but carefully. "Has she changed her mind, Clint?"

He hesitated. "I don't know. She says she's missed me."

"And you've missed her." It wasn't a question.

"I've already told you I did," he said impatiently, "but now I have you."

"No, you don't. I broke our engagement, remember? You no longer have to consider me. There's nothing dishonorable now about asking her to marry you. You don't owe me anything."

He stood and began to pace. "Maybe not, but you owe me something. You told me you loved me and accepted my proposal of marriage. You owe it to me to honor that acceptance unless you can give me a lot better reason than you have so far for not doing so."

Elyse knew she should be elated. He not only wanted to marry her, he was practically blackmailing her into it. So why was she holding back? Something was wrong, but she couldn't quite identify it.

"I still don't understand why you let Dinah come to see you three days in a row when you not only didn't tell me but wouldn't let me anywhere near you."

He clamped his hand around the back of his neck. "You know why I wouldn't let you come over. I didn't want to expose you and Janey to the flu. As for telling you about Dinah's visits, I would have when I saw you. I just didn't see a need to discuss it over the phone."

"Because you knew it would upset me?"

He looked sheepish. "Yes."

"Then why did you encourage her?"

He started to pace again. "I... I don't know. Curiosity, I guess. I wanted to talk to her, to know what she'd been doing these past four years, how she was getting along."

"Did you find out?"

"Yes, she worked at the United Nations for a year, then was offered the job with the embassy in France. That's where she's living now."

"And she's still in love with you?"

He looked startled. "Love was never the problem with us—she always said she loved me. But she wouldn't marry me."

"Would she marry you now?"

"I don't know. I didn't ask her."

"Why didn't you?"

He glared at her. "Oh, knock it off, dammit. I didn't ask her because I want to marry you, and the sooner the better."

She was pushing him and she didn't mean to, but for both their sakes she had to know what his true feelings were.

"Why the rush? Until this week you weren't in any hurry. You weren't even anxious to announce the engagement."

He ran his fingers through his hair. "That's not true."

"All right," she said wearily. "I'll concede the point. It's not worth arguing about."

She walked over and stood in front of him. "Why do you want to marry me, Clint? Is it because you love me, or is it because you want me to protect you from yourself?"

He blinked in astonishment. "That's the craziest thing I ever heard."

She looked away. "Is it? The love you felt for Dinah was very deep and very special, and when she rejected you the pain and loneliness were shattering. Then you met me, and I would have married you anywhere, anytime. I was safe, and you dared to open up to me and let yourself feel strongly again. But Dinah came back, and as you said, no man would let himself be hurt twice by the same woman, so you're determined not to examine your feelings for her."

"That's nonsense."

She put her hand to his mouth to silence him. "No, just listen to me. You think that if you were married to me you wouldn't be so tempted by her, but I'm not willing to take that chance. You've avoided this question every time it's come up, but I'm going to ask it straight this time, and I want an honest answer.''

She looked into his anxious green eyes, and her gaze never wavered. ''Clint, are you still in love with Dinah Jefferson?''

Chapter Twelve

Clint caught his breath. He was staggered by the enormity of Elyse's question. It sounded so simple, but had such far-reaching consequences.

Was he still in love with Dinah? Dear God, how could he answer that? He hadn't even let himself think about it this past week, and now if he didn't give a satisfactory answer he was going to lose Elyse!

The thought made him shudder. Elyse, with her sunny smile that lit all the dark corners of his soul and her shimmering eyes that were incapable of harboring secrets. Even now she looked at him with the love he knew she'd prefer to hide.

That love had melted the cold wall he'd built around his heart, and her soft hands had worked magic at healing the wounds that had tormented him for so long. She was his light, his warmth, his comfort and his pleasure, so why did he hesitate to give her the resounding *no* he knew she was demanding in answer to her question?

He'd sell his soul to be able to do that, but she was too perceptive and he was a poor liar. Oh, he was an expert at evading the truth—all good politicians were—but every time he'd tried to tell a deliberate lie he'd flubbed it. The tragedy was that he honestly didn't know if saying he no longer loved Dinah would be a lie.

Clint knew he'd hesitated too long when he saw the anguish creep into Elyse's pinched face and heard the quickly stifled sob in her voice. "I guess I have the answer to my question," she said, and turned away. "Please leave, Clint."

He couldn't let her go. "Elyse, wait!"

He didn't try to touch her, but she stopped and stood still. "I don't know how I feel about Dinah," he said raggedly. "This has all happened too quickly and for several days I was too sick to worry about it. The only thing I know for sure is that I love you."

Very carefully he put his arms around her waist. He felt her tense, but she didn't move away. "I know I'm not making sense. I've never believed it possible for a man to love two women at the same time, but now I'm not sure. For six years Dinah was my one and only love. My obsession. I firmly believed she was the only woman in the world for me, and even after she left I never stopped loving her. Then just a few weeks ago you came along and awakened needs in me I hadn't had in years. It was you I wanted, you who made me long for a wife and children."

She was less tense than before, more pliable in his arms and he knew she was listening and considering what he was saying. If only he could make her understand . . . But how could he, when he didn't understand himself?

Her untamed hair tickled his chin, and he rubbed his face in the soft clean texture of it. An unwelcome stirring in his groin reminded him that this lady was dynamite and he'd better be careful or he'd ache for hours. Clint had always considered comparisons odious, but now he realized that Elyse's trusting and uninhibited response to his advances had always excited him more than Dinah's more experienced and deliberate seduction ever had.

The stirrings quickened, and he forced his mind back to the discussion.

He gathered the loose ends of his thoughts and continued. "After we made love the first time I knew you were special and that I wanted you around for good. Then when you made me tell you about my relationship with Dinah before you'd agree to marry me, I nearly blew it. I'd never talked about our broken engagement before with anyone, and it was incredibly painful—"

"I'm sorry," Elyse murmured, leaning back more fully into his embrace. "I didn't mean to cause you pain."

He couldn't resist the overwhelming urge to nuzzle the pulse at the side of her throat, although it made desire surge within him. "I'm glad you did," he said, fighting the need to press against her exquisitely firm bottom. "It brought everything into much clearer focus, and I realized I was wasting years of my life waiting for a woman who didn't love me enough to come to me."

Elyse tensed again. "So you decided to go for second best and proposed to me." Her tone was bitter, and she tried to pull away.

Clint could have bitten his tongue. Dammit, why did everything always come out wrong when he tried to talk to her?

He tightened his hold on her. "I didn't mean it that way. I don't think I've ever in my life been as inarticulate as I am with you. You've got me so confused and upset and half-crazy with the fear of losing you that it's a wonder I can talk at all."

"Why are you afraid of losing me if you're still in love with Dinah?" Elyse asked with undeniable logic.

Clint grunted derisively. "That's a good question. The obvious answer is that I'm no longer in love with Dinah, so why won't you accept it?"

"I would if you would," Elyse said in little more than a whisper, "but you said yourself that you're not sure. How do you feel about her?"

Clint searched his memory and his emotions. He didn't want to hurt Elyse, but she insisted on the truth and he owed her no less. "I was overjoyed to see her again. For years I'd prayed for that moment, and I was so stunned when it finally happened that I wasn't aware of anything but the fact that she was back. Once the shock wore off, though, my only thought was to find you and undo any pain I might have caused you.

"Apparently I was already coming down with the flu, because as the afternoon went on I felt miserable. I thought it was just shock, but I was irritable and bad tempered, and we wound up quarreling. After that I was too sick to care about anything, and when Dinah called on Wednesday I have to admit I wanted to see her."

Elyse tried to squirm out of his embrace, but he tightened his arms around her. "No, I'm not going to release you. You asked for the truth and you're going to get it. When she came to see me that evening I was still too sick to get out of bed, so she sat by me and held my hand.''

He hadn't even thought about Elyse until after Dinah had left, but then he'd been racked with guilt.

"I told Dinah about us," he said, "but I also invited her to come back the next day."

He felt Elyse flinch and hated himself for what he was doing to her. Why in hell didn't he just tell her he felt nothing for Dinah and sort his real feelings out later?

He took a deep breath and continued. "She spent all day at the house on Thursday. We talked practically nonstop, and there were times when it got pretty personal."

This time Elyse took him by surprise, pulling away with such force he couldn't hang on to her. "Damn you, Clint," she cried. "Just shut up and go away. I don't want to hear this."

She turned from him, but not before he'd seen the anguish on her face. He knew he couldn't put her through any more.

"I knew you wouldn't," he said, "but you insisted. I guess what I'm trying to say is that loving Dinah was a habit that I've probably broken, but I can't be sure yet. All I know for certain is that I no longer want to marry her."

Elyse walked to the fireplace and stood with her back to him. "Then I suggest you figure out how you do feel about her, and please, have enough respect for my feelings to stay away from me while you're doing it."

A sob shook her, and he had to fight to keep himself from going to her. "All right, sweetheart," he said, and he could hear the defeat in his tone. "I can't expect you to put up with my stupidity. If I didn't care for you so much I'd lie to you and use any means to get you to marry me."

She whirled around then, and her features were twisted with anger. "Oh, stop it!" she grated. "If you suspect you're still in love with Dinah, then why would you want to marry me?"

He walked over to her and took her white face in his hands. "Because, no matter what my mixed-up feelings for her may be, you're the one I want to spend the rest of my life with."

He kissed her warm quivering lips, then tore himself away and walked out of the room.

Elyse stood listening to his footsteps retreating down the hall, but instead of the sound of the outside door opening, she heard the footsteps climbing up the stairs.

Clint was keeping his promise to Janey not to leave without seeing her again!

A soft cry of pain escaped from Elyse as she crumpled into a chair and buried her face in her hands. What was the matter with her? Why was she demanding perfection when no one was perfect? So he didn't love her with all his heart and soul. He cared for her, and he was considerate and loving with Janey. What right did she have to demand more?

Elyse knew Clint would cherish her, even if a portion of his heart did belong to another woman. Why couldn't she be content with that much? It was more than many women had.

Shortly after noon the following day, Sunday, Elyse's phone rang and it was Liz. With all the other things she'd had on her mind, Elyse had forgotten that Paul and Liz were due back today from their honeymoon trip abroad. Fortunately her sister was so excited and happy she didn't notice when Elyse wasn't exactly coherent for the first few minutes.

They'd talked for about half an hour, when Liz suddenly exclaimed, "Oh, heavens, I forgot this is a toll call. I'll have to float a loan to pay the phone bill if I don't hang up."

They both laughed at the absurdity of Paul Sterling worrying about paying for a toll call from Sacramento to Placerville.

"Look, honey," Liz continued, "I want to see you. We brought gifts for you and Janey, and we still have so much to tell you, but I've got to unpack and get things straightened up around here. Why don't you and Janey drive in and spend the afternoon and we'll take you out to dinner. By the way, is Clint there?"

Elyse stiffened. "No." She didn't elaborate.

"If he's in the area, why don't you call him and ask him to come, too."

Elyse gripped the phone. "I don't know where he is." She tried to keep her voice from breaking. "Besides, I'd rather talk to you and Paul alone, if you don't mind."

She had to tell them about her broken engagement before they heard that Dinah was back, but she wanted to do it in person.

"Well, sure," Liz said, puzzled. "If that's what you want. Elyse, is anything wrong?"

"There have been some . . . developments. I'll tell you all about it when I see you." She hung up and went to find Janey.

An hour later Elyse and Janey were joyously greeted by Paul and Liz in their Sacramento apartment. There were gifts of Swiss musical toys for Janey and French perfume and handmade frilly lingerie for Elyse. "For

your honeymoon,'' Liz said with a teasing smile, and
Elyse bit her lip to keep it from trembling.

This had been Liz's first trip out of the country, and
she chatted nonstop about art galleries in Paris, pag-
eantry in London and gondola rides on the canals of
Venice. It was late afternoon and Janey was napping
before she finally got to the question Elyse had been
dreading. ''Now tell me about you and what you've been
doing for the past three weeks. I notice you're not wearing your ring yet. When are you and Clint going to announce your engagement?''

Elyse hated to put a damper on her sister's enthusiasm, but there was no way to avoid it. She braced herself before she spoke. ''There won't be an
announcement. I've given Clint's ring back to him.''

''What!'' The exclamation rang from both Liz and
Paul simultaneously.

Paul was the first to recover. ''Good Lord, Elyse,
what happened? You two were so happy together.''

There was no way she could soften the truth. ''Dinah
Jefferson is back.''

Liz gasped. ''No!''

Paul's sudden oath betrayed the depth of his shock.
''Are you saying that my idiot brother dropped you for
her?''

Elyse shook her head. ''Not exactly.''

She told them about the Ogdens' party and Dinah's
surprise appearance. About Clint's illness, her quarrels
with him and Dinah's presence at Clint's house. She
tried to give them a clear account of her last discussion
with Clint the day before, but it was so confused in her
own mind that she bewildered her listeners, too.

"Now wait a minute," Paul said. "I don't understand. If Clint still wants to marry you, what makes you think he's in love with Dinah?"

Elyse sighed and raised her palms in a gesture of uncertainty. "He doesn't deny it, Paul. He claims he doesn't know himself how he feels about her, but he does have strong feelings for her. Maybe it's not love anymore, but until he finds out whether it is, I can't marry him. It would be disastrous."

Liz took Elyse's hand and held it. "Of course you can't, honey," she said angrily, "and when I see him I'm going to give him a tongue-lashing that'll blister his hide."

"Oh, no, Liz." Elyse's dismay was clear in her tone. "You mustn't do that. He can't help how he feels, and he didn't want me to break the engagement. If you take sides it will only cause trouble in the Sterling family. After all, he's Paul's brother, your brother-in-law."

Liz wasn't about to be appeased. "Well, you're my sister, and I'm not going to stand by and let him hurt you without a protest. What's the matter with the man? It sounds to me as though this woman doesn't know what she wants."

"I'm sure Clint realizes that," Elyse explained. "But we seldom get to choose who we're going to fall in love with. Look how hard you fought against loving Paul."

"Well, yes, but . . ." There was a shade of uncertainty in Liz's tone.

"Actually, I think that's the reason Clint wants to marry me. He says he loves me and I believe him, but it's a love born of desperation. I came along when he'd given up hope of getting Dinah back, and I filled a large void in his life. I gave him the love, companionship and the warm physical intimacy he so badly needed. He liked it, and he knows that if we married I'd continue to give of myself. He also knows he can't trust Dinah not to desert him again."

"That's for damn sure," Paul growled. "I used to like Dinah. The whole family did. She was beautiful, bright, well educated, the perfect wife for Clint—or so we thought. Then after they'd announced their engagement and were planning a wedding, she changed her mind and walked out. Just turned tail and ran. Wouldn't even make an effort to solve her problem, even though she knew how much Clint loved her and what her leaving would do to him. He'd be out of his mind to take her back now."

Elyse winced. It was an automatic reflex against the pain she felt when anyone talked about how much Clint had loved Dinah. "I'm certain he realizes that, but I don't think he trusts himself to remember it if she stays around and he's free. Try to put yourself in his place, Paul. Liz was adamant about not marrying you. If she'd gone away instead of relenting, could you have just turned off your love for her?"

Paul shook his head. "I wouldn't have let that happen. I knew Liz loved me in spite of her fears about the difference in our ages, and if she'd run away I'd have gone after her. I had no intention of letting her go, no matter how long it took or how much trouble it was to make her see that we belonged together."

His gaze locked with his wife's across the room, and Elyse could feel the warm happiness that radiated between them.

"That's what Clint should have done," he continued, "and I'm convinced he would have if he'd really wanted her as badly as I wanted Liz."

Elyse wanted to believe that, but she knew Clint far more intimately than Paul ever would. It wasn't out of character for Clint to put Dinah's feelings ahead of his own.

"I'm not so sure," she said. "Clint is a sensitive man. Probably too much so for his own good. He didn't try to find her because he respected her feelings. He didn't want to force her into marriage if she honestly didn't want it. He told me so. That may have been a mistake, but he'll have to come to terms with his feelings for her on his own. I refuse to be his shield."

Elyse kept busy with her doll-making. She was working on Christmas stock and already had several orders for personalized dolls from friends of Paul's who had seen Liz's collection of her work. She didn't have time to brood during the day, and at night she fell into bed, exhausted, and slept.

It was early the weekend after Paul and Liz's return that she saw the item in the Around the Town column in one of Sacramento's newspapers, to the effect that the handsome bachelor senator, Clinton Sterling, had been seen in various places with the beautiful former administrative assistant, Dinah Jefferson, who had been living in Paris. The writer reminded her readers that Clint and Dinah had been engaged at one time, and wondered in print if they were taking up where they'd left off four years before.

The next day Elyse accepted a date to go to a movie with Ferris Rogers, a teacher whom she'd dated occasionally before she'd met Clint. Not that she wanted to go out with anyone else, but she was determined to get back into the mainstream of life and not sit at home and brood.

On Tuesday the telephone rang, and it was Grace Sterling, Clint's mother. "We're at the house in Cameron Park," she said after introducing herself. "We arrived on Sunday and are looking forward to meeting you and Janey."

"But, Mrs. Sterling," Elyse said, trying to overcome the jolt this surprise call had given her. "Didn't Clint tell you—"

"He told me the story of your broken engagement, yes, and I'm truly sorry about it, but whether you marry our son or not, you're still a part of the family. We're totally captivated by Liz, and we want to know her sister and little niece. My husband and I are having a cocktail party on Saturday to get together with family and friends we haven't seen for nearly a year, and we'd like you to be there."

"Oh, but—"

"I realize it might seem a bit awkward for you, and I certainly don't want to cause you distress, but we're both especially anxious that you come."

Going to a party at the Sterlings' was the last thing Elyse wanted to do, but neither did she relish embarrassing Liz by seeming ungracious and standoffish to her sister's new in-laws.

"Does Clint know you're inviting me?" Surely he wouldn't want her there. It was too much to hope that Dinah wouldn't be invited, too.

"Yes, he does, and he asked me to make every effort to persuade you to accept."

Damn him! Why couldn't he leave her alone! Did he get some sort of perverted kick out of having two women falling at his feet? Well, she'd show him.

"Mrs. Sterling—"

"Please call me 'Grace.'"

"Grace, if I do come, may I bring an escort?"

There was a slight pause, but when Clint's mother answered there was approval in her tone. "Yes, of course you may, and bring Janey. This won't be a riotous affair. Several people are bringing children. We've arranged for a hostess and a clown so the little ones can have their own party around the wading pool. We'll expect you about six."

By Saturday evening Elyse was a bundle of nerves. She's spent the past three days trying to think of a socially acceptable excuse for not going to the Sterlings', but short of coming down with a communicable disease there was none. She was Liz's only family, and she couldn't let her sister down.

Ferris Rogers had readily agreed to escort her. He knew she'd dated Clint a few times, but not that they'd been engaged.

With Liz's more knowledgeable help she'd chosen a long oyster-colored pleated skirt with a loose-fitting sleeveless overblouse in a whisper-soft gray floral print. With the outfit she wore matching hose and high-heeled sandals. The only contrast was a chunky necklace of black and oyster, and a wide black satin bow that caught her hair in the back and tamed it to cascade down between her shoulder blades.

When Ferris arrived his eyes lit with admiration, and his long, low sexy whistle made her grin. "Hey now," he said in his pleasant tenor voice, "I always knew you were beautiful, but I never realized you were elegant, as well. What happened to the gypsy maid in the quilted skirt and wild curls who went to a movie with me Monday night?"

Elyse laughed. "She turned into Cinderella for a few hours, but she'll be back at the stroke of midnight. Elegant just isn't the real me. It suits you, though. I've never seen you looking more handsome, Ferris. I'm proud to be with you."

She'd spoken the truth. His dark slacks and white coat were well tailored and accentuated his blond good looks.

When they arrived at the Sterling home the small parking lot was full of luxury cars, and more were parked along the shoulder between the road and the creek. Ferris parked his well-used but still classy black Datsun 280ZX about a block past the house in the first empty space, and they walked back.

When they came to the bridge and steps Ferris reached down and scooped Janey into his arms. "Come on, sweetie, I'd better carry you so you don't fall into the creek or skin your pretty knees on the stairs."

Janey, who was dressed up, too, in a navy-and-white cotton dress with a white ruffled pinafore, giggled and threw her arms around his neck.

The door was opened by Grover, Alice's handyman husband, who apparently doubled as butler. He directed them into the great room. The place was alive with people and they filled the large space and spilled over onto the terrace. Soft background music accompanied the sounds of conversation and laughter.

As the trio started to move toward the crowd Elyse looked up and saw Clint coming toward them. Her heart sped up, and her calm was shaken. He was so handsome in his beige linen coat and dark trousers. But his wide smile changed to a frown when he noticed Ferris standing beside her, holding Janey.

For a moment he glared at them. Then apparently remembering his manners, he managed a reluctant half smile. "I've been watching for you, darling," he said with just a slight emphasis on the word *darling*, as though he wanted to be sure Ferris heard.

Ferris eyed Elyse warily, but before she could speak Clint turned and held out his arms to Janey. "Hey, sweetheart, don't I get a hug?"

To Elyse's surprise Janey tightened her hold on Ferris and buried her face in his shoulder.

Ferris looked startled, and the shadow of pain in Clint's eyes was so strong it almost tore Elyse's breath from her. "Janey—" his voice couldn't completely disguise his anguish. "—what's the matter?" He put his hand gently on her small back. "What have I done? Why won't you come to me?"

Elyse was as shocked as Clint. For a while after he'd stopped coming over Janey had asked about him every day. Elyse had made excuses—he was busy, out of town or whatever—and soon she'd stopped asking. When Elyse had told her about this party at Clint's home, Janey had shown only mild interest instead of the wild enthusiasm Elyse had expected at the prospect of her seeing her beloved Clint again. It had surprised Elyse, but she'd been so upset at the same prospect that she hadn't registered a problem.

She was almost undone by the effect Janey's rejection had on Clint, and she spoke more sharply than she'd intended. "Janey, you're being rude. Answer Clint."

"No, Elyse, please let me handle this." Clint tenderly lifted Janey out of Ferris's arms and cradled her against him. "Now tell me, baby, what did I do to make you angry with me?"

Janey wouldn't look at him. "You didn't come and see me. You don't like me anymore."

Clint quickly turned his back on Elyse and Ferris, but not before she caught the torment her daughter's re-

mark had caused him. "Excuse me," he said in a choked
tone, and walked away with Janey clutched in his arms.

Ferris looked at Elyse. "Is there something I should
know about?"

Elyse pressed her lips together to keep them from
trembling. "It—it's just that Janey got very attached to
Clint while he and I were going together, and I guess
when we stopped dating she was more upset than I realized."

Ferris took her arm. "It looks as though all three of
you are pretty upset," he murmured. "Come on, let's
find our host and hostess and introduce ourselves."

They waded into the crowd, but got only halfway
across the room before Liz caught up with them. "Hi,"
she said, looking radiant in peach chiffon, "I didn't see
you come in. Did you bring Janey?"

It was Ferris who answered. "Hello, Liz. Yes, we
brought her, but Senator Sterling ran off with her.... I
haven't had a chance to wish you and your husband
happiness."

Liz smiled. "Thanks, Ferris. Paul's around here
somewhere. Come and let me introduce you to my fa-
ther- and mother-in-law."

They elbowed their way through the press of people,
and out to the terrace, where an older couple were surrounded by guests. The woman reached out to Liz as she
approached them and took her hand. "Elizabeth, my
dear," she said, "this has got to be your sister, Elyse. I
recognize her from Clint's description."

"Yes," Liz said, "this is my baby sister and her friend
Ferris Rogers."

Grace Sterling was in her early sixties, but her delicate face was unlined and there was only a trace of gray
in her dark hair. Her eyes were as green as Clint's, and

her mint green designer gown couldn't be larger than a size six.

Shyly Elyse shook hands. "I've looked forward to meeting you, Mrs. Sterling. I do hope Clint's description was kind."

The other woman's eyes twinkled. "I thought we'd agreed that you'd call me 'Grace,' and Clint's description wasn't kind, it was truthful. He said you were the most beautiful woman he'd ever known."

Elyse could feel her face flush and tears sting her eyes, but Grace quickly changed the subject and introduced her to her husband, Burton, then greeted Ferris.

Burton Sterling was an older version of Clint, but with brown eyes and white hair. He sat in a wheelchair and made no apology for not standing. "So you're Elyse," he boomed. "Welcome to the family. Lean down here and give me a hug. I'm not so old yet that I can't enjoy kissing a pretty girl."

Elyse laughed and leaned down into his embrace as she kissed him on the cheek. "Now I know where the Sterling sons get their charm," she teased.

A familiar voice from behind made her jump and straighten. "And this is the third gorgeous Haley female. Janey say hello to my dad and mom."

It was Clint, still holding Janey, but now she was all smiles, although Clint still looked shaken.

He put the child down, and while the Sterlings visited with her and with Ferris, Clint took Elyse by the arm. "I want to talk to you," he said grimly.

"But I—"

"Now." His tone brooked no opposition. "Dad and Mother will introduce Janey to the party director, and your boyfriend can damn well look after himself."

Elyse groaned. So it was going to be like that. Surely he couldn't be jealous! And too bad if he was—she wasn't going to be a martyr for any man.

As they made their way slowly through the crowded great room she caught a glimpse of Dinah Jefferson talking to one of Sacramento's TV anchormen. She also recognized the secretary of state, a woman who had championed several women's rights issues, and the colorful and controversial speaker of the assembly.

Clint ushered her into the den and shut the door. "Sit down," he said tightly, and motioned toward the couch.

She sat on a chair, instead, but he continued to stand.

"Elyse, I'm surprised and disappointed. I wouldn't have believed that you'd turn Janey against me. You know how special she is to me."

Elyse gasped and her eyes widened with disbelief. "I don't know what you're talking about."

He walked away from her and looked out the window. "Why did you tell her I was too busy to see her?"

"I didn't. I . . ." Yes, she had, but not in those words. "Clint," she said softly, "if that's what she thought, I'm truly sorry. She kept asking why you didn't come, and I just couldn't tell her that you wouldn't be coming to see us anymore—"

He whirled around to face her. "Why would you even consider telling her a thing like that? The only reason I didn't come was that you asked me not to. It certainly wasn't because I didn't want to see her or you."

He ran his hand through his hair. "My God, I'm beginning to wonder if women ever know what they want. First Dinah tells me she expected me to come looking for her after she told me emphatically she wouldn't marry me, then left the state. Now I find out that you've let

Janey think I was too busy to come and see her after you told me to stay away. Dammit, I'm not a mind reader!''

"You mean Dinah was just playing games with you when she left?" Elyse asked, outrage in every syllable.

He shrugged. "Not exactly, but when I made no effort to find her she didn't feel she could come back, even though she now admits she wanted to."

He smacked his fist into the palm of his hand. "It's such a waste. If she'd just picked up the phone and told me where she was I'd have gone to her and brought her back, but without any sign from her I assumed she was staying away because that's how she wanted it."

Elyse hadn't realized she'd still retained a glimmer of hope until that hope was shattered along with her heart. Dinah still wanted Clint. She'd come back to repair the damage she'd done to their relationship earlier, and Elyse had stood back meekly and let her do it.

She didn't notice that Clint had moved until she realized he was standing directly in front of her. She lifted her head and met his cold gaze. "Now," he said, "suppose you tell me your excuse. Why didn't you call and tell me Janey wanted to see me? I would have made arrangements to spend time with her. In fact, I'd have insisted on it."

Elyse didn't like the feeling of guilt that assailed her. After all, she wasn't the one who was in love with someone else. "How was I to know you'd be interested? According to the newspaper you've been spending most of your time squiring Dinah around Sacramento."

She couldn't miss the look of disgust that settled in his eyes. "And you believe everything you read in the papers?"

She jutted out her chin. "Usually, yes, unless I have reason to believe otherwise. And I didn't notice a retraction."

"It wasn't important enough to bother making a fuss." He turned away. "I notice you didn't waste any time replacing me in both your life and Janey's. Who's Ferris Rogers and how long have you known him?"

Elyse stood. They were just hurting each other and getting nowhere. "I don't think that's any of your business, Clint. You've got what you've wanted for so long. Dinah's back and willing to marry you, so grab her before she changes her mind again."

She walked past him and out of the room.

The next day Elyse painted faces on dolls. Slow delicate work that took every ounce of her concentration and left no time for what-ifs and could-have-beens. She knew she'd have to get a firm grip on her emotions and steel herself to see Clint occasionally without coming unglued. It would be unforgivable of her to destroy the loving relationship between him and Janey, and since he was also a member of Liz's family now, it would be impossible to avoid him without seeming childish.

On Monday she cut out clothes for the dolls, and in the afternoon she sat down in front of the television to sew. This was a restful job since she could stitch and watch television or listen to the radio at the same time. Janey had been put down later than usual for her nap, so she was still sleeping at four o'clock when Elyse switched the channel to the popular interview program that aired on a Sacramento station at that hour.

She was only paying partial attention, when suddenly the screen went black and big bold letters that spelled NEWS BULLETIN appeared. A male voice broke in.

"We interrupt this program to bring you a news bulletin. State Senator Clinton Sterling was shot as he left the Capitol View Restaurant, where he had earlier given a speech on the need for gun control legislation at a luncheon meeting sponsored by a local businessmen's association."

Elyse's cry of horror was drowned out by the loud, rapid voice of the announcer.

"The senator has been taken by ambulance to Sutter General Hospital, but as yet there is no word on his condition.

"Repeat. Senator Clinton Sterling has been shot and taken by ambulance to a hospital, but as yet there is no word on his condition. We'll keep you posted on events as we learn of them."

Chapter Thirteen

For a moment Elyse sat rooted to the chair. Clint shot! God, no! They didn't say whether he was alive or—

She jumped up and ran for the telephone. She had to call somebody. The police? The television station? Liz! Of course she'd call Liz. Liz would know if anybody did.

She grabbed the telephone, but when she started to dial the number she couldn't remember it. She slammed the phone back in the cradle and reached for her index file. It slipped out of her trembling fingers and fell to the floor, scattering the little cards in all directions.

She wailed a curse and dropped to her knees as hysteria clawed at her quivering nerve ends. If anything happened to Clint she couldn't bear it. *Dear God, don't let him die!*

She scooped the cards into a pile, but her hands were shaking so that she scattered them again when she tried to pick them up. She was crying hysterically, too shaken to reason, when the phone rang.

It was Liz. But Elyse was too upset to do more than scream Clint's name into the phone.

"He's alive, Elyse," her sister assured her. "Now calm down and listen to me. He's at the hospital and he's unconscious, but the bullet didn't hit anything vital. Honey, please, try to stop crying. They'll be taking him into surgery almost immediately. Paul and I are leaving for the hospital, and Grover Irwin is driving Dad and Mother Sterling in. Sweetie, don't cry so hard. Maybe I should send Paul on to the hospital and come up there to be with you."

"No!" Elyse shouted. "I want you...to go...to the hospital. That's the only way...I have of...knowing what's going on." She was making a massive effort to get control of herself.

"Will you be all right?" Liz sounded worried and indecisive.

"Yes, just call me as soon as you know anything. Promise, Liz!"

"Of course. I've got to run now. Paul's waiting to leave."

For a long time after she hung up the phone, Elyse sat huddled on the floor with her face buried in her knees and her arms wrapped around her legs. Her whole body shook with deep hurting sobs that nearly tore her apart.

What a fool she'd been. What a blind, stupid idiot. She'd behaved as though time were a friend instead of the enemy. She of all people should have known that there's no guarantee of tomorrow. Hadn't she already had her nice secure future blasted all to hell once?

When Jerry had died she'd vowed she would never again put off what she could do immediately, but then

Clint had come into her life, and she'd felt secure again. She forgot that you had to grab what you wanted and hold on to it. That tomorrow might be too late.

Why hadn't she just accepted Clint's assurance that he loved her and gone ahead with the engagement announcement? What difference did it make if he loved Dinah, too? Once they were married she could have made him forget about the other woman. She'd have loved him so much that he wouldn't have needed anyone else. But no. She had to have it all. She'd insisted on all or nothing, without ever stopping to think that nothing could be so irrevocably permanent.

No, Clint wasn't going to die. Life couldn't be that cruel. She couldn't lose Clint as she had Jerry. She could eventually heal, even if Clint married Dinah, if she knew he was healthy and happy. But if he died, a large part of her would die with him.

Her sobs finally spent, she got up and went into the bathroom, where she blew her nose and washed her face. Her skin was blotchy and her eyes were red with weeping, but she couldn't stay here and wait for the phone to ring. She was going to the hospital in Sacramento. She had to be there, even if she couldn't see Clint.

Half an hour later Elyse was tearing down the freeway in her blue Mustang at well over the legal speed limit. Her most trusted baby-sitter had been available and had responded immediately when Elyse had called. Elyse had changed from her paint-spattered jeans into a cotton skirt and blouse, hastily applied lipstick to her colorless lips and arranged for the sitter to spend the night if necessary.

It seemed to her that the drive took forever, yet it was only little more than an hour from the time the news bulletin broke into the television program until she turned off the highway in downtown Sacramento and drove to the hospital where Clint was battling for his life.

The area around the building was chaotic. Aside from the normal rush-hour traffic, the streets were clogged with news trucks, cars and equipment. Elyse parked in the public parking lot under the freeway and ran the block to the entrance, where she was stopped by a security guard. "Sorry, ma'am," he said, "but unless you have authorized business I'll have to ask you to come back later."

She had no intention of being turned away. She reached in her purse and extracted her wallet. "I'm Mary Elyse Haley, Senator Sterling's sister-in-law." A small lie, but almost true. She showed the officer her driver's license.

"Just a minute," he said, and spoke into the walkie-talkie he carried. A moment later there was a response, and the man said, "An officer will be right down to take you to the family."

A few minutes later another man arrived. He escorted her to the third floor, where, he informed her, a room had been set up for Senator Sterling's relatives.

As she entered, Liz, who had been sitting on the couch by Grace Sterling, jumped up and rushed over to embrace Elyse. "Honey, how did you get here? Where's Janey?"

"Terri's with her. I couldn't just sit at home and wait. How's Clint? Have you heard anything more yet?"

Liz shook her head. "Not much. The bullet entered the right side of his chest, but thank God it missed any vital organs. He's in surgery now, so all we can do is wait."

Elyse greeted Paul and his parents with hugs and words of condolence, and it was only then that she realized Dinah wasn't there. For the first time it occurred to her that exactly what the other woman had feared all along had happened—another assassination attempt. Her husband had died this very same way, and that's why she'd refused to marry Clint.

But she'd come back. Was she going to desert him now that it had happened to him, too?

"Where's Dinah?" Elyse asked, fully aware it wasn't the most diplomatic thing to do.

The four other people hesitated for a moment and looked at one another, before Paul spoke. "She's out of town. Our two sisters have been notified and will be arriving as soon as they can make airline connections. One lives in New Hampshire and the other in Georgia, and its the height of the vacation rush, so it may take them a while to get here."

Obviously he didn't want to talk about Dinah Jefferson's absence and was hoping to change the subject by switching to his sisters. Elyse didn't push. They all had enough on their minds right now; she'd make Liz tell her about Dinah later.

She switched to questions about the shooting. "What happened? Why would anyone want to shoot Clint? Did they get the person who did it?"

Again Paul, who was obviously spokesperson for the family, answered. "The subject of gun control is a fiercely debated one and emotions run high. Clint had given his talk, answered the questions and spent a while socializing before leaving. He'd just walked out of the restaurant, when the shot was fired."

Elyse gasped and could almost feel Clint's pain in her own chest as Paul continued. "The police have a man in custody, but we don't know anything about him. There'll be time enough for that later after we find out how Clint is.''

Soon they received a call from the governor, who regretted that his security staff wouldn't allow him to come to the hospital but assured them that his prayers and those of his wife were with Clint.

The evening wore on, and they were joined by Clint's secretary, his administrative assistant, Bill and Reba Ogden and several other people, who were introduced to her as close friends of Burton and Grace Sterling. Visitors to the room were carefully screened by the security men, who had set up an office in the building. Only those closest to the senator and his family were allowed on the third floor.

Meanwhile reporters, photographers, anchorpeople and other members of the news media crowded the lobby and waiting rooms on the first floor, all anxious for a medical report on the fallen senator. Still there was no word from Dinah. None of the Sterlings seemed surprised by her silence or her absence. Nothing was said about her, and Elyse bit back her own questions.

By seven-thirty she could no longer tolerate the small crowded noisy room. She felt hemmed in, claustrophobic. A buffet of sandwiches and salads had been brought up and set out earlier, but she knew better than to try to force food into her queasy stomach. Besides, she'd already consumed a gallon of coffee.

She took Liz aside and told her she was going to the chapel.

The small peaceful sanctuary on the third floor, with its oak pews, stained glass windows and large wooden cross in back of the altar, offered a haven of quiet and solitude. Elyse leaned back in one of the pews and closed her eyes.

Unless there were unforeseen complications during the surgery Clint would live. She had to believe that. Anything else was unthinkable. But what was in the future for her? Was there a place for her in his life?

Where was Dinah? Was it possible that she'd run away when she'd heard that Clint had been shot? Such a reaction was incomprehensible to Elyse. No woman could be that selfish and cruel.

Still, Dinah had been through an identical experience before, and she'd suffered a breakdown because of it. Maybe her nervous system simply couldn't cope with the same shattering situation twice. Who could say what another person's breaking point was? Elyse had been through a similar experience, but she was more fortunate than Dinah. Elyse had Janey, who needed her. Janey, whose helplessness and dependency gave Elyse the will and the purpose to survive.

A hand on her shoulder made Elyse jump, and she opened her eyes to see Liz standing beside her, smiling. "The surgery's over," she said, her voice tremulous, "and Clint's been taken to the recovery room. The bullet's been removed and there are a couple of broken ribs, but he'll recover completely."

Elyse collapsed against the back of the seat as joy replaced the terror and pain. "Oh, thank God," she moaned as Liz sat down and gathered her close in a loving maternal embrace.

For a moment Elyse clung to her sister, drawing on Liz's strength until she could recoup her own. "The doctor says Paul and his parents can go in and see Clint for a few minutes," Liz said, "but he's still coming out of the anesthetic. They'll be moving him to a private room in an hour or so, and then you can see him."

Elyse nodded and sat up. "Is Dinah here yet?"

"Dinah isn't coming," Liz said firmly as she stood up. "Look, I've got to get back to Paul. He wants me with him when he sees Clint, but we can't stay long. Wait for us in the family waiting room. There's nobody there now. Everyone took off after being assured that Clint would be all right. We'll talk later."

Liz left, but Elyse continued to huddle in the pew. For a moment she was too light-headed with relief to think or move, but her mind wasn't blank for long. Liz had said Dinah wasn't coming to the hospital, which meant that she was still running from her problems.

Poor dear sweet Clint. He was probably going to have to go through losing Dinah all over again, and at a time when he was most vulnerable. A stab of pain for him made Elyse wince.

Would she be willing to be second best if Clint still wanted her? Damn right she would. She'd take him any way she could get him and count her blessings. But there was one thing she couldn't do. She couldn't be there when Paul told him that Dinah had deserted him again. She couldn't watch the anguish he wouldn't have the strength to hide. If there was a chance that she would be taking Dinah's place in his life she didn't want to know the depth of his pain when he heard the news.

So okay, she was a coward, but this was one time she couldn't comfort him. Clint of all people wouldn't expect it. He wouldn't want her put through something like that.

She picked up her purse and walked slowly out of the chapel. In the family waiting room she found a pad of paper and wrote: *I've decided to go on home. Janey needs me. Please give Clint my love and my best wishes for a speedy recovery. Tell him I'll come to see him when he's feeling up to having visitors.*

She signed it and left it on the coffee table, where it couldn't be missed, then took an elevator to the ground floor and walked out of the hospital, unnoticed.

Physically and emotionally spent, Elyse slept soundly all night, but woke in time to catch the six o'clock early-morning news broadcast on one of the Sacramento television stations. According to the report Clint's condition was good and he was resting comfortably. She'd call Liz later and get a more detailed account.

That is, if Liz were still speaking to her. Elyse had known her sister would be upset with her for leaving the hospital when she'd been told to wait, and she hadn't felt up to arguing about it, so when she'd arrived home last night she'd unplugged the telephones before taking a shower and dropping into bed. She'd been uneasy about it, but Liz had assured her that Clint's life was no longer in danger. His family was with him, so he'd be well cared for, and she'd desperately needed sleep before facing him the next day.

She'd plugged in the phones again when she'd gotten up, but so far they hadn't rung.

She curled up on the sofa and sipped her coffee, not hearing a word of the news as the broadcast continued. Her thoughts were with Clint. How was he really? Would he be in the hospital long? How had he taken the news of Dinah's defection, if that's what it was?

Her heart ached for him. Hadn't he suffered enough? Why hadn't Dinah just stayed away and left him alone?

Elyse longed to go to him. They should have been married the same weekend Paul and Liz had been, then nothing would have kept Elyse away. If she were given a second chance with him she was going to marry him and let tomorrow take care of itself. She loved him enough for both of them, and eventually she'd make him forget Dinah.

Janey came downstairs at seven-thirty. She and Elyse had just finished breakfast, both still clad in their nighties, when they heard the front door open and close. Elyse got up and went into the hall, where she met Liz coming toward her, her eyes blazing.

Before she could speak Liz lit into her. "What's the matter with your telephones?"

Elyse had been afraid her sister would react like this. "Nothing. I unplugged them."

Liz was furious. "Oh, that's just great. I've been trying to get you all night. If you ever do a thing like that to me again I'm going to turn you across my knee and give you the spanking I should have administered at intervals years ago."

By this time they were back in the kitchen, and Janey was watching them, wide-eyed with amazement at her aunt's uncharacteristic anger.

Elyse sighed. "I'm sorry, Liz, but I knew you'd be upset with me for leaving without telling you, and—"

"You're damn right I am. Clint's been asking for you—"

"For me?" Elyse blinked with surprise.

"Yes, you, although why he wants such a blind, stubborn little fool, I'll never know."

"But I thought it was Dinah he'd want."

"I told you Dinah wasn't coming. Now, dammit, get your clothes on while I dress Janey. I'm taking you back to the hospital if I have to tie you in the car."

Without another word Elyse turned and ran upstairs and into her bedroom. She heard Liz dressing Janey in the next room as she quickly donned a breezy turquoise gauze dress with a wide flounce and multicolored rickrack trim. Her pulse was pounding, and she didn't take the time to put on makeup—except for a rich berry shade of lipstick—before sliding her bare feet into white pumps. She hurried toward the door just as Liz and Janey came out of Janey's room.

Liz carried a small overnight case. "I'm taking a change of clothes for Janey," she explained. "She and I are going to spend the day together, aren't we, pumpkin?"

The child clutched her aunt's hand and nodded vigorously.

Downstairs Elyse headed for the garage, but Liz stopped her. "We're going in my car," she said flatly.

"But how will I get home?"

"I'll bring you, but not until Clint tells me to. Now get in and don't give me any more trouble."

From long experience Elyse knew better than to argue with Liz when her elder sister had her mind made up. She and Janey got into Liz's gray Chrysler.

By the time they were on the freeway and headed for Sacramento Elyse had regained some of her composure and was determined to find out what was going on. "Liz, I want to know where Dinah Jefferson is and why she hasn't been to the hospital. Does she know Clint's been shot?"

Liz was driving ten miles over the speed limit, and she kept her eyes on the road as she answered. "I'd have given you a detailed explanation last night if you'd waited as I'd asked you to do. Now I'll let Clint do it. He'd prefer it that way."

Elyse's protest was met by stony silence, and neither spoke again until Liz pulled up in front of the hospital. "When you're ready to leave, call me and I'll come and get you. And Elyse—"

Elyse looked at her sister and saw that Liz was smiling.

"He's in room 426. For the love of God, marry the man."

Elyse nodded and managed an uncertain grin. "I intend to if he'll still have me."

She kissed Janey goodbye and walked into the lobby.

Chapter Fourteen

Elyse saw the uniformed police officer as soon as she rounded the corner of the nursing station on the fourth floor. He was sitting outside the door of the room at the end of the long hall, which she knew would be number 426. When there was an attempted assassination of a state senator, law enforcement was conspicuous.

Her stomach churned as she hurried toward him. How was Clint? Would he be glad to see her? Would the officer even let her in?

He stood as she approached him. "I'd like to see Senator Sterling," she said.

"Your name, please, and family affiliation."

"Elyse Haley. I'm his brother's sister-in-law."

"Wait here." He pushed open the door and walked into the room, only to reappear within seconds. "You can go in, but I'll have to search your purse. Sorry."

She nodded and handed the white crushed leather bag to him, but he didn't take it. "Open it and empty the contents out on the table." He motioned to a cart that stood next to his chair.

She did as she was told, and he eyed the assortment of makeup, wallet, pens, credit card holder and keys.

"Okay, you can put everything back and go in," he said, still not touching anything.

She scooped the items into her purse and walked through the swinging door.

The room was fairly large and the furnishings were polished hardwood instead of metal, but there was no mistaking the place for anything but a hospital room. Clint lay on the partially raised bed, his eyes open, watching her. He was wearing a navy cotton pajama coat with white piping, and the sheet covered him to the waist. There were no IVs or other needles or tubes, and any bandaging was covered by the coat, but he looked white and tired.

Elyse's first impulse was to run to him and hold him, but his grim expression didn't encourage such familiarity. Liz must have been mistaken. He didn't want to see her, after all.

She stood rooted to the floor, drowning in his cool green eyes. "Since you've finally decided to visit me, you might as well come all the way in," he said, and beckoned her with his left hand, while keeping the right one at his side.

He was angry. She'd hurt him—the last thing she'd wanted to do.

She walked over to the bed and stood on the left side, away from his injury. "Clint, I'm so sorry—"

Her voice broke, and she reached out and took his hand in hers.

His fingers closed over hers in a firm grip. "Sorry about what? That I've been injured? Or that you didn't come to me last night when I needed you so?" There was bitterness in his tone.

Her knees gave way and she dropped down on the side of the bed, careful not to jar him. "Oh, darling, what I'm sorry about are all the misunderstandings that seem to plague us constantly," she wailed. "If I'd known you wanted me with you, nothing could have kept me away." Her voice shook and her features twisted with anguish.

With a groan Clint pulled her to him and cradled her against the uninjured side of his chest. She put her hand to his neck and caressed him.

"Why would you think I didn't want you?" he murmured, his voice as shaky as hers.

"I—I knew how upset you'd be because Dinah wasn't here. I guess I just couldn't face you, knowing I was second choice."

"Second choice!" His arm tightened around her. "You mean you didn't know? But I thought someone would have told you."

She raised her head to look at him. "Told me what?"

He uttered a low growl of regret as he kissed her on the forehead. "That Dinah left yesterday morning to go back to France. I was hurrying out of that luncheon on my way to you when some idiot took a shot at me."

Elyse's eyes widened with surprise. "You mean she left *before* you were shot?"

Clint nodded. "She went back to a man she'd been seeing in Paris, and I was trying to get to you. It's as I told you all along, you little skeptic. It isn't Dinah I want—it's you."

Elyse collapsed against him, too relieved to argue. Dinah was gone. She didn't even know of the assassination attempt, and Clint didn't seem at all upset about her leaving.

He continued to speak. "I'm afraid it's my own damn fault you weren't with me last night." There was strong self-disgust in his tone. "I should have told you on Saturday that she was leaving."

This time Elyse sat up. "You had this all settled on Saturday and you didn't tell me?"

He nodded, and in spite of her burgeoning anger she could see the toll this discussion was taking on him. His face was drawn and his eyes reflected the physical pain he wouldn't admit to. "I'd intended to tell you at the cocktail party, and you'll never know how eagerly I was looking forward to the big reconciliation scene that was to follow. I was going to haul you off to my bedroom, lock the door and keep you there all weekend."

Clint closed his eyes and shuddered. "Then you waltzed in on the arm of another man, and I went crazy with jealousy."

The anger drained from her. "Jealousy? You were jealous of Ferris?"

"Damn right I was. He had his hand on you, and he was carrying *my* daughter. It was all I could do to keep from throwing him out."

My daughter! He was already thinking of Janey as his.

Elyse couldn't help grinning. "But I told your mother I was bringing an escort."

"Well, she didn't tell me," he grumbled, "and when you walked in with him I lost all my celebrated cool. Then Janey turned away from me, and the whole thing got nightmarish."

He reached for her and hugged her to him again. "I'm ashamed to say it wasn't until then that I fully understood how you felt about my relationship with Dinah. I'd never been jealous before, not even when she and I

were engaged. She had a lot of men friends, and sometimes they'd take her to parties or receptions when I
wasn't able to. It never bothered me, but when you
showed up at my house with another man I felt as if I'd
been stabbed in the gut."

She kissed the pulse that was hammering under his
jaw. "I'm glad. I like the idea of your being jealous of
me, and besides, it served you right."

He nibbled her earlobe. "You little devil. You're not
going to sympathize with me at all, are you?"

"No," she whispered, "not about that. And I still
don't know why you didn't tell me Dinah was leaving."

Clint sighed. "Because I was too bullheaded. Also, I
was so mad I couldn't think or reason. I decided that if
you were going to flaunt another man at me you could
damn well wait a while longer before I proposed to you
again."

Elyse burrowed her face in his shoulder. "That wasn't
very nice," she chided. "I've been going through hell."

"So have I, my darling," he murmured as he nuzzled
her hair. "Unfortunately I'm only human, and there are
a lot of things about me that aren't very nice—I'm sure
you'll discover all of them during the next fifty or so
years. But I love you with a passion I never asked for,
and sometimes it just plain scares the hell out of me."

She couldn't very well argue with that. "Speaking of
scared," she said, "I hope you never have to feel what I
did when I heard on TV that you'd been shot. I didn't
know if you were dead or alive, and—" Her voice broke
and she shivered and clung to him.

Clint held her close. "Take off your shoes and lie on
the bed with me," he said.

There was nowhere she wanted to be more, but she
hesitated. "I might hurt you."

"Sweetheart, I already hurt. You take my mind off the pain—and besides, I need you as close as I can get you. I've spent too much time in bed alone these past few weeks, tormented with dreams of holding you and loving you, only to wake and find the bed and my arms empty."

She slipped out of her pumps and adjusted her position so she was lying full length next to him on top of the sheet. He put his arm around her and cuddled her against him. "Mmm, that's better," he murmured. "Now raise up and give me a kiss. I can't move around much."

She leaned over him and stroked his temple. "You mean this time you want me to take charge?"

He rubbed his cheek against the soft rise of her breast. "Are you sure you know how?" There was amusement in his tone.

"I'll improvise," she whispered into his ear, then traced the inside of it with the tip of her tongue.

"You're learning fast," he said approvingly as she kissed first one side of his mouth, then the other.

She touched her lips to his fleetingly, then returned to brush them again. The third time she settled her mouth squarely on his and felt the blood pound through her veins at his quick, heated response.

"Mmmmmm," she murmured, and ran her tongue around his lips. He parted them, inviting her penetration as the hand that was holding her searched for and found her bare thigh. She bent her leg and brought it up to rest gently against his sheet-covered groin.

Unexpectedly her knee nestled beside the hard ridge of his desire, and she quickly moved it. She hadn't meant to arouse him. "Oh, my, I didn't mean to—"

He chuckled. "Honey, all you have to do is come into the room to get that kind of response from me. Now come on, put your knee back up. It feels so good."

"But you can't—"

"No, I can't. Not yet. But it's sure as hell reassuring to know it's not because of any...uh...structural damage. Meanwhile we can fool around a little. It'll just be that much sweeter and more satisfying when we do make love completely. Besides, this will relieve some of the frustration that's been driving me out of my mind."

He tugged at her thigh, and she returned to the position he wanted.

He sighed contentedly and moved his left arm to caress her knee. The effort caused him to cringe and swear with pain.

Elyse raised herself on her elbow, frightened that he might have injured himself. "Clint, be careful!"

He relaxed as the discomfort subsided. "It's all right. The muscles in my chest are sore on that side, and moving my arm pulls them. I'll just have to get used to it."

She snuggled closer against him and put her hand on his stomach. "Can I see what they did to you?"

"If you want. There's not much to see."

She unfastened the buttons of his pajama top and pushed it aside. There was a large dressing covering part of his chest, extending around to his back. "The bullet must have hit you to one side," she said as she carefully caressed the part of his shaved chest that wasn't bandaged.

"Lucky for me it did. Otherwise it would have damaged my lung and I'd have to stay here longer. I'm going home tomorrow."

"Oh? Isn't that awfully soon? Did the doctor say it was all right?"

"I didn't ask him—I told him. I'm going to take you and Janey home with me, and we're going to be a family. If you'd rather get married first there's a chaplain here at the hospital who will do the honors, but I'm not going to let you get away from me ever again. There's been enough shilly-shallying about this. I love you. You're the *only* woman I love, and I intend to spend the rest of my life proving it to you."

He sounded so confident, but Elyse saw the cloud of uncertainty on his face as he searched hers. "Will you marry me, love? I really, truly can't live without you."

She raised herself up to once more cover his mouth with hers, and their kiss was long and hot and wonderfully satisfying. "Of course I'll marry you," she said when they'd finally pulled apart. "I love you and I want you, and if you still have unresolved feelings for Dinah I'll marry you anyway, because even second best is better than not having you at all."

His good arm crushed her against him, and with a strangled moan he lowered his head to bury his face in her hair. For a moment he said nothing, but she could feel his muscles clench with the effort he was making to control his runaway feelings.

She put her arm around his neck and nuzzled his shoulder. "I don't deserve you," he murmured brokenly, "but you'll never ever be second best with me. As I told you earlier, Dinah was a habit I had to break. It wasn't hard. Actually, it happened fast once I knew I'd lose you if I didn't. But then you flaunted another man at me, and I behaved like a jealous teenager."

"We've both acted like spoiled brats," she said as she continued the nuzzling, this time on his bare chest.

He pulled her loose-fitting dress up with his left hand and rubbed his palm over the silky panties that covered her bottom. His low sound of approval was almost a purr, and she arched against his side and hoped it wouldn't be long before he could move around enough to tend the fire he was building deep inside her.

It was time for a little distraction, and there was a question that had to be asked. "Clint, are you going to tell me what happened between you and Dinah?"

His hand stilled, but remained where it was. "The conclusion was simple, actually, but it took us both years to arrive at it. I'd always thought of love as eternal. But now I realize there are different kinds of love. Romantic love, the passionate love of a man for a woman, needs to be returned and nurtured in order to grow and flourish. Like a flowering desert cactus it will survive a lot of neglect and mistreatment, but eventually if it's not nourished it will wither and die."

He rubbed his lips across her forehead. "That's what happened to the love Dinah and I once shared. It died of neglect. But it happened so gradually that neither of us noticed until we were forced to."

Elyse thought for a moment before she spoke. "You may be right. When Jerry died I was sure I'd never love again, but as the shock wore off and the pain and loneliness lessened I was able to accept dates with other men."

She tenderly ran her hand around the outside of his bandage, wanting desperately either to take away his pain or share it. "When you first came to the house I was surprised at the wallop my emotions took. It caught me off guard, and from then on I didn't have a prayer of resisting you. I think I fell in love with you before I even knew you, and no matter how hard I tried to prevent it that love just grew stronger and deeper."

Clint's fingers slid under the leg of her skimpy panties and stroked her soft skin. "That's because it was returned. Even when I thought you were Paul's girl, I wanted you, and I knew I was in trouble. Lust could have been toned down or turned off, but I couldn't do anything about the feelings I had for you except yearn.''

His fingers crept closer to her heat and she squirmed. He shivered and clutched the inside of her thigh.

She started to move away, but he protested. ''I want you to touch me. It's just that it's been far too long since we made love, and when I hold you like this my whole body responds.''

''I'm having the same problem,'' she confessed. ''When I crawl into bed with you all thought of sleep goes up in smoke.''

His thumb explored upward, making her sigh with pleasure. ''There are ways, you know . . .''

She put her hand over his to stop its upward spiral. ''I know, darling, and tomorrow when you get home I'll let you teach me, but for now we'd better not think about it. We'd not only shock the nurse if she walked in, but you don't need that kind of excitement. We don't want to take the chance of your tearing something loose and having to stay here any longer—''

''I'm afraid you're probably right,'' he said regretfully, moving his hand to her breast, ''but keep your knee where it is. I promise to behave.''

''I was afraid of that,'' she said playfully.

He swatted her gently. ''Watch what you're implying, young lady, or I'll disregard bullet holes, broken ribs and outraged nurses and make love to you in all the ways I can think of right here and now.''

''Tomorrow,'' she whispered against his cheek.

''Is that a promise?'' he murmured.

''Cross my heart.''

* * * * *

Silhouette Special Edition

COMING NEXT MONTH

#433 ALL THE RIGHT REASONS—Emilie Richards
Crack attorney Brett Terrill wasn't looking for love—just an obedient wife who'd bear his children. Meek, maternal Olivia LeBlanc seemed the perfect match . . . till she developed her own case of ambition.

#434 HEART OF THE TIGER—Lindsay McKenna
After her marriage failed, Layne Hamilton vowed never to get involved with a CIA man again. But agent Matt Talbot had a mission . . . and enough charisma to hijack Layne's heart.

#435 ONCE BURNED . . .—Karen Keast
Morning Skye Farenthall and Brandon Bear Hunter had once pledged eternal love . . . then betrayed their youthful vows. Now a raging forest fire reunited them, and their burning passion—and blistering pride—threatened to consume them.

#436 SAY HELLO AGAIN—Barbara Faith
When Miguel Rivas met his high school heartthrob, Brianna Petersen, at their fifteen-year reunion, the old feeling was back. And this time he wasn't looking for a prom date, but a partner for always.

#437 CANDLES IN THE NIGHT—Kathleen Eagle
For practical Morgan Kramer, falling in love with idealistic dreamer Mikal Romanov was sheer insanity. Driven by his humanitarian causes, would he ever notice *her* very human needs?

#438 SHADY LADY—Patricia Coughlin
On Diamond Cay, Kara McFarland found the privacy her past demanded. Celebrity Max Ellis sought precious solitude himself. But as they trespassed on each other's turf, proximity led to dangerous passion.

AVAILABLE THIS MONTH:

#427 LOCAL HERO
Nora Roberts

#428 SAY IT WITH FLOWERS
Andrea Edwards

#429 ARMY DAUGHTER
Maggi Charles

#430 CROSS MY HEART
Phyllis Halldorson

#431 NEPTUNE SUMMER
Jeanne Stephens

#432 GREEK TO ME
Jennifer West

Silhouette Romance™
Legendary Lovers Trilogy

BY DEBBIE MACOMBER....

ONCE UPON A TIME, in a land not so far away, there lived a girl, Debbie Macomber, who grew up dreaming of castles, white knights and princes on fiery steeds. Her family was an ordinary one with a mother and father and one wicked brother, who sold copies of her diary to all the boys in her junior high class.

One day, when Debbie was only nineteen, a handsome electrician drove by in a shiny black convertible. Now Debbie knew a prince when she saw one, and before long they lived in a two-bedroom cottage surrounded by a white picket fence.

As often happens when a damsel fair meets her prince charming, children followed, and soon the two-bedroom cottage became a four-bedroom castle. The kingdom flourished and prospered, and between soccer games and car pools, ballet classes and clarinet lessons, Debbie thought about love and enchantment and the magic of romance.

One day Debbie said, "What this country needs is a good fairy tale." She remembered how well her diary had sold and she dreamed again of castles, white knights and princes on fiery steeds. And so the stories of Cinderella, Beauty and the Beast, and Snow White were reborn....

Look for Debbie Macomber's *Legendary Lovers* trilogy from Silhouette Romance: *Cindy and the Prince* (January, 1988); *Some Kind of Wonderful* (March, 1988); *Almost Paradise* (May, 1988). Don't miss them!